# THE GIRL FROM NORMANDY

RACHEL SWEASEY

Boldwood

First published in Great Britain in 2025 by Boldwood Books Ltd.

Copyright © Rachel Sweasey, 2025

Cover Design by JD Smith Design Ltd

Cover Images: Shutterstock

The moral right of Rachel Sweasey to be identified as the author of this work has been asserted in accordance with the Copyright, Designs and Patents Act 1988.

A CIP catalogue record for this book is available from the British Library.

Paperback ISBN 978-1-83533-117-0

Large Print ISBN 978-1-83533-116-3

Hardback ISBN 978-1-83533-118-7

Ebook ISBN 978-1-83533-115-6

Kindle ISBN 978-1-83533-114-9

Audio CD ISBN 978-1-83533-123-1

MP3 CD ISBN 978-1-83533-122-4

Digital audio download ISBN 978-1-83533-119-4

This book is printed on certified sustainable paper. Boldwood Books is dedicated to putting sustainability at the heart of our business. For more information please visit https://www.boldwoodbooks.com/about-us/sustainability/

Boldwood Books Ltd, 23 Bowerdean Street, London, SW6 3TN

www.boldwoodbooks.com

*For all those who've risked their own lives for the sake of others. May we never take our freedom, or your sacrifice, for granted.*

# PROLOGUE

As Marie-Claire held her precious baby in her arms, and Benjamin wrapped them both in his embrace, the new parents quietly cried, overwhelmed with relief and gratitude that mother and child had both survived the delivery. And yet, the same night that this light had come into their lives, a deathly darkness had fallen, with the sound of crashing glass, over thousands of this little one's brothers and sisters in nearby Germany.

But here in the little Paris attic apartment that Marie-Claire and Benjamin Dubois called home, on this night, in their world, all was calm, and peaceful, and hopeful, at last. Baby Antoine sucked noisily at his fists and his mother began to whisper to him about who he was, and all he might do and see one day, where he fit into the world, and mostly of the beautiful blue bay that she loved in the south, where the Mediterranean lapped the shores.

It wasn't until some days later when they left the cocoon of their home and ventured into the streets with their new baby in his pram that they learned of the horrors that had occurred on the night of Antoine's birth, and the threat this brought closer to their little family. For Benjamin Dubois, through his mother's line, was Jewish.

The evil had been spreading through Germany like a malignant cancer over the last decade, but the root of the disease had begun right here in Paris, in Versailles, almost twenty years ago in 1919. And the bitterness harboured by one angry little man was now poisoning all of Europe. And little Antoine Dubois had been born on Kristallnacht.

# 1

## PARIS, DECEMBER 1940

Benjamin snapped shut the textbook from which he'd been reading aloud and regarded his students as they began to pack their satchels. He knew this would be the last time he saw them all but, because so many of them were Jewish like him, he chose not to alarm them. They would learn after the holidays that Mr Dubois had left his position at the school for family reasons and, in no time at all, they would accept his replacement. But he scanned the room again and looked for those he knew to be Jews like him: Esther, Reuben, Deborah, Joseph. The father in him was torn in two as he wanted to scoop them up and take them with him to safety, away from Paris, away from the rise of the Third Reich. But if he and his own family were to survive, they had to get out of here now, and quietly.

They had all known how real the threat of German invasion was, two years back when baby Antoine was born. And the horror was that antisemitic violence had become accepted behaviour by so many otherwise good people. Good German people were being propagandised to believe a lie, and so their leader had been empowered on his mission to take over Europe.

Benjamin remembered that day in June, six months ago, when the sky had turned black with soot, and the French government had turned and run. The invasion had been a silent one, not accompanied by an attack and desperate defence that might normally go along with the fall of a great city. The soot that filled the air was only the detritus from burning fuel, some distance from the city. The French government had just given in and left the city open for the peaceful arrival of Hitler's troops.

Benjamin had gone out on 14 June, leaving Marie-Claire at home with Antoine, to watch with a dreadful hunger for news as the display of steel-grey uniforms marched down the Champs-Élysées. There had been hundreds of vehicles, tank after tank and then motorcycles with sidecars, and trucks towing huge guns, in a line that never seemed to end. And then thousands of infantry officers followed, all grim-faced and determinedly looking to their generals, who wore breeches with side-stripes of red to match the splash of red on their collars. Soon the red Nazi flag was hung from every major building in Paris, so that there was nowhere one could go to avoid the reminder that Paris was now owned by the Nazis.

Thousands of Parisians had fled in scenes like those from the biblical exodus, fearing the destruction they expected would follow. But Benjamin and Marie-Claire had chosen to stay, foreseeing the nightmare that would be faced on the roads, and hoping there would be a better chance to get out later.

The atmosphere of the city had changed completely over those first terrible days, and the soul of Paris seemed to leave with the exodus. Just going out of the apartment to buy food had been frightening, as hundreds of soldiers in their severe grey-toned uniforms could be found on every street, and in each café. So Marie-Claire mostly stayed indoors, and Benjamin walked to school every day, buying provisions while he was out. Before the invasion, Marie-Claire had enjoyed spending hours searching for new ingredients and cooking up wonderful new dishes. She'd worked in restaurants before having Antoine, and had learned from some of the best chefs in Paris, though as a woman she was only ever a lowly cook, with no hope of advancing to the status of a chef.

And her love for cooking had led to the creation of dozens of new recipes, which she'd been writing into a journal she hoped one day could become a published cookbook. Marie-Claire treasured her ancient copy of *L'art du Cuisinier*, but she harboured a dream of writing a more practical guide for the woman at home: women like her who longed to serve delicious and interesting cuisine, but who didn't have a whole kitchen of staff and the budget of a princely *comte* to play with. The occupation of Paris had put a stop to her daily walks where she'd visited markets and wandered down the back lanes of Paris visiting various exquisite and well-stocked *boucheries, fromageries*, and intimate little *marchés,* hunting for the finest ingredients.

Benjamin had been walking to school one day just after the arrival of the Germans, when he heard a tremendous explosion that made him duck into a doorway for cover, his heart racing and hands shaking. Was the expected violence about to start? But there was no danger in this street. No sudden rushing of soldiers, or gunfire as he'd expected. He later learned that the invaders had been instructed by Hitler to destroy the statue of Charles Mangin – a figure who represented German defeat. They'd blown up the plinth and then melted down the statue for scrap metal.

There was always the threat of possible violence everywhere, in every gun slung over the shoulder of every soldier, but this expectation of danger started to seem far-fetched. Paris was peaceful. Soon, it was clear that the German army intended to take the best of Paris as their private playground. They took over the Ritz as the chosen watering hole of generals and officers, and they started emptying the Louvre of any artworks that hadn't been removed to safety by the time of the occupation. But there was no fighting, at least not obviously. So those who'd fled – and found there was nowhere to go – had started coming back. The people of Paris relaxed, a little, into this new normal.

And then, the Nazis began their systematic attack on the dignity of every Jew, with the Law on the Status of Jews being passed in October.

'See you after Hanukkah, sir,' called Deborah as she left the room. He smiled and waved, giving a little nod, but hating himself for the lie in his demeanour.

Benjamin checked his desk to see if there was anything particularly personal he would like to take with him. The rows of books on the shelves that he'd collected through his youth and university years would have to stay, sadly. And he would never need to read any of these old exam papers again. He opened his second drawer, and took out his favourite pens and the inkwell he'd inherited from his father, closing it tightly and wrapping it in a dust cloth before popping it safely into his bag. And there was the letter he'd had from Reuben last term, apologising for his laziness and promising to make better use of the education he'd been granted. Benjamin tucked it into his bag but, saddened now by the hopelessness of a future where these bright children were not wanted, he turned and, taking one last look at his schoolroom, shut the door behind him. He walked out alongside other staff, nodding in greeting to a few, touching his cap to them, as if his life were not about to change completely.

It had been two months now since the Law on the Status of Jews had been passed, and Benjamin had discovered his head-master had lost his position the very next day. Under the new law, Jews – who could be defined that way simply by having a Jewish mother, whether or not they identified with the religious rituals of the faith – were prohibited from holding any position in government or the legal system, medicine, journalism and teaching. His headmaster, Mr Cohen, had been removed from his position immediately, but somehow Benjamin had stayed hidden among the other, non-Jewish, teachers in his school. It surely wouldn't be long before he was found out and removed too.

Teaching was the only vocation that he'd trained for, and all he'd ever hoped to do. But there were precious little other occupations open to him now, even if he'd tried to remain employed. He had waited for someone to come and tell him he had to leave the school. He stayed quiet in the staffroom and was grateful for every day that he seemed to be left alone to get on with his job. But it couldn't last. He'd heard of schools where the occupying Germans had carried out raids and any Jewish teachers were thrown out on the spot. Perhaps it was because he was only half Jew, on his mother's side. Maybe the fact that his father's name was very firmly French and not Jewish stood in his favour. But the talk of restrictions to come, for all Jews, could not be ignored.

Law firms had been shut down. Countless friends of his who worked in the government, or the police force, or wrote for newspapers had all lost their jobs. Their livelihoods. Their reason for being in Paris. And yet, they were beginning to realise that soon they'd be banned from leaving as well. Their independence was slipping away.

\* \* \*

For some weeks now, Marie-Claire and Benjamin had been planning to get out of Paris. Marie-Claire had been carefully sorting through their belongings, packing into two suitcases a greatly reduced assortment of their most precious things – a task made a little more complicated by two-year-old Antoine who felt that taking things out of cases was more fun than putting them in. She had made room for her treasured little journal of recipes in her small shoulder bag, but the old cookbook would have to stay behind.

The cases had to appear light enough that the Dubois trio might just be going on a short trip south to distant family, where Marie-Claire had holidayed with cousins on the Côte d'Azur, and the apartment was to be left as if they'd be back in just a short while, in time for the new school term to start. The issue of what to do about Minette had been of real concern. They couldn't just leave without placing her in someone's care, and yet they couldn't tell anyone they would be leaving forever. In the end, Marie-Claire had told their neighbour just this afternoon that they needed to visit her father as she'd heard he was unwell. She'd asked Madame Bernard to feed the cat for a few days while they were away.

The travelling group, made up of Marie-Claire, Benjamin and Antoine, and their newly married friends Philippe and Juliette, had chosen this Wednesday night to leave, knowing it was generally quieter, and Marie-Claire had bought the tickets a few days earlier. Philippe and Juliette were not Jewish, but they'd seen enough of the Nazis in these last six months to know they wanted to escape to the south, where there was more chance of staying out of danger. When they'd heard from Marie-Claire and Benjamin their plan, they'd eagerly offered to go with them to help with sweet little Antoine on the long journey. Philippe and Juliette had family further along the coast in Nice, so would travel with the Dubois family all the way to Saint-Christophe.

They were all due to catch the seven o'clock overnight train from Paris Gare de Lyon, all the way to Marseille in the south. Once there, they'd have to arrange another train east from Marseilles in the direction of Nice, stopping at Saint-Christophe, and they hoped that when they reached that great distance from Paris, the presence of German soldiers could not hinder them. Once safe in Marie-Claire's favourite spot by the sea on the Côte d'Azur, something would surely work out for them. Teachers were always needed, and Marie-Claire's distant family ran a restaurant there. She had sometimes holidayed with them from her home in the north, and it was on those visits to their restaurant where she had first learned to cook.

As she'd been packing the bags earlier on this dark and cold December day, she had remembered the warmth and sunshine of a summer spent beside the beach on the Côte d'Azur, and she had tried not to pack too many winter clothes, knowing the space would be better used by summer things. The long, balmy evenings of those summers were treasured in her memory along with the times she spent in the restaurant kitchen, creating magically buttery sauces and dishes under the guidance of the chef. Warmth, sunshine and good food had come to mean happiness to her. And she loved to cook for Benjamin and make him happy with good food.

At first, when she and Benjamin realised they must leave Paris, they'd wondered about reaching out to her own parents, whom she imagined must still be living in Fontainebleau, south of Paris, but the rift that had been driven between them when she'd chosen to marry a Jew was too deep to cross now. It wasn't that they were against Jews, they'd explained, but just that a Catholic should not marry one. It didn't matter to them that she only loosely considered herself Catholic – because they told her she was – or that Benjamin was Jewish only because his mother had been. No, they had stuck fast to their prejudiced and misguided opinions and so, when Marie-Claire last saw them, she packed up all her belongings from their home, and left for Paris knowing she never wanted to see them again. Now that her little family faced what she suspected could become a life and death situation, she wondered if they would have softened. But the danger always was that their prejudice against the Jews might be growing even stronger now and the Dubois trio might be in more danger under her parents' 'care' than they were hiding in Paris. So the only sensible option was to ignore their existence, and reach out to the distant cousins south, in Saint-Christophe.

She'd written ahead to Saint-Christophe saying they would try to get there soon but, here in Paris, they were hopeful that, apart from Philippe and Juliette who would leave with them, nobody except Madame Bernard was aware they were planning to leave.

* * *

Benjamin opened the front door to their apartment block and pushed inside, gratefully shutting out the cold wind that tried to follow him in. A flurry of dried brown leaves followed him in and scuttled around the foyer and he closed the door tight. The leaves came to rest and settled in silence. He checked his watch. Almost six o'clock. The time he usually arrived home each evening for his dinner. He took the steps up to their apartment two at a time, as he always did, his long legs seeming to need the extra stretch at the end of a day in the schoolroom.

At the landing he paused and looked around, knowing this was the last time he would come home here to this place, if all went to plan. He chastised himself for even considering that anything could go wrong. They had packed their bags. They were going on a short trip to visit Marie-Claire's father, the story went, although the truth was Marie-Claire only had distant family left in the south. Benjamin would eat a quick, cold meal with his family now, and they would say a fond farewell to Minette and stroke her fur for the last time. He drew a breath and readied himself to greet the darlings of his life, just as he always did.

'I'm home!' he called and braced himself for the onrushing ball of energy that was little Antoine.

'Papapapapapa!' shrieked the bouncing blond boy who rushed headlong into Benjamin's arms. He scooped up his son and covered his soft cheeks with kisses before walking over to Marie-Claire and reaching a strong arm around her waist.

'And how is my beautiful wife tonight? Excited?' he whispered into her hair.

'Terrified,' she breathed back, kissing him on the lips. 'But in a few hours, we will be miles from Paris and on our way to safety in the south. Then, I will breathe freely again.' In reply, Benjamin squeezed her lightly around the waist and then spoke brightly to their little boy.

'And what are we feasting on tonight, hey? Ah – I see it all before me. Bread and cheese and a little ham. Perfect!' he cried, sitting at the table and placing Antoine on his high chair. He poured two glasses of wine from the carafe and tore off a small hunk of bread, buttering it and slicing a piece of cheese for Antoine who took hold of the food with both hands.

They ate quietly, thoughtfully, and after the meal Benjamin went into their bedroom to check the bags and see if there was anything else to add. There was a little room, and perhaps space for one or two small books. He scanned his shelves, and took his mother's Jewish prayer book and her copy of the *Haggadah* and felt he could hear her quiet voice then, saying, 'Next year in Jerusalem.'

'Perhaps not Jerusalem, *Maman*, but maybe in Saint-Christophe,' he said under his breath as he kissed the books and slipped them into the side of his bag. He closed the bags and carried them out to the dining room where Marie-Claire had just finished wiping Antoine's hands and face and was buttoning him into his winter coat.

'Come on, little man, we're going out for a walk,' she said, and then as an afterthought, 'Give Minette a cuddle, darling,' and they all bent to stroke and kiss the cat goodbye.

The night was now fully dark in the street and Benjamin was grateful that they lived in the 12th arrondissement, so there wasn't far to walk in this bitter wind.

'*Froid, Maman, j'ai froid*,' whimpered Antoine as he buried his face in his mother's chest to hide from the freezing cold. Benjamin carried the bags, and they walked on, not daring to stop and draw any attention to themselves. There were few German soldiers around, and those they did see seemed too busy huddling around fires and smoking to keep warm to notice them, but anything and everything at all different or suspicious was always noticed, they'd learned in these strange, dark months. Look straight ahead, keep walking, both parents repeated internally, over and over again.

As they came in sight of the grand archways and imposing clock tower of the Gare de Lyon, they both became aware of noise like rushing water inside the station. Benjamin looked up to see the clock showed ten to seven. There was still plenty of time to find their train, and Philippe and Juliette who were going to meet them here, but there was no time at all to stand still. Once inside the station they were both overwhelmed by a heaving mass of people like they had never seen in the station before. There were hundreds of people queuing at the ticket office, some waving fistfuls of banknotes, far in excess of the cost of a ticket.

'Something has happened,' said Marie-Claire in a high-pitched tone that Benjamin didn't recognise.

'Just keep walking. We have our ticket. There's our train ahead, see?' he said, nodding in the direction of a train that already seemed to be full to overloaded. The voice, when it came over the megaphone, had a terrifyingly imperious sound to it.

'*Keine Juden an Bord! Alle Juden melden sich an der Kasse.*'

'Oh Lord, no,' breathed Benjamin, trying to school his face to remain calm and his legs to keep walking.

'What do they mean, "*no Jews aboard*", Benjamin? They don't want us here, and now they don't want us to leave either? We have our tickets already. Nobody asked for identity when I bought the tickets, and I'm not Jewish anyway. Why do they want us to report to the ticket office?' asked Marie-Claire in rapid fire.

'Shush, my love. Then don't give them reason to think anything at all about us. I'm only half Jewish myself, and they can't possibly know that.'

'Marie-Claire! Benjamin!' called the friendly voice of Juliette from the train window. 'We're in here already! We thought you weren't coming.'

'Oh Juliette, you are here!' called Marie-Claire with relief. 'But the train is so full! How will we fit?' she shouted through the din and chaos of the station.

'Here, pass Antoine through the window to me,' Juliette called, reaching out her arms to take the little chap in her arms. Marie-Claire passed him up, and he giggled as he was squeezed through the window, knowing he was safe with this 'auntie' he loved.

'Now the bags, and then you two will fit easier through the

doors!' Juliette called, after handing Antoine to Philippe beside her.

Benjamin passed the first piece of luggage in. The second case was a little larger and it stuck as he tried to push it through.

'Hold on, let me take it back and try another way,' he said and, pulling it back too forcefully, the bag fell to the ground and the catch snapped open. Benjamin and Marie-Claire both bent to pick up the few items that had fallen out and froze as they saw a pair of black boots, polished to a shine like the moon on a calm lake, stop right beside them. A black leather-gloved hand reached to pick up the two small books that had fallen from the bag, and the couple dared to look up into the soldier's face as he studied the books. He snapped them shut and pointed to the front of the station.

'*Alle Juden melden sich an der Kasse*. All Jews to ticket office!'

Marie-Claire and Benjamin locked eyes and in that fleeting moment decided, without saying a word, who should speak first. Marie-Claire stood slowly and pasted her smoothest smile onto her face.

'*Bonsoir, Monsieur*. There seems to be a misunderstanding. My husband and I are not Jewish. We are French and we are Catholic. We have tickets for this train, and our son is already aboard, so if you don't mind,' Marie-Claire crooned in her most sweetly seductive voice, as she bent with Benjamin to put the belongings back into the case.

'*Halt!*' came the imperious command. Both looked up to him as he opened one of the books. 'These are Jewish books. You are Jews!' he cried.

'Oh, no, sir. I study literature of all languages. Neither of us is Jewish,' explained Benjamin as the train whistle sounded.

'You lie! All Jews lie!' yelled the soldier, unwittingly repeating the lies he'd been told himself. 'All Jews must report to the ticket office!'

Benjamin had finished repacking the bag and stood now, turning to glance at their friends on the train whose faces reflected the horror he felt. He made his decision and turned immediately, passing the case up neatly through the window and pulling Marie-Claire away from the soldier. He pushed her ahead of him toward the train door as the whistle sounded again, low and long, like a moan on the wind, and then he heard another sound – the last sound he would ever hear.

## 2

POOLE, APRIL 1998

Esther leant against the glass, staring through the Georgian criss-crossed pattern on the window of the half landing at the back of the main staircase of Upton House, where the Dorset Chamber of Commerce had its offices. The rain had been light and drizzly for days, but now it pelted and hammered, and the wind blew through the trees in the park as if it meant to rip them up by the roots. She couldn't even see the waters of the harbour, the rain was so intense. Her coffee cup warmed her hands, and the steam made wispy patterns on the cold glass of the window. As she looked through the patterns to the wind and rain outside, she imagined she could see the face in the rain that she'd not seen in person for nearly thirteen years now. Whenever Esther was feeling even just a little bit glum, when she stared into a blank space – and especially in the rain – it always took her to him, and what might have been.

She wondered what Jules Joubert was doing now. The last time she'd seen him, he was about to leave the rural farm in Normandy where he'd grown up, and go off to Paris to start university. She'd only been sixteen years old, and must have seemed so young to him. And though any adult would have called it a teenage crush, for Esther, it had been as real and lasting – even more so – than any relationship she'd had with a man since then.

Esther remembered how she'd been longing for that French exchange trip all year – for the previous four years, really, ever since she'd started learning French at secondary school. The fifth-year French exchange trip had been the reward for sticking with conjugating verbs in French lessons long enough to be in the O-level programme, and then, in her final year of school, she had well and truly earned her right to go.

Esther had been about to finally meet Giselle, the penfriend she'd been matched with from her school's twin in Normandy. The girls had been writing to each other every few months for the previous few years and Esther was finally going to see the farmhouse she'd heard so much about. Giselle's letters had given Esther so much information about the farm in Sainte-Mère-Église where she lived, in the middle of the Norman peninsula, that she'd felt almost like she'd be going home even on her very first trip. Esther even knew the names of the cats – Minette, Coco, and Fifi – but there'd been details Giselle had never thought to mention. Like the fact that her older brother Jules was drop-dead gorgeous. Or the tiny detail that the farmhouse didn't have any plumbing – no shower, no toilet, no running water even in the kitchen. Just a centuries-old cast-iron hand pump over a well, in the 'water room'.

She laughed to herself now, as she watched the rain falling outside, remembering her shock when she'd arrived and been shown the bucket under her bed, and the washstand that looked as if it had come right out of a Jane Austen movie.

The first time she'd seen Jules, he was working in the little café-bar in the centre of Sainte-Mère-Église. He'd stepped outside to help his father carry Esther's case, and his gloriously long and shiny dark hair had covered the blue of his eyes until he flicked it aside and she'd seen clouds of intensity in his brow. She'd fallen for him then, she knew.

The last full day Esther had spent at Giselle's home on that first trip was warm and sunny. Her walk to the church and back with Jules, after they'd got to know each other, had opened her eyes and her heart to a future where she might get to kiss this dreamboat every day of her life. She sometimes wondered now if he'd ever really kissed her, or if she'd just chosen to remember it that way. But no, she knew he had. Because every time she'd kissed another man she'd compared it to that first – and only – kiss with Jules.

Her last meal with the family that trip, a long lunch on the rustic table outside in the kitchen garden, had been a divine bombardment of her senses. The scent of the garden, the garlic, the slow-cooked meats, and the fruity red wine – watered down a little for herself and Giselle – had all filled her soul to the brim with happiness. She and Jules had stolen secret looks across the table and she knew that it was his ankle that found hers and stayed connected through the duration of the lunch.

But the next morning had dawned with a thunderstorm and the grey clouds and rain didn't let up. Because of the rain, they'd not used the horse and cart that she'd been brought to the farmhouse in and she'd had a rare ride in a car to get to the village square with her bags and, while everyone else was rushing to get aboard the coach before they got too wet, she hung back and said a long farewell to Giselle, looking hard towards the café-bar on the edge of the square where she knew Jules was working that morning.

At the last moment he'd stepped out onto the pavement and stood in the rain to wave to her. She had smiled and waved back and, eventually, climbed aboard the coach. The driver had to go right around the square and back past the café-bar to get onto the road north out of town, and Jules stood there in the rain the whole time. As the coach drew past him Esther saw that he was drenched, his long, floppy hair wet and stuck to his soaking face. But she wondered if he was crying too, as she was. She'd always liked to remember it that way – the boy who'd cried when she left him.

Esther shook herself back to the present and drained the coffee cup. She had work to do. Always. She really should be getting back to her desk. But this spot, in this window seat, with her coffee, was one place she often chose to take a break from the day, the people, the phone calls. And the phone was ringing off the hook today.

The new Condor Vitesse high-speed catamaran ferry service between Weymouth, Saint-Malo, and the Channel Islands was proving very popular and various business developers, seamen, and frequent cross-Channel ferry customers were all keen to push for a similar service between Poole and Cherbourg. Esther's job, as the resident fluent French speaker, had been to speak with all kinds of interested parties on both sides of the Channel and form a business plan for the best option. With the upcoming summer season about to kick off, everyone was keen for something to get off the ground sooner rather than later – especially those who travelled frequently into Normandy for business. The Channel Tunnel had been operating for four years now, but with the extra time it took to travel by train from Dorset and into London to catch it, the journey to Paris could take five hours or more, with changeovers.

With the high-speed catamaran to Cherbourg travelling the distance in only two and a quarter hours, and a further train on to Paris, the travel time was similar, but the flexibility of being able to break the journey in Normandy was what excited Dorset businesspeople. At the moment, their only option for that trip was on the cross-Channel ferry, *Barfleur*, which took more than twice that time.

Esther had travelled to meet Giselle that first time on the *Barfleur*, and would always remember the excitement of the trip. As soon as she'd been allowed off the coach, Esther raced up to the deck so she could watch the harbour pass by beneath them as they made their way out past Brownsea Island and through the harbour entrance. For Esther, who'd grown up sailing these waters on weekends, it was fascinating to see it all from such a height that the *Barfleur* allowed. She moved from one side of the ferry to the other, getting a good look at all the views, and remembered in the nick of time to look at the people waving from the Haven Hotel at the harbour entrance. Yes, there was her mum, stood in front of their red Renault, waving with both arms and enthusiasm enough to warm anyone's heart. Esther smiled to herself and sent back her own two-armed wave, hoping her mum would be able to pick her out from all the other kids waving. Even then as a young girl of sixteen, Esther had been worried about leaving her mum alone for a week. She'd have Grandad, of course, but ever since her dad had left them when she was just four years old, Esther and Lucy Holt had become so close, by necessity. All they had was each other and Lucy needed Esther as much as Esther needed her mum.

It had been Mum who'd encouraged Esther with her French, right back then when she was not even at school. Lucy had taken Esther to a pre-school French club, and helped her all the way through school, encouraging her finally to study French and Business at Royal Holloway in London, which had led her to this job at the Dorset Chamber of Commerce as a translator.

The town of Poole had been twinned with Cherbourg since

1977, and Esther had been working closely with the twinning association, making connections between the group and businesses on both sides of the Channel.

By the time she'd started university, all direct contact with Jules was over. For the first few months after her trip, they wrote to each other every couple of weeks, and into the next year they began to wait until there was real news of changes in their lives. Esther was excited to hear of all the adventures Jules had when he moved away to Paris, but within a year of him starting his degree, a period of three months went by, and she hadn't heard a reply to her last letter. She wrote again, wondering if it had been lost in the mail, but still no reply came. All this time, Esther kept up her correspondence with Giselle and tried to ask discreet questions that might help her understand why he had stopped writing.

'*My brother is too busy with all the women of Paris to write to his family,*' Giselle had written as a side note once, complaining about his lack of interest in the farm. The blunt truth, delivered so innocently by Giselle, had dug into her young and impressionable heart like an ice-cold dagger. He had moved on. Jules had forgotten her. She had probably always been too young for him and was just imagining that he even liked her at all. He probably kissed every girl that way.

Over the years she had been to Cherbourg several times, as well as some of the other smaller towns in Normandy, many of them also twinned with villages in Dorset, and many times she'd extended her trips to go back to visit Giselle, and the family. She'd come to love the town of Sainte-Mère-Église, and the Joubert family. But for reasons she wasn't keen to explore, Jules had always stayed in Paris whenever she visited. He was working in a large corporation, so the family told her, and rarely had time to visit them.

She had seen him once, at Giselle's wedding to Hugo, when Jules had brought his latest Parisienne glamorous girlfriend as a date, and he hadn't made eye contact with Esther once.

There'd been half a dozen different men in Esther's life, and even one who wanted to marry her. But she used her career as an excuse to say no – she wasn't ready to be tied down, and couldn't see herself as a mother anyway.

Watching her own mum bring her up alone, with no help from her dad, had turned her off any ideas of having children. Her dad had left them and disappeared to America with a young woman he'd met at work, without a care for the woman and child who had to cope without him. Parenthood was a mug's game, as far as she could tell. She liked the company of a man, and the fun side of a relationship, but she would probably never marry and certainly wouldn't have children.

Now, the closest thing she had to a permanent relationship with a man – unless she counted Archie, her cat – was with the Mayor of Cherbourg, who had chosen this moment to ring her.

'Esther, *ma chérie,*' he cried, as he did every time she answered the work telephone to him. 'When are you coming over to see us again, eh? We have some new projects to share with you. And I haven't had lunch with you for months! Come and see us – stay a while!' he crooned, and though she knew he meant nothing untoward, as he dearly loved his wife and children, it almost sounded as if he was trying to entice her into a seduction.

Today, as she listened to the beautiful Norman accent of Monsieur le Maire, and looked out at the rain, she thought about the weekend ahead of her with nothing but grocery shopping and housework to do. She wondered if it was, in fact, time she took a holiday. She could go and stay in a gîte, eat too many crêpes, and perhaps stay in Paris for a few days. And of course, she would go and visit Giselle and her family, who all lived on the farm in Sainte-Mère-Église. There was a new baby she'd not met yet, after all, and the christening was coming up soon.

That evening, Esther poured herself a glass of wine and sat at the kitchen table to write a note to Giselle. Archie jumped up onto her lap and demanded that she stroke his back for a while until he curled up and settled to sleep there, purring like a baby, and keeping her lap warm like a blanket. Esther started her letter in the usual way. She asked Giselle how baby Julien was doing, and if little Elodie was being a good big sister. Was the date of the christening still set for the middle of May, and might it be alright if she came for a visit? She finished with a little wrap-up on the business meetings she needed to attend in Cherbourg and around Normandy but let Giselle know she could spare a week in Sainte-Mère-Église, if it suited the family.

Esther put down her pen and realised now how much she hoped that it would suit them. A visit to that idyllic farmhouse was just what she needed.

# 3

PARIS, 1940

Marie-Claire screamed and fell to the ground, cradling Benjamin's head in her arms and resting her hand on his bleeding chest, trying to stop the flow of blood that seemed to be pouring out of him like a flood. Chaos had broken out around them, and people ran in all directions panicking, once they'd heard the shot.

'You murderer! You've killed him!' she shrieked up at the stony face of the German soldier who was calmly replacing his revolver in its dark tan leather holster. He pointed to the front of the station.

'*Alle Juden melden sich an der Kasse*. All Jews to ticket office!' he repeated, and walked on.

Marie-Claire turned back to Benjamin, whose face had turned grey. His eyes were closed. The blood from the wound in his chest had now spread all over the marble-tiled floor of the station, and she heard the cries of Juliette and Philippe behind her as if in a dream. She turned slowly towards them and saw they were beckoning and calling her to board the train, but she was frozen, petrified, and unable even to make her thoughts connect to what was happening around her. The train was moving, and she was still kneeling on the floor cradling Benjamin's head. They screamed her name again and at the last moment she saw the face of Antoine at the window which woke her from her nightmare.

She stood and started to move towards the train but before she reached the door of the now moving carriage, she was grabbed back by strong hands.

'*Alle Juden melden sich an der Kasse*. All Jews to ticket office!'

'I am *not* Jewish!' she spat in the man's eyes and he slapped her face so hard that she saw black and heard nothing for several moments. When she opened her eyes and looked toward the train, she saw it disappearing out of the station, with Antoine aboard. Benjamin lay dead at her feet, her son was disappearing from her, and she was held firmly by a German soldier who now threw her to the floor. One more time, before he stomped away, he yelled his instruction.

'*Alle Juden melden sich an der Kasse*. All Jews to ticket office!'

Marie-Claire knelt on the floor and watched in horror as her stomach emptied, mixing with the blood of her husband. She sobbed into his chest and waited until the noise around her subsided a little.

Looking up she saw the train had fully left the station, the soldiers were all congregating around the ticket office, and there were hardly any passengers left on the platform. She bent and kissed Benjamin on the forehead.

'Goodbye, my love. I must go, and follow Antoine. I love you. I will always love you,' she sobbed and, kissing her fingers, placed them gently on his unresponsive lips.

Marie-Claire stayed seated on the floor for a moment, quietly observing the scene. There was a door out of the station on the side of the platform quite near her. No Germans stood there, as they had all gathered with the sad collection of Jews they'd forced up to the ticket office. There was nobody watching her.

Quickly, and without a sound, she stood and walked briskly to the door on the opposite site of the platform concourse. Once through it, she checked that no one was watching and then, at a run faster than she'd ever run in her life before, she pelted back to their apartment. At the top of the stairs, she reached under the mat for the key that had been left for Madame Bernard, and let herself in, locking the door behind her and falling to the floor where she rested her head on her knees and cried like a wounded animal.

Marie-Claire shook with fear, and shock, and outrage. Her entire world was gone – Antoine steaming away from her to the south coast, and hopefully towards safety, but Benjamin gone from her life forever, stolen from her by one bullet from a soldier who wasn't paid to listen. Wasn't expected to be human. Simply carried out the expectations of a machine that was on a path to world dominance at the expense of real people like Benjamin. Her only comfort in this dreadful moment was that Antoine was safe. He was with Philippe and Juliette who loved him and would protect him with their lives. He had identity papers which showed that his mother was Catholic, not Jewish. They were taking him to the safety of her distant relatives in Saint-Christophe. There were clothes for him, and some food for the journey in the bags that were now on board with him.

An hour later, Marie-Claire was still lying just inside the door, curled up tight, and beginning to drift into something like a sleep. Minette had curled up beside her, purring and sharing her warmth in the now cold and very dark apartment. The flood of tears had eased to an occasional trickle, and the blood on her hands and face had mingled with her tears and dried. Though her body was numb, she tried to make her mind think.

She had to leave. She had to find a way to get south and catch up with Antoine. But getting out by train on a route to the south now looked impossible. She could not go back to the Gare de Lyon and risk being caught up in that fiasco again, or worse, recognised by her husband's murderer. Her own identity papers that were safely stowed in the small shoulder bag that she was still wearing across her body showed that she was French, hailing from Fontainebleau, but they linked her by marriage to Benjamin whose identity, if anybody cared to look it up now that he was dead, showed that he was half Jewish. She opened the bag now to check what else was there.

With a rush of relief that belied the enormity of what else she had lost on this night, Marie-Claire pulled out the little journal of recipes that she had been building for the last few years. She opened it to the last page, where she'd written her latest creation and described the expression that she'd seen on Benjamin's face when he'd tasted the meal. Silent tears rolled down her face again and she laid the journal on the mat beside her. Her identity papers were safe, and there was a little loose change in her purse along with half their meagre savings; the other half was inside Bemjamin's jacket pocket. She realised at that moment that whatever they had done with her husband's body, they would have been sure to ransack his pockets first.

There was also a small photograph of her with Benjamin and Antoine. But her selection of better clothes, spare shoes and basic toiletries were all on the train with Antoine.

A few months earlier, during the summer when the Germans had first invaded Paris, the exodus of those trying to get out was like something from the Bible. Hundreds of thousands had left, some driving and sitting in traffic jams until their fuel eventually ran out, others starting on foot. They'd scattered as far as they could, many getting away into Normandy, or to the west and south. But wherever they'd gone there had been limited food, no accommodation. Even water was scarce. Some had camped out as best they could, the rich surviving on huge amounts of cash that still had value to those outside of Paris at that stage.

Over time, many families had gradually dribbled back into Paris. News had reached them that it wasn't so bad, things were going on as normal for the most part. There was work, and food, and their homes were waiting for them. And life had begun to feel almost normal – except for the presence of a multitude of German soldiers and the dreaded swastika flag hanging all over Paris.

If she was going to get out, she had to do it without bringing any attention to herself. On foot, she might be too conspicuous, and it was undoubtedly dangerous as a lone woman. But what choice did she have? The plan formed quickly, and she stood and moved around the apartment nimbly, packing a small holdall with a sorry assortment of her old clothes. She found a few biscuits and a small piece of sausage left over from dinner and wrapped these in a cloth together with the last hunk of bread and a couple of apples.

The idea of going back to the Gare de Lyon was out of the question, and it was highly unlikely that any other trains would be going south from there tonight after the disturbance there earlier. She had to get out of the city fast and into the country-side on the south, where there would be, she hoped, less of a German presence, as soon as possible. She decided to use *le metro* to get as far south as possible, and work it out from there, even if she had to walk a great distance. Or all the way.

Marie-Claire checked her bag again. It must be light enough for her to carry without a struggle, as she might be walking for miles before she could get on another train or hitch a lift. But she wondered now if she could manage to add the old recipe book that she'd initially left behind. It had always been a font of such deep knowledge when she'd been playing with ideas and this book seemed to offer a sense of security, and a link to her real life – instead of this dreadful new reality she was now living. She dropped it into the holdall.

Marie-Claire bent and scooped up the cat for her second farewell of the evening and for a fleeting moment considered putting Minette into her bag, so she'd at least have one member of her family with her. She scoffed at the stupidity of the idea.

'I will always miss you, my sweet,' she whispered into Minette's deep fur. 'Perhaps you will follow me, *non?*' she said, then put the cat down and, with what she knew must be her very last look at this place, went back outside, locked the door and tucked the key under the mat again.

The night was even colder now, but thankfully there were even fewer people around and no soldiers on the street corner any more. She walked in the opposite direction to what they'd taken earlier, this time heading for *le metro* station at Nation, where she would take the line south towards Porte de Charenton. It was only a few stops but was further from the centre of the city and on the way south, at least. From there she would simply start walking towards Lyon, and hopefully either catch a train or hitch a ride at some stage.

At the Nation metro station, Marie-Claire trotted down the stairs into the underground world without a look over her shoulder to farewell her Paris home. All seemed quiet on the street with just a few people out and no sign of soldiers.

She stepped onto the platform to wait for the southbound train and was horrified to see a half dozen or so soldiers in the now all too familiar grey uniform of the *Wehrmacht* all huddled together, laughing at something. One of them turned to look at her and the terror went through her body like a rush of ice water and for a second it froze her feet to the floor. Her mind was filled with the image of Benjamin lying dead on the platform, while that harsh grey uniform had hovered near, the shiny black boots just inches from Benjamin's body, and the brass buttons reflecting the station lights. This appearance of six copies of the same uniform was unbearable. In a heartbeat, and without thinking what she was doing, she turned around and went back across to the northbound platform, where a train was just pulling into the station, her heart racing with fear that she would feel the soldier's hand on her shoulder at any moment.

Marie-Claire stepped aboard, took a seat in a quiet part of the carriage and took out her journal, hiding her face in it. The train set off – in the opposite direction from where she wanted to travel. She saw the group of soldiers, still where she'd seen them on the other platform. None of them had followed.

Marie-Claire, now coming to her senses, groaned. She was going to have to find a way to act as though she didn't care about their presence, these soldiers who now represented so much pain for her. This was all going to be harder than she'd imagined. She kept her head down for two stops and glanced up to see that the train had reached the Gare de Lyon metro stop. Somewhere above her the body of her husband was probably still lying, unceremoniously pulled to one side of the station, possibly covered over by a tarpaulin, until he could be collected. And dumped. Probably burned.

A small, rebellious tear escaped, and she wiped it away at once, sniffing and setting her face like stone. She could not let anyone notice her. She remained still and refused to look up at any other passengers, or to notice the names of the stations she was passing, trying to remember to turn the pages of her book from time to time so that she looked as though she was reading.

She could not think what to do next. She should get off this underground train and try to get south. But the exhaustion of shock washed over her and she couldn't move. Couldn't think. Instead, as she sat on this train that was racing her in the opposite direction from where she wanted to be, her mind was showing her a film of her life with Benjamin, their meeting in the summer of 1935, their marriage here in Paris, and the birth of Antoine. The days they had spent together walking, playing, eating. That time each night that he came home from work and showered her and Antoine with his deep love. The details of a life that was over.

The train had stopped. The passengers had all left. The doors remained opened. Marie-Claire realised she had come to the end of the line. She picked up her bag and walked up to the outside world. She was at the Pont de Neuilly station, on the far north-western side of Paris – in exactly the opposite direction from where she wanted to be.

Marie-Claire looked around her, lost for inspiration on what to do next. The exhaustion made her feel as though she were dropping into a kind of coma, and she just wanted to lie down and sleep. Marie-Claire fought with herself to keep going. She had to get out of Paris – far out of Paris – if she was ever going to get to Antoine. She walked until she reached an overground train station and looked at the map on the wall for routes. There would usually have been several trains south, to Dijon, Montpellier, even Monaco, ultimately, but these had all been cancelled.

There was still one train due into the station that night, arriving in the next half hour, headed north-west to Caen. This was so far in the opposite direction to Antoine that she wanted to weep. But her only other option was to take *le metro* back to the southern side of Paris again, and hope to get out that way. And if all trains south were being cancelled from here, they were more than likely cancelled everywhere. Marie-Claire wondered now if it might be easier to get south from somewhere else – some-where other than Paris. Perhaps heading north-west and away from Paris was a better choice.

She approached the ticket office. Was there a train from Caen to the south? There was, daily, the ticket officer told her. The next one would leave Caen in the morning, headed for Montpel-lier. She bought a ticket to Caen and waited to board the train. The ticket master spoke kindly to her, indicating the small café on the edge of the station.

'*Avez-vous faim, madame? Peut-être un petit café ou de la soupe?*' Yes, she realised now. She was hungry, and yes, hot coffee and a bowl of soup would fill her.

'*Merci beaucoup, Monsieur,*' she said, paying for her order and sitting in a corner to hide. As she sat and put her face in her hands she realised now how weak she felt. She had only been travelling for a couple of hours, but the weather was bitterly cold and it was taking all her effort to keep going, already.

The last meal she'd eaten had been a happy though nervous one with both Benjamin and Antoine. Marie-Claire whimpered quietly, remembering the scene, and wiped the tears away fast so she wouldn't be seen. Since that simple meal, her world had become this nightmare. The turmoil of grief and pain in her heart was almost overwhelming, and so why was her body thinking of food at such a time? Antoine. Because of Antoine. She had to stay strong, follow him south, and find him. He was her only reason for living now. Thank God he was with Juliette and Philippe. They could understand his childish garble. They knew that he didn't like to drink cold milk, but adored it warm. They'd understand how to hold him close and keep him warm and safe. And they even knew the address of her relatives in Saint-Christophe where the Dubois family had been headed. He would be fine with them.

Marie-Claire ate the soup and drank the coffee fast. The warmth of the food was good for her, and she began to feel her blood revive a little. The soup had been served with two small bread rolls. She buttered them both, and then wrapped them in the napkin, and, checking that she wasn't seen, tucked them into her pocket. She would need them later.

The engine let off steam as the train pulled in, and the stationmaster blew his whistle and called the destinations along the route.

Marie-Claire boarded the train and, leaving Paris firmly behind her, thought only of Antoine as she settled into a quiet corner and formed her coat into a pillow to sleep against the window. The train pulled out of the station, headed west towards Caen, Normandy, her first stop on this reimagined route south.

# 4

POOLE, MAY 1998

Just as April had been true to the expectation of 'April showers', it seemed that May was determined to live up to its standard as the start of summer. Warmer days, longer evenings, and a shock of colourful blooms in every garden gave the clear sign that the long winter, and often dismal spring, were at an end. As Esther walked up her garden path on the evening of the last Friday before her break, she stopped to run a hand through the wisteria that bloomed like bunches of grapes along the wall, and to enjoy the tulips and late bluebells that still blossomed. Her home was small, and modern, in the new development close to the harbour shore in Poole, but Esther had filled the tiny gardens with all the best of the English cottage garden flowers she could fit in.

Esther was going to be away for three weeks altogether, the first week not a holiday but a business trip, the next week in Sainte-Mère-Église for the christening and time with the Joubert family, and one last week she was leaving open for whatever adventure she felt like – perhaps some time in Paris. The big bonus was having the Chamber of Commerce pay for her ferry fare from Poole to Cherbourg and back on the *Barfleur*.

That night, full of the senses of summer, and excited to revisit the part of France she loved the most, Esther packed her bag with a pretty dress for the christening, one that she'd bought especially. She'd been thrilled by Giselle's excitement that she would be there and very touched that she'd even been asked to be godmother to baby Julien. Esther packed plenty of summer frocks, shorts, T-shirts, and strappy tops, as well as the light business suits she would need for her meetings. But she was a realist. So there were jeans and sweatshirts too. The weather might give her just about anything but snow in the next three weeks. Almost as an afterthought, she added in a couple of dressy outfits that would do for dinner in Paris, in case she got that far.

Early the next morning, as she waited in line to drive her car aboard the ferry, Esther plugged her new mobile phone into the car to save the battery, and called her mum.

'Hi Esther love, how's it all going?' Lucy Holt said as soon as she heard her daughter's voice.

'Good! Exciting. Lots to get through in the first week, but these French business meetings are nothing like the boring English ones,' she laughed. 'Long lunches, lots of drinks, and a whole lot of talking before we get down to discussing a few tiny details of business. It's all about the networking really, which is why they love me going over there,' Esther explained.

'And you're going to visit Giselle – and what is her husband's name?'

'Hugo – she married one of her brother's good friends from school.'

'Oh, that's right, I remember now she had a brother – he looked after you well when you visited, didn't he? What's he doing now? Married too, I suppose?' asked Lucy, in all innocence.

'To be honest, I don't know, Mum. He went away to Paris to

university, and I don't think he went back to live on the farm again after that. I've only seen him once since then, at Giselle's wedding. I haven't heard he's married but he might well be. I don't expect to see him. But Giselle's old *grand-mère* is still alive. She was getting on a bit even when I first met her back in 1985,' said Esther.

'Steady on, love, you probably thought *I* was getting on a bit in 1985, and I'm still here,' Lucy laughed. 'The French diet and all that good-quality milk you told me about has probably kept her hale and hearty.'

'Well, I will find out very soon and let you know, Mum. Listen, the cars are beginning to move ahead of me, so I'll have to go soon. Mrs Lindfield from next door is going to feed Archie for me, but if you could pop in and water the plants once and run the hose over the garden if it's dry while I'm gone, that would be great, please,' asked Esther.

'No problem, my love. Have a wonderful time, and drive safe,' said Lucy as they both rang off and Esther drove onto the ferry.

As she manoeuvred aboard and got herself settled for the trip, her mind was taken back to when she first met Giselle's grandmother. She had seemed very elderly to Giselle at the time, but thinking on what her mum said now, she was probably right. *Grand-mère* probably wasn't even seventy years old when Esther first met her.

She would always sit at a little table just in front of the farm-house, near the farm gate, and sell milk to the villagers. They would come with their bottles and churns and she'd pour out the milk for them from a big churn that they kept aside from the main pasteurising unit. The half-dozen or so cows were all milked by Giselle's parents and a couple of farmhands who lived with them, and the townsfolk preferred the unpasteurised Joubert farm milk to any they could buy at the *supermarché*. But they seemed to come for more than that. They would buy their milk but then sit and drink coffee and talk with *Grand-mère* for ages, huddled together as though they were sharing mysterious secrets.

Esther had grown fond of the older woman, but as a teenager she'd found it hard to understand her thick, rural accent, so they'd rarely spoken. Over the years since, on Esther's later visits when her French had improved, they'd talked more. But since old Monsieur Joubert had died, five or so years ago, *Grand-mère* had become much more reserved.

On her last trip over, Esther had found an ancient recipe book, and pressed between its pages was a handwritten sheet, on which was written in a loopy old-fashioned hand a recipe for preserving wild garlic, complete with wonderful descriptions of the woods behind the farmhouse where the wild garlic grew. When Esther turned the page over, she saw that on the other side was a poem, written in French and then translated into English. Esther'd kept it and taken it home with her. Once she had it at home she noticed a tiny note, written in such small script that, at first, she thought it was just a scribble. She'd had to take out a magnifying glass to check it. It was written in English, and some words were too hard to read, but from what she could make out it read:

*G – you restarted my heart, restored my soul, came back to die and live a moment long enough to save my love for me. I will never forget you. M-C*

She'd had it for three years and now Esther wondered if she'd taken a treasure that should be returned. So she'd packed it and hoped to find a chance to talk to *Grand-mère*. Even if the poem was just a way to open a conversation and find out more about the old lady, it would be worthwhile bringing it up. And she would love to know what that message meant, and whom it was written for.

The week in and around Cherbourg and some of the other towns of Normandy went just as she'd expected: busy, but happy – lots of food and laughter, and a good chance to immerse herself in speaking French again all the time. It was so easy to grow rusty when she didn't get much opportunity at home, but here she insisted that all her business counterparts talked to her in French to help her stretch and strengthen her linguistic muscles again.

By the end of the week she felt as if she was a part of the close family in which Monsieur le Maire lived. He had insisted on allowing her to stay in the little gîte on his property, but eat with the family whenever possible. His kind and thoughtful wife had made her feel at home, and the children were all calling her *tata Esther*, they felt so close to her.

When she drove off on her adventure a little further south to visit Giselle in Sainte-Mère-Église, Esther was almost regretting it and wondered if she should have stayed where she was. But it would be good to see Giselle, and all the family again, though she was frustrated with herself that she still always wondered if she would see Jules there. *Ridiculous*, she chastised herself, for thinking that way about an insignificant moment with a boy who probably didn't even remember she existed after all this time. When she thought about it, he probably hadn't spoken to her at Giselle's wedding because he didn't even remember meeting her before.

When she arrived in the town centre of Sainte-Mère-Église,

Esther was thrilled to see that nothing seemed to have changed since her last visit. The place seemed stuck in a wonderful time warp. The café-bar on the corner had been painted and was a brighter shade of green than it had been last time, but the chestnut trees still grew in the churchyard, the aroma of coffee was still strong, and 'Big Jim' still hung from the church clock tower.

She had learned all about the effigy of a paratrooper that hung from the church tower on her first visit in 1985. Apparently, during the D-Day landings, a paratrooper's parachute had caught on the tower and he'd hung there for hours. Everyone thought he was dead, but it had turned out he was just playing dead so he wouldn't be shot. His history had been recorded along with all the other details of how this little town had been the first to be liberated after the D-Day landings, and much had been made of his few hours hanging up there. He'd been known as 'Big Jim' ever since.

Esther parked and walked into the café-bar to get a cup of delicious French coffee before driving off to the farmhouse, as she'd arrived a little early for the lunch Giselle had invited her to.

The bell tinkled on the door as she walked in, and she saw, stooped behind the counter, the shape of a boy with long, floppy dark hair that fell over his eyes. He wore a black apron and for a moment her heart stopped, and she wondered if she'd somehow time-travelled here, back to 1985 when she'd first met Jules. On hearing the bell, the boy stood up, and she saw how very different he looked to Jules. Of course it was not him. Jules was a grown man of thirty now, living in the city, probably in a high-powered business role. He couldn't possibly still be working in this little café-bar. It must have been the sight of the church that made her think of him but, she told herself firmly now, this kind of reminiscing had to stop. She was not here to see Jules, but Giselle, and to have a delightful holiday in the country, become a godmother to Julien, and take a good rest from work.

'*Bonjour, mademoiselle, que souhaitez-vous commander?*' he asked, and Esther was happy to know that she still looked as young as an unmarried 'Miss' when most friends her age were well and truly married with children by this time. She looked over the delectable sweet treats in the counter and ordered a café-au-lait and a Florentine, then went to sit outside at a table on the pavement to enjoy the sunshine.

The boy brought the coffee and Florentine and as she bit into the delicious, sweet crunchiness, licking the stray bits of chocolate that threatened to fall, Esther remembered the first time she'd tasted Madame Joubert's rich hot chocolate. Her first breakfast in the farmhouse had been the delicious hot chocolate made on thick and creamy unpasteurised milk, with fresh hot croissants to dip into the deep bowl of heavenly chocolate. The flavours were divine and the memory had stayed with her all this time. The meal had been repeated each time she'd visited Giselle, *but you always remember your first time*, Esther thought to herself with a secret smile.

She couldn't wait to see all the family again, and once she'd drained her coffee cup, she checked the time and decided it would be okay to arrive now.

Esther was hit by a delightful sense of déjà vu as she drove into the farmyard and pulled to a stop. Stepping out of the car, the country air, the scent of farm life and the sounds of a happy family filled her senses. The front door opened, releasing a whole gaggle of smiling Joubert family members, Giselle leading the way with her arms outstretched.

'Esther, *bienvenue à la maison!*' she cried, and Esther was warmed to her soul to hear Giselle call this place, so full of happy memories from over the years, her 'home'.

'Oh, it is so good to see you, Giselle, and don't you look marvellous!' said Esther, giving Giselle a tight hug and then pulling back to look at her properly. 'Motherhood suits you!'

'Motherhood has made me plump, you mean, but yes, I am very happy. Come, meet the little ones,' Giselle said and there stood Hugo, holding in his arms Julien, only a few months old, with Elodie, suddenly shy of the visitor, hiding behind her daddy's legs. Elodie had only been a baby herself the last time Esther was here, and now she was a beautiful little girl, with long, dark hair, and sparkling eyes.

'It has been too long. I really should have come to see you sooner,' Esther said, going forward to greet Madame *et* Monsieur Joubert.

And there, sitting at the little table outside the front of the farmhouse was *Grand-mère*, who barely looked any older than she had done thirteen years ago, the very first time Esther had met her. She never aged. She was a little more stooped, and her hair was finer, and perhaps she'd lost some of her plumpness, but otherwise it was as if time had stood still. Esther went over to greet her, bending to give the old lady a kiss.

'Welcome back, Esther *chèrie*, it is so good to see you. Perhaps with Giselle so busy with the children, and Jules away, you and I will have more chance to get to know each other this time?'

'I would like that very much, *Grand-mère*, and I can't wait to taste some of that beautiful, creamy milk. Do you still sell it to the villagers here?' Esther asked, grateful that she now spoke such fluent French, and understood the Norman accent so well, that language was no barrier any more.

'Many of the old ones have gone on now, but yes, I still have a lot of customers. But my old friends who came to talk with me?

Not so much any more,' she said with a sad smile. Esther squeezed her hand and helped the old lady stand so she could come inside where Madame Joubert was finishing the preparations for a grand lunch they were all to eat outside in the garden.

\* \* \*

By the time Esther fell into the deep, soft mattress of her bed that night – in the room that was perfectly unchanged in the whole thirteen years since she had first stayed here – she felt full to the top of her heart. The company had been warm and welcoming, the food divine, the children delightful and the Joubert family had truly made her feel that she'd come home. Over lunch, they'd caught up on the news that had been missed out in letters through the last three years, and Giselle had reeled off the names of all the wider family who would be coming to the christening the next day.

'Will Jules be here?' Esther asked, kicking herself for even being interested. But no, Giselle assured her, while he was of course invited, he was far too busy to leave Paris these days. They would probably see him next at Christmas.

'We did ask him to be godfather, but instead Hugo's brother will take that place, as he did for Elodie. But, we are all so thrilled that you are here to be godmother to Julien.'

'Thank you, Giselle, it really is such an honour to be asked. You do know that I'm not terribly religious?' Esther asked, suddenly wondering if this mattered.

'Ah, puh!' Giselle said with a wave of her hand. 'It is not about religion. It is about family. You are a special auntie to him, this is what matters,' she said.

As Esther drifted into the deepest sleep she'd had in months, she dreamed of sunshine and butterflies in the kitchen garden, laughter, family – even by special adoption, and of the rich, creamy hot chocolate she'd been promised for breakfast in the morning on the day of the christening. And she thanked her lucky stars that she wouldn't have to face what could have been an awkward reunion with Jules, and could simply enjoy this holiday with the rest of the family.

## 5

### NEAR CAEN, NORMANDY, 1940

Marie-Claire cuddled little Antoine tight, smelling his hair and kissing him gently on the cheeks so as not to wake him. She whispered his name and sensed Benjamin nearby, drawing her out of the world where only she and Antoine existed together.

'*Réveillez-vous,*' he said quietly. '*Il est temps de se réveiller maintenant,*' he repeated gently, urging her that it was time to wake up. And then he cleared his throat and spoke with more authority.

'*Mademoiselle, réveillez-vous,*' he said and shook her by the shoulder. Marie-Claire's eyes shot open and she started, fearing she would drop the baby. But it was not Antoine she held in her arms. It was her coat. And this man who spoke to her now was not her husband, but a stranger on the train.

The dawn of this new reality slashed open the wounds already created many hours earlier and her face began to crumple as she almost succumbed to the grief again. But she covered her face with her hands and fought for control. She had to go on. This was the only way.

'I'm sorry, I must have fallen asleep,' she said, rubbing her face dry from the tears that had begun to flow again, and then she looked around her. The train had come to a stop but not at a station. Outside was in pitch darkness.

'Where are we?' she asked the stranger.

'The train needed to stop before reaching Caen. There is a problem with the track. They are bringing a bus for us, but we need to get off the train now,' he said and offered to help her up.

'I'm fine, thank you, I can manage,' said Marie-Claire as she picked up her bag and headed down the corridor to the train door.

Outside was utterly dark but a bus was slowing a little way along the tracks and soon passengers began to board.

'Where exactly are we?' she asked the young man who still walked beside her.

'I think we are near Canon – much closer to Caen than Paris, but a little to the south,' he said.

'South? So Caen is to the north of us here?' she asked, stopping in her tracks and looking back in the direction from which she'd just come.

'Yes, that's right. But you were on a journey to Caen, *non*?' he asked her. 'We must hurry, or the bus may become full before we reach it. Then we will have a cold wait for another,' he said, urging her along with a hand at the small of the back.

'No! I want to travel south from here, not north into Caen. Is there a village nearby?' she asked him, and he shrugged.

'I do not know the area, but we can ask. Come – let's get to the bus first,' he said, and she held back, not wanting to take a single step further away from Antoine than she had already come. He regarded her quizzically, and was about to speak again, but at once Marie-Claire realised how ungrateful she had been to this gentleman who was doing his best to help her. If he'd not woken her, she'd have stayed on the train, and might well have ended up back in Paris.

'I'm so sorry – I've been rude. Thank you for helping me. I'm Marie-Claire Dubois,' she said, and held out her gloved hand.

'Pleased to meet you, Mademoiselle Dubois,' he said, and Marie-Claire was about to correct him as she was a married woman. But her wedding ring was hidden under her glove, and she wondered at the point of explaining that now. After all, she was no longer a wife. She was a widow. The word galled her to even think it, and a fresh wave of grief and anger threatened to overwhelm her.

'My name is Jean-Baptiste. Let me help you, Marie-Claire,' he said and signalled to the bus again. They walked that way, and it was clear that the bus was full to overflowing already. He leant in and spoke to the driver, then came back out to Marie-Claire and the few passengers who were left.

'There will be another bus within the hour, but it is going straight into Caen,' he explained to everyone waiting. 'Those of you who need to reach Caen might like to take shelter in that barn there. The wind is too cold to wait out here,' he said, and all the other passengers walked that way.

'Marie-Claire, there will be no way to travel south from here tonight. What do you want to do?' he asked, and she looked about her in despair.

'Perhaps there is a house, or an inn at a village nearby that I could spend the night, and then set off in the morning?' she wondered. 'Look, there are lights that way – somebody is awake there, at least,' she said, then checked her watch. It was past midnight.

'You cannot simply walk out in the dark night towards a light, alone, Marie-Claire. Let me come with you. I am in no hurry to reach Caen in particular. My journey is headed north, but I have no deadline,' he said. She hesitated and looked towards the lights again, trying to gauge the distance. It was impossible to tell. Marie-Claire looked from the lights to the stopped train, and watched the crammed bus disappearing into the distance. She looked up again into the face of this stranger who regarded her with a steady gaze. His eyes were locked on hers and something in their depth said to her, *It's okay. I've got you. You're safe with me.* She took a deep breath and chose to trust him.

'If you are to come with me, Monsieur, at least let me share some food.' She took out the sausage and bread from her bag. He had a knife in his pocket and cut the sausage in half, giving a piece back to her as she tore the bread in two and gave him half of that. They ate in silence as if they were sharing a form of communion meal. Something about it held the importance of a ritual: a covenant. He would care for her, and she would trust him, she knew. They turned and began the walk across the fields towards the light.

They crossed three fields, finding their way along hedges until they came across gates or places where they could climb over the stone walls or stiles. The fields were bare and muddy, and occasionally they slipped a little on frozen puddles. Jean-Baptiste had quick reflexes and would reach out to catch her arm and stop her from stumbling almost before she knew she'd begun to slip. Marie-Claire was glad to be moving. The night was cold, and they had no protection from the wind that blew across the plains here. The idea of warmth that was promised by the lights ahead kept her moving. That, and the possibility of finding a way south to catch up to Antoine.

They reached the end of the fourth field and crossed a wall onto a narrow road. Opposite them were two enormous iron gates, decorated with an intricate pattern of swirls on the top. The gates were affixed to tall sandstone pillars, and the iron fence ran away to the right into the black night. To the left of the gates stood a small stone gate lodge, in total darkness. The lights were coming from ahead, presumably at the main château they had reached.

'Not quite the village inn you were expecting?' asked Jean-Baptiste with a raised eyebrow.

'Not quite. But there are lights, and people – presumably humans, not Nazi soldiers,' she spat, revealing more than she'd meant to about her reasons for being on this road, this night.

'They haven't come this far west yet – at least not in their hordes, and only in the cities is there an obvious presence. We should be safe here,' he encouraged her, and she wondered how he could feel so confident. He couldn't have seen anyone shot dead with no good reason, as she had, only hours earlier.

Jean-Baptiste found a small gate to a footpath beside the large carriage gates and stepped through, closing it quietly after Marie-Claire followed so as not to awaken the lodge keeper, if there was one. The walk up the gravelled drive must have been nearly another half a mile, and they found their way to the servants' entrance on the side of what must be a magnificent two- or three-storey building in the daylight. It was huge, and had dozens of arched windows on all sides. A fountain in a large basin played in front of the château, creating a centrepiece that cars and carriages must drive around.

They stood at the closed side door, bathed in the warm yellow light that shone from inside. Jean-Baptiste knocked on the door and was answered by an immediate exclamation of surprised but hushed voices from inside, the sound of multiple chairs scraping on slate tiles and then a silence. In time, a cautious footstep came to the door, and it opened, slightly ajar. A frowning face peered out into the darkness.

'*Qui est là?*' came the gruff demand.

'Excuse me, we are so sorry to disturb you. We are travellers, and need shelter for the night, if that's alright. We will be on our way again tomorrow,' explained Jean-Baptiste.

There was silence and then hushed whispers.

'How many of you?' asked the voice.

'Just two: myself and a young lady,' he replied, glancing toward Marie-Claire, who for the first time understood the vulnerability she had placed herself in.

The door opened wide, and a large hand was extended towards Jean-Baptiste, followed by hearty laughter that stunned Marie-Claire.

'And where did you manage to find a young lady who would spend the night in the country with you, Jean-Baptiste, eh, you old rascal?'

Marie-Claire's fear then turned to anger as she regarded Jean-Baptiste – the man she'd thought so innocent and kind just moments before – and wondered exactly who he was. He must have seen what she was feeling.

'I'm sorry, Marie-Claire – but it is all okay. I know these people. We are safe here, you see?' he said and opened the door wide to show her inside.

The room was a kitchen, with a vast wooden table around which sat a half dozen or so men and two women. A fire blazed in an enormous, deep hearth, warming the room to a temperature Marie-Claire had begun to wonder if she would ever feel again.

'Come in, my dears, and warm yourselves. There is hot coffee, and something a little stronger for it if you wish,' said the older of the two women.

On the table, at one end, was spread the remnants of a meal: a leg of lamb, a dish of vegetables. Wine glasses and three empty wine bottles. In the centre of the table was a large map, held down by cutlery at the corners and with the salt and pepper shakers positioned at different points.

'All is well, I assume, Jean-Baptiste?' asked the man who had opened the door to them. Jean-Baptiste had taken a seat at the table and was carving himself a lump of meat while one of the men poured him a glass of red wine. He was about to answer when Marie-Claire interrupted, dropping her bag with a thump and holding up one index finger towards him.

'I'm sorry, but all is *not* well. And Jean-Baptiste has some fast talking to do now to explain exactly what is going on, who he is, and why you are all here, because I have been going through the end of my world over the last few hours, and I have used the last shred of any patience I ever had!' She spoke with such authority that every jaw in the room dropped open.

# 6

The morning of the christening dawned as bright and beautiful as only the best of summer's days can. The shutters on the bedroom window had been opened before six o'clock, reminding Esther of her very first visit when she'd discovered there were no drapes to block out the sunlight. Each room had net curtains at the windows, but on the outside of the farmhouse were timber shutters which Monsieur Joubert went around and shut, using a long pole, last thing at night, and he opened them again when it was time for everyone to wake up in the morning.

Monsieur *et* Madame Joubert had already been out to milk the cows early, as usual, and Esther had volunteered to go and collect the hens' eggs, for old time's sake, and had encouraged little Elodie to take her hand and lead the way.

And then it was time for breakfast, where *Grand-mère* was helping to stir the warming milk, and Giselle was feeding the baby in the old rocking chair beside the range. Elodie climbed up and took her place at the table, making a start on a hunk of buttery bread before the hot chocolate arrived. *Grand-mère* was also turning some of the eggs into crêpes, so they had some extra sustenance to see them through the day.

'We got those eggs from up on the ladder, didn't we, Esther?' mumbled Elodie with a mouthful of bread.

'You went up into the hayloft?' asked *Grand-mère* with a look of some alarm.

'Don't worry, *Grand-mère*, I held her very steady. She was determined there were eggs up there, and she was right,' said Esther, anxious to show how much care she'd taken of the little girl.

'Of course you did, Esther. But Elodie, there are all kinds of dangerous tools and things up there. You must never go up on your own, hmm?' *Grand-mère* told the little girl, who nodded meekly in response.

Esther was glad of the warm summery day and went up to her room to dress for the christening in her beautiful new frock. It was made of fine white linen, printed all over with blue delphiniums. The bodice was fitted and shaped, and the skirt full and long, reaching to her calves. The straps were simple ribbons that tied in bows on her shoulders. She did a happy little twirl when she'd put it on then sat on the bed to buckle her strappy silver sandals.

Esther brushed out her long hair and wondered if she should tie it up but decided instead to add a few ringlets with her curling tongs – noting with a chuckle that the farmhouse had been through an upgrade in its electrics and there were now power points in the bedroom. On her first visit the only electricity was for the overhead light in each room. She'd also been amazed to discover, on one of her earlier trips, they'd built a full bathroom at the back of the farmhouse as well. Times had changed since she'd had to wash at the washstand, using just a basin and jug of water that had been heated on the old range in the kitchen.

For fun and for old time's sake, Monsieur Joubert had decorated the old cart with flowers and ribbons, and hitched up the farm horse, to take the family into town. They laughed and talked all the way and Esther felt as if she was in some kind of magical old romance of all that is wonderful about France. There was something so special about being a part of a full and complete family.

Esther knew that these families had always existed, that some people managed to stay happily married forever, but it was so different to her own experience that she'd almost blanked it off as a fairy tale and not possible in real life. Her own experience was living with a mum who was so hurt by the abandonment of her husband, that she'd never recovered. Never loved again. Never let herself get close to anyone who might then have the power to hurt her, leave her. And that had impacted Esther far more than Lucy probably imagined. Esther knew her number one responsibility was to care for her mum, to be there and take care of her. And she felt the generational trauma of that abandonment so strongly, that despite a few dalliances with men, and her early crush on Jules, Esther had never seriously considered committing herself to anyone. Commitment was just too dangerous.

Inside the cool and quiet church, there were already several other friends and family waiting, and after warm and loud greetings, they gathered at the font where the priest began the happy ceremony, naming the baby Julien Jules Hugo Cartier, which Esther felt made him sound like a little prince. She was warmed by the way he'd been given his uncle's name, and loved the way that, though Giselle had not always been so fond of her brother as a teenager, they must have a deep and lasting bond now.

The priest signalled it was time for the godparents to step forward and Esther took her place at the font beside Giselle, reaching out to put her finger into baby Julien's cute little grasp. Behind them, the big church doors clanked open, allowing the strong summer light to stream in and up the aisle to where they all stood, a little blinded by the brightness. Brisk footsteps followed and then the family, one by one, seemed to recognise who had arrived. Esther felt the lifeblood in her heart drop into her feet where the weight seemed to anchor her to the spot, just as her mouth fell inelegantly open in shock. The name on everyone's delighted lips echoed around the cavernous church, multiplying it out of all proportion, and burning Esther's ears. She had never in her life felt as though a shock could cause her to faint, but at this moment she felt positively swoonish.

'Jules!' cried Giselle, one of the last to see him, as she'd been focussed on baby Julien in her arms. 'You made it after all!' she said and, handing the baby into Esther's arms, rushed over to greet her brother with a tight hug and a kiss.

'Ah well, *Grand-mère* reminded me that it really was a very important event, didn't you?' he said, going next to his grandmother to give her a kiss, before greeting his parents. Esther saw now by the satisfied smile on her face that the old lady wasn't a bit surprised that he was here and that she had, in fact, orchestrated his arrival.

'But Hugo's brother, Robert, is standing in for you now, Jules – we arranged it when we knew you weren't coming,' said Giselle, looking a little flustered.

'Ah *non*,' said Robert with a classically French wave of his hands. 'I already 'ave Elodie as my goddaughter. It is only fair that Jules has Julien, eh?' he said with a shrug. 'Come, Jules, take your place 'ere beside the lovely Esther. You will make an excellent pair of godparents together.'

And this was, for Esther, the first time in her life that she realised men could also have a propensity to swoon, as Jules visibly stumbled and the colour drained from his face faster than she knew she was going to drain a very stiff drink, just as soon as she could get hold of one.

# 7

## CHÂTEAU DE CANON, NORMANDY, DECEMBER 1940

Marie-Claire waited for Jean-Baptiste to answer her, folding her arms and frowning at him. She glanced around the others who sat at the table, all looking somewhat sheepish and waiting for him to make the next move.

He paused with a sizeable lump of cold roast lamb hung on the end of a fork, just as he was about to stuff it into his mouth. Letting out a deep breath, he put the fork down and turned back to face Marie-Claire.

'I think you should sit down. Make yourself warm. Eat, drink,' he said, waving an arm over the table, 'and then I will explain.'

Marie-Claire could already feel the lifeblood coming back into her feet, and the smell of good food was divine. She took a seat next to the older woman who poured her some wine and brought a plate of food. Marie-Claire ate a few small mouthfuls and drank a long draught of wine before turning to Jean-Baptiste again, the questions still in her eyes.

'Okay, I will explain, but you understand that the more you know the longer you will be here, yes?'

She nodded, although she had no idea what he meant. Surely, she would be leaving the next morning, even if she had to walk south alone. Between now and morning she had no interest in going back outside into the cold night.

'The train we were on tonight from Paris to Caen – it was always going to stop where it did,' he began.

'Because of the fault on the line?' she asked.

'Not exactly. There was no fault on the line. Not this time. We engineered the stopping of the train as a practice exercise,' he went on.

'Practice for what, exactly? And who is "we"?' she asked, looking around the table again. The group seemed to be made of people of all ages, some younger men, some older, a younger woman and a middle-aged one. They wore workers' clothes, as if they might be the servants and gardeners of this château.

'We have formed a small group who desire to fight the Germans back again. Our government has given up, but General Charles de Gaulle has called to us from England through his messages on the wireless. If enough of us work together, we can fight back. We can at least slow them down and upset their plans,' he explained.

'And what exactly does that have to do with our train this evening?' she asked, not sure if the picture was becoming clearer or murkier by the moment.

'In time, we will need to halt trains to prevent innocent citizens from being killed when we destroy train lines and bridges, roads and checkpoints. We are already establishing a network of people who can infiltrate the infrastructure systems and tonight we successfully halted a train on a perfectly operational railway line.'

'Everything went to plan then, Jean-Baptiste? And the buses?' asked one of the younger men.

'Yes, the buses arrived on cue to take passengers, but Marie-Claire here was not keen to go all the way to Caen. She saw your lights,' he said accusingly, 'from as far away as the railway line, and wanted to come and find your warm and welcoming "inn". We are going to have to work better at blacking out windows. With the winter fully upon us now, there is no foliage on the trees and the view through to the château this way is clear.' There were sounds of acknowledgement and agreement from all sides of the table.

'We cannot be too careful. If we can stay hidden here, we will achieve much, but if they rout us out...' The young man didn't finish his thought, but it was clear from everyone's reactions that this would be disastrous. Marie-Claire now knew, first-hand, exactly how brutal the German soldiers could be if anyone stood up against them.

'So, Marie-Claire, tell us what has brought you to Caen from Paris if you are headed south, hmm?' asked the middle-aged lady who had helped her with food and drink.

Marie-Claire looked around the table and recognised that these well-informed people who were sworn enemies of the German *Wehrmacht* would very likely be able to help her find her way to Antoine, undetected. She took a deep breath and began her story, starting with the fact that Benjamin was half Jewish and needed to leave his school before he was forced out, and get out of Paris fast – a comment that drew whistles of shock from some of the party – and leading up to the moment that the German soldier had shot him dead, and the train had left the station with Antoine aboard.

Saying it out loud now, for the first time, somehow made it more real, more of a concrete moment in time – less of a terrible nightmare that she might wake from – and her tears flowed again in an agony of grief. Her chest heaved and she gasped for breath between sobs as the woman beside her engulfed her in a large and comforting hug against her ample bosom. The company gathered in the kitchen stayed quiet until, at last, Jean-Baptiste spoke again.

'And your son, Antoine, where is he now?'

She sniffed and wiped her eyes on her sleeve. 'He is on the train, with my good friends. He will be safe with them and with my family in the south, but I must get to him,' she said.

'This was the train from Gare de Lyon, to Lyon, and then on to Marseilles?' Jean-Baptiste asked. She nodded.

'We will do what we can tomorrow to find him. But until then, you really must sleep, Marie-Claire. You are exhausted,' he said, and Marie-Claire made no objections when the tender-hearted lady beside her helped her up and led her to a room to spend the night. As the two women left the room, Marie-Claire saw the others gather in more closely around the table and begin a deep but hushed conversation.

Once out of the cosy kitchen, the rest of the great house was quite cold, and she shivered as they walked down corridors lined with portraits of aristocrats from through the ages. The rooms off to the sides were all closed, and any furniture in the corridor was covered in dust cloths.

'Where are the family who own the château?' she asked.

'America. They have money, and they got out early. Saw it coming. Left us all here to "manage things". I think we are doing quite well on our own, so far.' She winked. 'The servants' quarters are cosier and closer to the kitchen, but I'm afraid they're all taken now that Jean-Baptiste is here tonight. You'll have to make do with one of the state rooms,' she said, as she opened a door into the most enormous room Marie-Claire had ever seen.

Madame Le Goff – Adeline – as she had introduced herself on the walk through the halls, went over to the full-height windows and drew the curtains shut before lighting a candle on the small bed stand. Then she removed dust sheets from all the furniture and held the candle to the fireplace, where a fire was set and ready to roar into life. In an instant the room was alive with the flicker of flames on the walls and Marie-Claire saw then that she would be sleeping in a four-poster bed tonight. She felt that she would sleep herself to death as soon as she laid down, and for a moment that was what she wished for until, again, she saw the face of Antoine before her and sensed the scent of his hair. He must be desperate for his *Maman et Papa* by now, she knew.

Adeline must have understood that Marie-Claire had frozen in thought again, and she dropped the folded dust sheets onto a chair in the corner. She came across and gently took the bag from Marie-Claire's hands, placing it on the bed and talking softly.

'Now then, *chérie*, let's see what you have here. A nightgown, hairbrush and toothbrush. Perfect. Let me help you get into this and pop you between the sheets,' she soothed, just as she had done for all the little girls who'd grown up in this house for decades. She gently undressed Marie-Claire, brushed her hair out for her and guided her to the bathroom along the corridor. Back in the bedroom again, Marie-Claire watched as Adeline turned down the sheets, removing the warming pan she'd managed miraculously to warm and slip into the bed when she'd first lit the fire.

'In you get then, poppet, and I'll wait here to blow your candle out,' she said as Marie-Claire dreamily did as she was told. She lay still and cried silent tears while being vaguely aware that Adeline sat beside her on the bed, brushed her hair on the pillow and hummed until the moment of oblivion arrived.

# 8

## SAINTE-MÈRE-ÉGLISE, MAY 1998

At the conclusion of the christening ceremony, the whole happy family went outside in a noisy celebration of chatter to pose for photos in front of the church doors. Esther found herself at one end, but was soon called back to the centre of things so she could pose close to the family as godmother.

'Esther, you are *la marraine*, and must stand here beside *le parrain*,' called *Grand-mère,* and Giselle agreed.

'Yes, come into the centre with us, godparents together,' she called, beckoning Esther over. Esther saw there was no way around it, so she moved into the space that had been made for her besides Jules, who looked at her as though she were a ghost. They both seemed unable to say a single word of greeting.

Everyone smiled happily for the camera and then, when the shots were all taken and the young children were running about the churchyard chasing each other, Giselle instructed the gathering to walk over to the café-bar where tables had been reserved for them.

'*Maman* wanted to prepare a feast at home, but there are so many people and this way nobody must work to cook or clean dishes. The manager is a good old friend of *Grand-mère,* and so we have a special family rate,' Giselle explained to Esther.

'Thank you so much for including me, Giselle. Your family is beautiful. And what a surprise for you all that Jules is here now!' she added, wanting to dig to find out more about his situation now. 'His family couldn't come with him?' she asked, looking around to see if he had attached himself to any of the women or young children she didn't recognise.

'His family? Ahh, you mean a wife, yes? *Non,* Jules has no wife. He is married to his business, he says.' Giselle groaned with a roll of her eyes. 'At least he will have Elodie and Julien to look after him when he is old and lonely.' She laughed and turned away to help guests find their seats at the table.

Esther should not have been surprised to find that she was seated at the same table as Jules, yet it was obvious by the look of panic on his face that he was as shocked as her that the day was turning out this way. Not only was he in a state of panic, she saw, but he looked as if there was anywhere else in the world he would rather be than at a table with her.

She listened to the chatter around her, but her mind drifted back to those happy months after her visit here, when his friendly letters had made her hopeful of a future that might involve him. But they had been so young, hardly more than children, and she had never meant anything to him romantically, despite what she'd first thought of as passion in that kiss of his. He probably just remembered her as an irritating little girl who'd hung around him when he would have preferred to be with his friends.

With a great effort of will, Esther shook away the gloomy thoughts and did what she always did when any kind of sadness threatened to darken her days: she counted everything she had to be grateful for. She had her mum – her ever-steadfast friend and supporter in life, and she hoped now that Mum was okay without her. Then there was this lovely holiday, and the rekindling of friendship with Giselle. The liberty she had to go where she pleased, and not be tied to anyone else's plans. This gorgeous lunch that was being laid out before her now. The warm sunshine that lit up the square outside and brought all the townsfolk out to play in its glow. And the presence of the old *grand-mère* whom she had taken so much for granted when she was a young girl of sixteen. Esther intended to get to know the lovely old lady very much better on this trip, and especially to find out more about that little note. She turned to listen to her now as *Grand-mère* was telling a story to her neighbour.

'It was laid out more simply in my day, of course, but the function of the place is still much the same,' she said.

'And didn't you live in a room above at one stage?' asked the cousin sitting beside *Grand-mère.*

'At the very beginning, yes, when I first arrived in Sainte-Mère-Église. But later, after the war, when your uncle and I opened *la crêperie*, we let the rooms above to tenants. There were many people made homeless by the war, you see, and rooms to rent were hard to come by. We only needed the café below for our business.'

'You were a chef, *Grand-mère*? I didn't know that,' said Esther, joining the conversation.

'Not a trained chef, not in the proper sense. But I was a cook, and I learned from my cousins who ran a restaurant where I used to spend my holidays in the south,' the old lady explained.

'And crêpes were a speciality?' asked Esther.

'They became one, yes, and so after the war we opened *la crêperie* right here in this building. It has always been somewhere for food and drink, and for people to meet and share stories. And now here we all are, a big family reunion in honour of little

Julien,' she said, reaching out to take the baby from his father across the table.

Esther watched as she planted luscious kisses on the baby's cheeks and held him close, taking in the scent of his beautiful little head.

'I wonder, *Grand-mère*, would you be able to teach me how to make crêpes, please? I can manage English pancakes quite well, but I've never had success making the thin crêpes the way you French make them,' Esther said.

'It would be my pleasure, *ma chérie*. And Jules, you can help too,' she said, catching her grandson by surprise so much that he choked on his wine.

'I can?' he asked.

'*Oui*, you made excellent crêpes when I taught you as a child. I'm sure you can remember how, and if not, you can have a lesson to refresh you, hmm?' she said in a tone that helped Esther understand just what a powerhouse of a woman she was. It was impossible to refuse her, but Jules tried anyway.

'You don't think I'd be in the way of you ladies? I'm sure Esther would prefer to have you to herself,' he said, looking down at his plate, but Esther noticed him taking a quick glance in her direction from underneath his dark eyelashes. Damn, he was still gorgeous. Dark and broody, with beautiful eyes and something almost pretty about his mouth. And yet there was a gentleness in his character. He seemed shy of her, right now. Not cocky and confident like most men of his age with good looks.

'Not at all, Jules. It's been so long since I saw you, I'd be glad to spend a little time with you,' she said graciously, and in all honesty meaning it with kindness.

Esther tried to fathom the expression on his face then. The panic had passed, and for a moment she saw something of the boy she'd known when he was only eighteen years old. And she was reminded again of the very first time she'd seen him.

'You used to work in this place, didn't you, Jules?'

'I did. I was just here to wait tables, and clean dishes. Nothing special. But it was the connection *Grand-mère* had with the place that got me the job. How did you remember that, Esther?' he asked, looking at her now properly for the first time.

For a moment, the intensity of his gaze took Esther's breath away and she felt like a teenage girl again, melting like chocolate in the sun under the burn of his eyes.

'I remember the first time I saw you, that day I arrived on the school bus right out there, in the square. Your father brought the horse and cart, and you came out of the café-bar to help lift my suitcase,' she said, and wondered if he would remember that day in the church, when they'd kissed for the first time. He did remember. She could see it in his face, and with the way his eyes darted across to the church and back to hers again. But then he seemed to shake himself back into sense, and coughed lightly.

'Will you be heading back to Paris later today, or tomorrow?' she asked, helping him to move on and forget the past, if that was what he wanted. She picked up her wine glass and made room on the table in front of her for the delicious plate of food the waitress had brought over.

'I was going to leave tomorrow, but as *Grand-mère* has big plans for a cooking class, I may need to leave it a couple more days. I'm due a break, anyway, and it's been a long time since I spent a good while at the farm. Paris can wait. There will always be work,' he said with a wave of his hand, and he picked up his fork to tuck into the dish of shellfish and pasta placed before him.

\* \* \*

Later that afternoon, when the group of wider friends and family had all dispersed, amidst greatly affectionate hugs and kisses, and the residents of the farm were all delivered safely home, each one took to their bed for a much-needed afternoon siesta. Whether or not it was the exhaustion of the morning, the heaviness of the long lunch, or the great quantity of wine consumed, Esther was not certain, but she couldn't keep her eyes open a moment longer. She fell onto the bed and sank into the eiderdown, feeling as though she was floating on clouds, and was soon drifting off to sleep, though she could hear occasional voices in distant parts of the farmhouse and farmyard. Dairy cows in the neighbouring field began to low, and there were hens scratching and clucking outside.

The sun moved around and the shadows in the room became longer, but Esther felt the full warmth of the late afternoon sun on her skin. Ideas and images filled her senses and with the warmth came the sensation of skin on skin, and she dreamed that she was being warmed by the body heat of another. She tried to form his name in her mind but couldn't grasp it, and the face was elusive. But the sense of his presence was real. In time, when the shadows moved and she was no longer bathed in sunshine, the coolness roused her. She woke with a sense of loss. Something had been close enough almost to touch but she didn't know what it had been. She lay still, in that moment after sleeping but before fully waking, trying to claw back the dream. And then, finally fully awake, she knew. She'd been dreaming of Jules.

Esther stretched and sat up, her mouth feeling dry as a dusty farmyard on a hot day. She needed a drink – water – and then perhaps a cup of tea. She went over to the window and looked out into the farmyard below. There was a little movement at one end of the farmyard and she saw that Hugo was outside with

Elodie, helping her to ride a bike. Then she heard a clatter from the kitchen below and thought perhaps she would find Giselle in the kitchen. She was just about to turn and head downstairs when she saw that Hugo was talking to someone who was inside the barn. He laughed heartily and looked up to the very top of the barn, and then she saw who he'd been talking to as Jules walked outside, stretching and rubbing his hands through his hair. He looked as though he'd just woken up, but surely he hadn't been sleeping in the barn, had he?

Then both men turned at once and looked up at the window where she stood, and though she was shielded by a net curtain she jumped away, not wanting them to see she was watching them. Strange that they should choose to look in the direction of her bedroom window though, she thought. But she shook it off, and went downstairs in search of a cool glass of water.

Esther found Giselle in the kitchen, feeding the baby, and Madame Joubert – who was insisting she call her *Maman* – was at the stove. She reached a glass down from the cupboard for Esther who took it to the jug they now kept cold in the fridge.

'This place has changed so much since I was first here,' she said as she poured a second glass, having drained the first in one go. 'I don't think I'd ever seen a working water pump until I came to visit you, and here it was your only source of water! Now look at all the mod cons – running hot and cold water in the kitchen, and even a shower and a plumbed toilet,' she said, laughing.

'You have me to thank for all of that, Esther,' said Giselle with a grin. 'When Hugo and I married, we were all set to move to an apartment in Caen, or perhaps Bayeux, but *Maman et Grand-mère* were so sad about me leaving that they convinced *Papa* to make the alterations here and extend the farmhouse so that Hugo and I could come and live here instead. We live in the rooms that the farmhands used to occupy, and we have our own small kitchen and bathroom down there. But I spend most of my time here with *Maman* now that I have the children. And because we don't have to pay rent, it means we can stay here in Sainte-Mère-Église where there is little work,' she explained.

'It sounds like a wonderful arrangement,' said Esther, taking a seat at the big table. 'And I suppose Jules had already moved to Paris?'

'Yes, and he's unlikely to ever come back. He's so engrossed with his business there that we rarely see him. I'm amazed that he's here at all today, and even more surprised that he has said he will stay on for a few days. I hope he doesn't get in your way, Esther. You mustn't take any notice if he's irritating.'

'If who's irritating?' asked a gravelly-voiced Jules who had also come in search of cold water.

'You, you big oaf,' laughed Giselle, without a shadow of the extreme embarrassment that Esther felt. 'Esther is here on holiday, and didn't know you'd be hanging around,' she said as cuttingly as only a little sister can.

'Oh no, Jules – don't mind me at all. I'm only here for a week and I'm glad to spend as much time as I can with all the family,' she said.

'And what are your family doing without you all this time?' he said, going to the stove and getting a pot of coffee ready.

'I don't live with my mum any more, and I'm sure Archie will be fine. My neighbour is making sure he gets plenty to eat,' she said and waited a few heartbeats of silence wondering quite what Jules was doing as he seemed frozen to the spot with a scoop of coffee grounds suspended over the pot. He cleared his throat and shook his head a little.

'Can Archie not cook himself a few meals while you are gone?' he asked, turning now to question her with a frown of puzzlement.

And now it was Esther's turn to feel puzzled, until the penny dropped.

'Oh, I see! No, Archie is not a man, Jules, he's my cat. So no, he cannot cook himself any meals and can't even open a tin of cat food on his own,' she said with a laugh. She saw Jules straighten his shoulders and take a deep breath before making sure he had eye contact with her.

'So, you live alone with your cat? You are not married?' he asked, now making it sound as though that was the most bizarre possibility.

'No, just like you, Jules, I am not married. I live alone.' And now Esther felt as though she'd been attacked, somehow, for the indiscretion of having reached the ripe old age of twenty-eight without having had the ability to tie a man down to marriage, as if this was some kind of failing. She prickled at the idea that he felt it was perfectly reasonable for a man of thirty to be unattached and yet she was some kind of a relationship pariah for being single. Honestly, what gave men the right to such arrogance, and why was the arithmetic so hard for them to understand? When the world is roughly fifty-fifty men and women, there is always going to be a ratio of roughly 1:1 unmarried men and women. Stupid idiot.

'Actually, I see you're making coffee, but I'd rather have a tea if that's okay, please?' Esther said to Jules and jumped up to reach down the tea caddy from the shelf behind her, just as *Grand-mère* came in.

'Ahh, I am pleased to see you two getting busy in the kitchen together,' she said, just as Esther was handing over the tea caddy to Jules.

'Just making a cup of tea and coffee, *Grand-mère*. This is hardly "getting busy",' Jules laughed.

'I'll have coffee as well please, Jules,' the old woman said, taking her seat in the easy armchair. 'And after coffee – or tea – I expect Esther would like you to take her for a little walk out in the fresh air, to revisit the places she will recognise from her previous trips, wouldn't you, Esther, *chérie*?'

Esther looked from *Grand-mère* to Jules and across to Giselle, wondering exactly what she was supposed to do with this suggestion. Giselle came to her rescue.

'I'm sure Esther can decide for herself how to spend her afternoon, *Grand-mère*. She is a busy businesswoman now, you know. She may have her own plans,' said Giselle helpfully.

'Is that right, Esther?' asked Jules as he handed her a cup of tea, and she told him, in a few short sentences, the kind of work that filled her days. His raised eyebrows told her that he was impressed, and she realised then how different she was now than she had been almost thirteen years earlier. Back then she'd been a young schoolgirl and he'd been heading off to university. But now, they were equals – independent adults, each successful in their own arenas and with substantial qualifications behind them. Something about that knowledge bolstered Esther's confidence.

'Actually, Jules, after I've had this drink, I would love to go for a walk, and you're welcome to come with me. But I'm sure I can remember my way alone, so don't trouble yourself,' she said dismissively, going to sit beside Giselle and making a fuss of baby Julien.

Jules stood awkwardly at the table, and looked around the room at the three women, and seemed as uncertain as a small boy might be about what to do. He sat at the kitchen table and sipped slowly at his coffee.

When Esther had finished her tea, and Giselle got up to go and change the baby, Esther made a move to go and swap her dress for a pair of shorts and a T-shirt for her afternoon walk.

She slipped on some trainers and trotted down the stairs, then, once in the farmyard, she headed for the stile behind the barn. Just as she stepped over it and hopped onto the path that led into the woods she heard her name called.

'Esther, wait!' called Jules, as he jogged out from the barn. 'I'd like to come with you, if that's okay with you?' he asked and, after a moment of hesitation, she smiled and gave him a nod.

'Sure, Jules. Let's walk together.' She smiled.

## 9

### CHÂTEAU DE CANON, NORMANDY, DECEMBER 1940

Marie-Claire stirred and stretched, enjoying the luxury of waking naturally. The room was silent and darkened by the heavy drapes, but bright sunlight burned through the tiny gaps around the curtains and shone onto the ceiling and into the room, highlighting a knife edge's width of dust motes that danced in the rays.

And then she remembered. She remembered where she was and why and, looking back to the empty pillow beside hers, the sharp dagger twisted again in her chest and the sobs came again in a wretched wave of new grief.

She got up and dressed herself hurriedly, packing her nightclothes back into the bag and carrying it downstairs to the kitchen, which took her some time to find, the château was so expansive.

When she eventually opened the door to the right room, she found the kitchen empty. A note rested on the big wooden table, held down by the salt cellar.

*Marie-Claire – there is bread and cheese in the pantry, and some cold pie. Please help yourself. We are all busy today but will meet back here for dinner after dark.*

*Adeline*

Marie-Claire was hungry, though she was frustrated at needing to take the time to eat. And she had no idea which direction to walk from here to get south, so the best thing was to sit and eat a while. Perhaps one of their maps was here somewhere and would help her work out which route to take, she thought as she buttered bread and cut a slice of cheese and a piece of the solid meat pie, thankful for the kindness of these people.

As she ate in the silence of the ancient kitchen, all she could hear was a few birds chirping outside in the gardens. And then she heard a clock strike in some distant hallway. The last ring of the chimes was still sounding, and she stopped chewing, thinking, calculating, assessing and coming to a decision. The clock had struck three. It was surely no more than nine in the morning, or possibly earlier, though the sun did seem to be fully up, and it was nearing midwinter's day, after all. Why would the clock be so out of time, with so many people here to keep it right?

Marie-Claire finished her small meal and poured a glass of milk from a steel churn she found in the cold store cupboard built deep into the stone walls of the château. She opened the door from the kitchen and drank the milk on the back step, surveying what she could see of the grounds. There seemed to be an enormous walled garden to this side of the main house, which she guessed must include a kitchen garden, and she wandered down to see.

Many of the beds were bare and being wintered, but there

were rows of cabbages, broccoli and cauliflower growing strong. In the middle of the kitchen garden was a sundial and she stepped towards it, eager to find out which way was south from here.

The day was bright and clear, though freezing cold again, naturally. She noted the points of the compass on the dial and looked over the horizon in the direction of south – not too far off the course she and Jean-Baptiste had taken the night before. They'd been walking in a north-easterly direction to get here. Thanks to the sunshine, the sundial had a clear shadow. The time showed as three in the afternoon. That couldn't be right – she'd only woken up from her night's sleep less than an hour earlier.

Marie-Claire went back indoors and, setting the empty milk glass down on the table, walked the corridors until she found the main entrance hall at the front of the château. It was grand and square, with a patterned tiled floor above the centre of which hung an enormous chandelier – currently covered in dust cloths – and hanging at the height of the balcony above. There was a pair of staircases which wound around the entrance hall in two opposing semicircles, meeting at a great gallery above, where, she presumed, she would find a ballroom if she went looking. And there at the back of this entrance hall, in the centre of the wall, was the most enormous clock. She walked up to it, touching the glass gently as if to check it was real, just as it was about to strike half past the hour. The time was now half past three in the afternoon, and the sun would be going down again soon. She'd slept all night and all day, and cursed herself for the wasted time.

She rushed back through the corridors to the kitchen and looked about her for where the others might have stored their maps. She opened drawers and cupboards but found nothing you would not expect to find in the kitchen of a grand, old house.

She tried some of the surrounding rooms, but couldn't find anything. In frustration she pulled on her coat, scarf and hat, and went outside to look around the grounds to find at least if there were other ways out and towards a main road. She walked all around the main house and discovered an enormous stables building, complete with a courtyard and paddock exercise area for horses – so many stables that there must have been race-horses here at one time. But now there were only a few horses grazing on the grass.

The gardens went on forever and were obviously being well maintained by gardeners – possibly some of the people she'd met last night.

Behind the château were expansive woods, and in front were fields and orchards. There were two main avenues leading up to the front of the house: the one that she and Jean-Baptiste had walked up last night, coming from the east, and another heading south. With no better information to go on from that, Marie-Claire decided the avenue to the south would be the start of her journey onwards. She would walk all the way to the Côte d'Azur if she had to, but she would get to her son.

Marie-Claire made her way back to the kitchen to collect her bag, meaning to set out at once, despite the late hour. She pushed open the door and staggered backwards in shock to find the room now heaving with almost as many people as had been here last night.

'Oh, *ma chérie*, here you are,' crooned Adeline, coming over to take Marie-Claire by the hand. 'We wondered where you could have gone.'

'I slept so late – all day! I need to leave. I must get to my son. I've been looking around the estate and I'm going to take the southbound avenue. Where does it lead? Is there a town that way? I need to know exactly where I am so I can plan my route. Do you have a map here? I saw maps on the table last night,' Marie-Claire fired at the room in general. There was no response. They all stood, mouths agape, and eventually turned to Jean-Baptiste, expecting their leader to take over. He cleared his throat.

'Marie-Claire, I think you should take a seat—'

'But no, I am leaving now, Jean-Baptiste,' she interrupted him, reaching for her bag. 'I thank you all for taking care of me, but I must get to my son,' she said.

'Marie-Claire, please, sit down,' he said, standing and pulling out a chair for her. 'There are things you need to know.'

His manner was so direct, and his face so grim, Marie-Claire found herself acquiescing quite without meaning to. She looked to him for answers. He sat opposite her and began to explain.

'We've been out today, meeting various others like ourselves, and we've heard news that we believe involves you.' Marie-Claire looked around the room at the other faces in confusion. What could they possibly know that had anything to do with her?

'Your son was on the train that left Paris, from the Gare de Lyon, at seven o'clock yesterday evening, yes?' Jean-Baptiste asked. She nodded.

'The train was brought to a halt just an hour into its journey. There had been a fault on the line ahead and the driver was responding to signals.'

'A real fault on the line, or was this your work as well?' she asked, a sharp tone of accusation in her voice. He raised his palms in defence.

'This was a genuine fault – nothing to do with us. But while the train was resting it seems there was a dogfight overhead. Two British

Hurricanes had been chasing a Luftwaffe Messerschmitt. The chase ended in the air just south of Paris. The dogfight ended badly for the Luftwaffe pilot who was shot down. The fault on the train line had been cleared, and the train continued. The wreck of the Messerschmitt crash-landed onto the train line, and before the driver could be alerted, the train was derailed as it hit the wreck at high speed.'

Jean-Baptiste remained calm, factual, relaying the incident as if for a news report on the wireless, with no emotion. It took a few moments for Marie-Claire to process, and then she stood up abruptly, knocking her chair backwards onto the slate tiled floor with a loud clatter in the otherwise silent room.

'My son might have been hurt! I have to get to him. Where did they take the passengers? If my friends, Juliette and Philippe, were injured there will be nobody to take care of him,' she said desperately.

'Marie-Claire, we have made enquiries at the hospital. There were a large number of deaths, and barely any survivors. There were no children who survived the accident. Do you understand me?' he asked, reaching out and taking hold of her hand. 'Marie-Claire, you must sit,' he said as he pulled up the chair and guided her to rest in it.

In Marie-Claire's mind a jumble of words and images tossed around and created a storm that she couldn't see through clearly. She saw the laughing face of her baby boy and then the same face, lifeless and grey, lying in a ditch of snow beside a railway line. She saw the mangled wreck of a crashed plane and the carriages of a train, tossed aside from the rail. She saw the beautiful eyes of her beloved Benjamin, warm and loving and then cold. Staring. Dead.

She looked around the room, and saw Adeline wipe a tear from her eye with the corner of her apron.

'This war is taking from us all that we love, *ma chérie*. It is why we must fight back.'

There were other words spoken that night. Kind words, and encouraging ones. Words of welcome and words meant to build her up and make her feel strong. But she felt the effect of none of them. Marie-Claire's heart had been shocked into a state of stone.

\* \* \*

It wasn't until a full month later that Marie-Claire felt herself smile again. For the first fortnight after she heard the news that she had not only lost her husband, but her son as well, she had spent her nights awake, sitting alone and crying at the kitchen table, or wandering the halls when she had tired of staring at the ornate ceiling in her bedroom. The days, she had mostly slept through, unable to face the sun, or the sky or the people who were caring for her so tenderly. Her life was over, and she felt that the existence of a soul lost between the worlds of life and death gave her the most comfort.

But by the third week, Adeline had begun to be more insistent that she come downstairs in the morning, at least before lunch. There was work to do and mouths to feed, and Adeline couldn't do it alone. Marie-Claire would be a help if she could manage to get up, she would say. It was then that Adeline discovered that Marie-Claire was extremely talented in a kitchen. There was virtually nothing she couldn't do, and she was particularly talented with pastries and brioche. Adeline had put her to work immediately as the house bread-chef, and soon Marie-Claire was involved in the kitchen garden as well, gathering ingredients to make some of the most delicious pies the little band at the château had ever tasted.

On this day in late January, Marie-Claire had discovered some apples in storage and offered to make a dish with them.

'Ah, yes, and there is some very good Calvados in the cellar too. We shall have *Poulet Vallée d'Auge*, a local speciality. I will teach you the recipe,' Adeline said.

The apples had been diced and fried in butter, and a sauce made with the Calvados and cream, to be poured over chicken breast also fried in butter with shallots. Marie-Claire had gone upstairs to bring her journal down to the kitchen and wrote the recipe out carefully, adding her own thoughts about the quality of ingredients, the specific flavours that were required and how the kitchen smelled while the dish was cooking.

'You've made it to perfection,' said Adeline as she tasted the sauce, and read over what Marie-Claire had written. 'And you make it sound so wonderful too. It is one thing to have the talent to cook like this, but to describe the process and the senses so perfectly – that is something I could never do. The men will all turn to goo when they taste this tonight, instead of the bread, cheese and ham they eat so often.'

Sure enough, as each one came in from their various day's work – some of it obvious, in the grounds of the château, and some of it entirely secretive – they took a deep sniff of the gorgeous aroma. Everyone sat at the table that night and ate in a kind of reverent silence which at first made Marie-Claire worry that there was something wrong with the flavouring. But then the sounds of appreciation began.

'Mmmmm, Marie-Claire, this is perfection!' exclaimed Jean-Baptiste. 'How did we not know you could cook like this?'

'She is a miracle worker!'

'I've never tasted food so good as this in all my life,' said old Henri, the husband of Adeline.

'Hey, what are you saying?' called Adeline in mock horror

and the whole table laughed, including Marie-Claire. It felt good, and she realised then how long it had been since something had even made her smile. Her old life was over, and while she knew she would never recover from her losses, a new kind of life was beginning. It was as if there were two Marie-Claires in the world. One from before, and one for the future.

'Marie-Claire,' began Jean-Baptiste. 'Your cooking skills are excellent. Are you a trained chef?'

'Trained by my cousins, yes. They ran a restaurant, and I learned at their sides when I was a young girl. I worked in kitchens when I first came to Paris, which helped me explore food for my writing, until I met Benjamin and we married,' she explained.

'What do you mean, your "writing"? What did you write?'

'I was a food writer. I collected recipes and wrote articles about the ingredients, the people who created the recipes, the areas they were from. Mostly I'm keeping my writing for a book I want to publish one day, but I also sold a few articles to magazines, and I wrote a little for newspapers,' she said, and sipped her glass of Calvados slowly.

'You should hear how she has described this meal, and the area where the ingredients are grown,' said Adeline, reaching for Marie-Claire's journal and asking for permission to read it with the merest question in her glance. Marie-Claire nodded in response, and the older woman read out the journal entry.

Jean-Baptiste regarded Marie-Claire, with a look she could not quite fathom, for some time. They sat on in silence, the only movement in the room being shadows caused by the flicker of firelight. In the silence, he drained his glass and put it down softly on the table, turning towards her.

'Marie-Claire, you are a wonder. And I have a proposition for you.' Marie-Claire turned to look at him, full of questions. He continued.

'You know that we are fighting here, and we have big plans to form something of an underground army to fight back and reclaim France for the French.' She nodded. Marie-Claire had little idea of the details of the work they were involved in yet but had been content to be among them – glad of the family they were all becoming around her in this desperate time of grief.

'You are a skilled cook, a gifted writer, and you are brave – so strong, determined and very, very courageous,' he said. She dipped her head, feeling unworthy of such high praise. She was just surviving, the only way she knew how.

'There is work for strong women like you. We are beginning to see that it is sometimes easier for a woman to become trusted in the places where we need to plant our operatives. Somehow, women are less suspected. Have you asked yourself why it was your husband who was shot, and not you? The German soldiers seem much more suspicious – frightened, perhaps – of men than women. So this makes women very powerful.' He paused a while, and this gave Marie-Claire a chance to take this on board, to consider the mind of the man who had shot her husband. She recalled again how he'd simply walked away and she'd quite easily left the station, undeterred. She looked back to Jean-Baptiste to see what else he had to say.

'There is a town further north of here, called Sainte-Mère-Église, which we have chosen because it is small and insignificant, but also on the main route between Cherbourg and Paris. It is surrounded by countryside, and we expect that soon contact will be established with a team in England and there will be operatives sent over to work covertly alongside us. And a restaurant in the town is the ideal place for us to collect and pass on information. Soon the Germans will be there, just as they are in Caen near here. In fact, it cannot be long until they come and discover this beautiful château and take it for their own purposes,' he said with a shrug, as if giving this place up was already a foregone conclusion. 'Once they arrive there, we hope they will not have much interest in the village. There is no industry that will draw them, no factories they can use, just farms. But they will keep a presence there, and the restaurant will likely be a common meeting place for them – especially if we engineer it so they are welcome.'

'And what would you want me to do?' Marie-Claire asked.

'You would work in the restaurant, cooking your beautiful food, and perhaps working to make the Germans feel comfortable—' He broke off suddenly and again raised his hands in defence as Marie-Claire was about to launch her objection to what she imagined he meant by making them 'comfortable'.

'Hear me out, please – I am not asking you to become fully *involved* with them, Marie-Claire. That would be too much, and I believe that is a role you would need to be trained more intensely for. I am simply suggesting that you cook, and serve, and smile, and talk, and write. And listen. And help us write messages – recipes and articles about food and wine, sprinkled with code, once we develop it – to help us with our missions.' He stopped, at last, and sat back in his chair watching Marie-Claire for her response. She took another sip of the delicious Calvados and savoured the heat and apple flavour as it trickled down her throat.

'I feel that I owe you all so much. You have cared for me like family, and I don't know what would have happened if I'd made my way south and discovered Antoine's death alone.' She paused to swallow the tears that threatened again before finding the strength to continue. 'Thank you, for everything. And if I can be of help – do something to give back the Germans some of what they deserve for the pain they have caused me – I am glad to help. But how do you know you can trust me?' she asked.

'Simple,' he said with a shrug. 'You have everything to gain by joining us, and nothing to lose. They've already taken everything dear to you, and I know in your heart you will never forgive them for that. You will be faithful to our cause until you've done everything in your power to bring them down.'

## 10

SAINTE-MÈRE-ÉGLISE, MAY 1998

Esther waited as Jules climbed over the stile to join her on the woodland path. The dappled sunlight flickered on the ferns and lichen growing around the base of the leafy trees that made this little path cooler. It felt a million miles away from the people who were only yards distant in the farmhouse. As they set off together, side by side on the wide path, she became aware of an intensely strong aroma that brought back bittersweet memories of their last walk this way.

'I love the smell of the wild garlic here. Does it grow all summer?' she asked him, stooping to pick a leaf and crush it, breathing in the deep aroma.

'No, in fact it only grows in spring. It is coming to its end now. My mother comes out here and harvests it in batches then preserves it in olive oil, so she can use it in her cooking all through the year,' he explained.

'Ah of course, that must be why it is so familiar. I was here in May for my first visit as well as this one,' she said, unwittingly introducing to him the memory of their walk together on that day they had kissed in the church. Jules nodded and cleared his throat, and they walked on in silence for a while.

'Actually, that does remind me of something. Does your mother write her own recipes? I think I may have found one on a previous trip. I took it home with me thinking it was nothing, but realised I should return it. I think it is more personal than just a recipe for preserving wild garlic. There's some poetry on the back, as well.'

'Poetry? My mother is a very straightforward rural woman, Esther. She might have written out one or two recipes in her time but I don't think she has ever been interested in poetry.' The pair walked on a while and Esther wondered if the paper she had really was something simple and meaningless after all, and then Jules spoke again. 'Is this note written in French or English?' he asked, stopping to look at her as an idea seemed to occur to him.

'Both, actually. The recipe is in French, and the poetry is written in French and translated into English, plus there is another small note in English,' she said.

'Well, that is interesting, and it tells us that *Maman* did not write it. She can speak reasonably good conversational English, but she cannot write it. Your note must be written by someone else. Are you sure it is not Giselle's? She has very good written English,' he suggested.

'No, it's definitely not her handwriting. I've been writing to Giselle half my life and I know every curve of her hand,' Esther explained and Jules nodded.

'Of course, yes. Well then, it is a mystery. Where did you find the note?'

'It was in an old recipe book, a very old book. Perhaps the book was second-hand when it was bought, and the note was simply left there by the previous owner,' she said thoughtfully.

'That sounds like the most likely answer,' he said and then stepped aside as a couple of children rode along the path on their bikes.

'So, tell me about life in Paris, Jules. Is it all you hoped it would be? I remember you were so excited to be going off to university and becoming a part of the big city,' she said.

'Paris is a wonderful place to study, and to be young with friends, and I did have everything I wanted from my years at university. And that, of course, led to my work, and Paris has become my home. I love the lights, and the restaurants, and the art. But it always does my soul good to come back here, home, as well. What about you, and London?' he asked.

'I did love being in London for uni. It was so great to be right there in the thick of it, just a few Tube stops away from the West End – all those shows at student discounts, and nights out with friends. But I've always preferred the country. I think that's why I fell in love with this place so much – the truly rural feel, the out-of-town peace.'

'There is a place for both, I think: the city and the country. But your hometown, Poole, it is not so much in the country as Sainte-Mère-Église, I think?' he probed.

'No, you're right. Poole is quite a bustling town, but it has a beautiful, peaceful harbour with quiet beaches, if you know where to find them, and it's surrounded by rolling countryside. But it's the countryside that I love more than the town – always. So I think Sainte-Mère-Église stayed in my heart much longer than any other school French trip might have done if we had just visited Paris instead,' she said.

They walked on for another minute or two in silence before Jules stopped and gently touched Esther's arm, causing her to stop and look at him.

'I think there is more reason than the peace and quiet of

Sainte-Mère-Église that made this place stay in your heart, and I think that is my fault. I'm sorry, Esther,' he said, and she could see that he'd been struggling to decide how to say this.

'No, no,' she said, laughing lightly and batting away the idea that he had anything to apologise for – despite the way she'd felt all those years ago. 'You don't need to be sorry. I'm not sorry. I was just a young girl, and it was a harmless little teenage thing, really.'

'No. It wasn't, Esther. It was more, to me at least. And I'm sorry that I stopped writing.'

Esther had thought he simply meant to apologise for kissing her, and getting up her hopes when she had never meant anything to him. This was the version of his story that she'd told herself all those years ago: that she meant nothing to him, and he'd just been caught up in the passion of a moment. But now, the way he was looking at her with real and mature regret, she wondered if she'd misunderstood all along.

'So why *did* you stop writing then?' she asked, and instantly regretted the tone of demand in her voice. 'I mean, I just assumed you had met someone else and moved on. That idea made sense to me at the time. Is that not what happened?' she asked him, eager to finally hear his response, but dreading it at the same time.

'I didn't meet anyone else, Esther. I was just young and stupid, and with all the excitement in Paris, and you so far away in England, I just stopped writing. It was immature of me, and I'm sorry,' he said.

Esther stared at him for what felt like hours, trying to decide if she believed him.

'So you didn't date anyone else then?' she asked, watching his eyes to find the truth. He shook his head slowly.

'At that time, I just studied. I know that sounds hard to

believe, and my friends all thought I was crazy, but I just didn't find anyone with a smile like yours,' he said with a shrug. 'They all tried to find me girls to go out with, and I went on plenty of double dates, but I didn't ever follow up with any of them. After I left university, and started work, I've had a few girlfriends, of course, but nothing ever seemed to last. But now, *oh mon Dieu*,' he said and rubbed his face in his hands, before continuing. 'This timing is awful, Esther. I did think about getting back in touch with you, did you know that? I asked Giselle about you and how you were, but I was certain that you'd settled down with someone else. She told me that you had moved out of home and shared a house with Archie. Once I heard that, I made myself forget you. And now – today – I discover that Archie is your cat? So tell me, Esther, what about you? Is there anyone except Archie in your life now?' he asked, smiling at his stupid mistake, and lack of intelligence to double-check his facts.

Esther turned and started walking again. His story was remarkably like hers, but she'd been getting over the loss of someone she thought had dumped her for someone else – or for the many women she had imagined him to be romancing in Paris.

'No, there's no one else. I mean, the Mayor of Cherbourg has always seemed pretty keen on me, but he's also very happily married, and I think his attentions are more in line with those of an older brother,' she said with a wink that made him laugh. 'I've been out with a few guys, but no one special,' she said, and he nodded as they continued to walk.

The rest of the walk into town was filled with small talk about life here in Sainte-Mère-Église, the various buildings that were coming into view as they neared the town centre, and what it had been like to grow up here. But Esther felt like they had made a new beginning. She understood – almost – the reason why he'd stopped writing. And she was certain that they'd both now made it quite clear that each one was single. And here they were, spending time together. Anything could happen.

As they arrived in the town square, Esther and Jules made their way around the shops where Esther bought a cute little souvenir for her mum, and they stopped at the café, choosing a table beside the window so they could watch the world go by. They ordered coffee and chatted through everything economics and business in terms of Paris and London, and Esther shared all the details of her work with the Chamber of Commerce, and especially about how pleased she was that she'd kept up such close connections with France and found ways to keep her language skills up.

'Mmmm, it smells delicious in here,' said Esther, looking around and noticing that the tables had begun to fill with dinner guests who were being served some delectable-looking dishes. 'Goodness, it's nearly seven o'clock! Where did that time go?' They'd been together now for nearly three hours, and the time had disappeared in moments.

'The food does smell good. Are you hungry?' asked Jules.

'After that glorious lunch today, I didn't think I would ever eat again, but yes, I guess I'm a little peckish,' she said, forgetting that she was slipping back into English slang.

'Peckish? What is this?' he asked.

'Sorry, it means I'm a little bit hungry. Like I could take a peck – a nibble.'

Jules found them a menu and they chose a share plate of breads, charcuterie meats, olives and cheese. And he ordered a carafe of fruity red wine with two glasses.

'Will they miss us back at the farm?' she asked, realising now that when she'd left for her walk, she'd told Giselle she was going alone.

'I'll let them know you're here, with me,' he said, slipping a little distance away from the café and making a call on his mobile. She watched him as he paced a little while he talked, now and then stopping and slipping his hand into his pocket, and then running it through his hair – a habit she knew he'd had ever since he was seventeen at least. And he was still gorgeous. A little more world-weary around the eyes, perhaps, but still the same guy she'd first fallen for right here, on this pavement, when he'd come out to help lift her bag thirteen years ago. She realised she was staring and turned to look across the square instead, but then was faced with the church. The place where it had all gone down.

It had started so innocently. Just a walk into town on the woodland path, and then Jules had suggested they go inside the church to look at the war memorial. They eventually sat in a pew together and, while gazing up at the stained-glass image of parachutes falling into Sainte-Mère-Église, Esther felt the shiver of emotion and the quiver of tears. Jules had wrapped his arm around her shoulder and she'd leant into him. She didn't remember how they'd started to kiss, but she knew she'd never wanted it to stop. She shivered again now as she remembered the passion of that moment.

*Oh, stop it, Esther. He moved on and so did you.*

Jules came back tucking his phone away and sat down, smiling. 'It is all okay. I told Giselle I was taking care of you, and they are not expecting us back soon.' And they set to eating the plate of goodies that lay on the table between them.

When it was all gone, Esther wiped her fingers and drained her glass of wine.

'Would you like anything else to eat? Perhaps a main course?' Jules asked.

'No thank you, and I certainly shouldn't drink any more,' she said with a laugh, realising they'd also emptied the carafe between them. 'Let's walk around the other side of town, shall we?' she suggested, with the intention of putting this café and the church out of her thoughts. Walking was always a good way to clear the mind.

But as they stood, Jules came to help her with her chair and touched a hand to the small of her back, sending tremors of pleasure through her. And as they stepped away from the table, he simply reached down and touched the back of her hand with the back of his. Where was this going?

\* \* \*

They'd wandered the back streets of Sainte-Mère-Église, and as they walked, they drew closer to one another, frequently bumping hands or shoulders. They passed down lanes, over bridges, and along a little stream to where they sat now under a tree, each sharing their memories about that time they'd spent together.

'I know I was young, and it might have seemed like it meant nothing. But – this is going to sound odd, Jules – there's never been another man who made me feel the way you did then,' she said, knowing she was opening herself up to deep hurt, but taking the leap anyway.

'I've always been quite capable of looking after myself, and making my own decisions,' she said firmly. 'So what is this now? What are we doing?' Esther asked him, twisting so she could see his face directly. He seemed to think long and hard before he spoke.

'Well, what is going on here is that we are spending time alone, and enjoying each other's company. And it's a free country, so...' he said and rubbed his face with his hand. 'I'm a klutz,

Esther. You're the clever one. Could we perhaps make this up as we go along, and see what happens? If I try to be less stupid this time?'

Esther watched his eyes flick over hers, searching for her answer, and she thought about how much she had tried to never get attached to a man. All men left, or were likely to, once you became dependent on them, in her opinion. Her own father had set the standard and she'd never been able to get past that. Trust a man, and you'll get left behind and hurt. This was the only mantra she knew. But the way she felt about Jules, it was so unreasonable. It was more than just the physical rush she'd felt with the other guys she'd dated. She'd never known anything like the 'love' her girlfriends talked of. There was fun, and sex, and then there was the time to move on – usually when they were getting too attached to her. But the heartache she'd felt when this teenage thing with Jules had been over, that had been real. She'd let him get into her soul and then, when she thought he'd rejected her for someone else, she'd allowed it to hurt her. She remembered all the other times she'd been with someone, and yet all they could do was remind her of Jules.

Esther gazed at the lips that she'd dreamed of while lying on her bed that afternoon, and quickly, before she could stop herself, she leant in, kissing him firmly and fully, but pulling away quickly to gauge his response. He gently reached out to stroke her cheek and his eyes gave her the answer she needed. He'd been longing for this all day, just as much as she had. She kissed him again and, this time, they both leant in and released the passion they remembered from their first kiss.

# 11

SAINTE-MÈRE-ÉGLISE, MAY 1941

Marie-Claire patiently stood over the stove as she browned the chunks of beef in butter and pork fat, turning each piece carefully, then setting them aside and starting again on the next batch. The process would take her a while but once the enormous pot of boeuf bourguignon was very slowly cooking in the oven, it wouldn't need her attention for hours, and then she could get busy with the bread, preparing vegetables, and making a leek and potato soup for tonight's menu.

She heard the door open and, glancing at the small mirror she kept on the bench to warn her what to expect from behind, saw there were two young men, dressed in civilian clothes, likely looking for their morning coffee. She didn't recognise them. She wiped her hands on her apron, and turned to greet them with a smile, and asked them how she could help.

'Marcel says that he has an extra delivery of eggs for you this week,' said the taller of the two, and Marie-Claire looked at them both again more clearly, startled. She was sure she'd never seen them before and yet they'd opened with the code to say they were leaving a message with her. To anyone else in the café who might have heard, the man was simply passing on a message about supplies for the café-bar. She smiled and nodded to table number nine.

'Thank you, Messieurs. Please, take a seat at the corner table and I'll bring it right over.'

As Marie-Claire prepared two cups of coffee she tried to think if she might have met these men before. She was growing better at remembering faces, but sometimes they would slip from her mind. Regardless, she was learning to operate based on the rules alone. If someone came in and used the expected code phrase, she would give the expected response.

As she carried the drinks over to the table, she saw there was a small piece of paper mostly hidden under a paper serviette. She scooped it up as if it was rubbish and headed back to the kitchen where she transferred it to her pocket. An hour later she sat outside in the sun, taking a much-needed rest. She checked there was nobody around to watch her in this little corner garden on a terrace at the back of the café-bar. She took the note from her pocket and saw it was from Jean-Baptiste.

'*Taking a short holiday. Plan to return in a week, but if I don't see you before Sunday, I hope you can find somewhere to publish your spring vegetable and lamb recipe, before it is summer – it is lovely, as are you,*' he wrote. She knew now how to interpret his messages. There was some kind of mission, which had a high element of danger. If he were not to return, there was code written into a recipe and journal entry she'd penned that must be put out so that others would know what to do without him.

Back in the kitchen again, she bent to open the door to the fire in the base of the oven, threw in an extra log, and the crumpled note with it.

As she prepared the soup for the evening menu, and then filled some tiny tart cases with custard and berries, Marie-Claire wondered exactly what Jean-Baptiste was getting up to this time. So far, their work seemed to be all about setting up safe places and lines of communication. There were very few German soldiers in Sainte-Mère-Église but they had made themselves very much at home. The mayor's home had been taken over, and he'd been demoted from his role, a *Wehrmacht* major now claiming his right to rule over the town. Two enormous flags with the swastika slashed through the middle of the blood-red background now hung from poles outside the mayor's home, where once the French and Norman flags had hung. There was a half dozen or so regular enlisted soldiers – *Schütze* – who came into the café-bar regularly through the day, and some non-commissioned officers together with a senior officer would often come in for dinner at night. Marie-Claire had learned now how to tell the subtle differences in their uniforms on sight, looking to their shoulders for the braided strap, or sleeves for a simple chevron, but it was very simple to see the difference in rank by the way they greeted each other when ranks were mixed in the same space. If there was anyone higher than a *Schütze* present, the others would lower their eyes and voices in reverence to the senior man.

Still, every single time she saw any of their uniforms she felt sick as she thought of Benjamin and the hateful soldier who had killed him, and separated her from Antoine. She had become skilled at masking her feelings and smiling at them all as though they were welcome customers.

For most of the time, Marie-Claire stayed close to the town centre, living above the café-bar in a room she rented at a reduced rate, as part of her pay. On her day off on Sundays she would go to church, and take a walk into the surrounding woods and fields, trying hard to fit in as a villager, but also not wanting to get too close to anyone. Half the week she worked in the restaurant late into the evening, but then didn't start work until late in the morning. The other half of the week she started at six o'clock and finished just after lunch, but she took a half day on Wednesday or Thursday most weeks as well. She had plenty of waking hours to work on her journal, perfecting her descriptions of recipes and researching some of the locally grown ingredients. At the end of that night, after the boeuf bourguignon was all gone, and she'd listened to countless customers give her their praise, she had cleaned the kitchen and, together with the wait-staff and the restaurant manager, helped to stack chairs so the floor could be swept and cleaned. When the door was locked and the lights finally turned out, she went up to her room to sleep. But first, she took out her journal and found the recipe she knew Jean-Baptiste referred to. It was in two forms, both containing a few words of code. The first was to be used in the event the next mission went well. The second version would be published in the town newsletter, alongside her recipe for her custard tarts, if things did not go to plan for Jean-Baptiste.

There were few critics of writing in Sainte-Mère-Église, very unlike the situation in Paris, and she knew nobody would take any notice of the style of her language or her choice of vocabulary – except those people who were looking for her coded messages. The standard of writing for the town parish newsletter was low. There was no newspaper any more – at least, not one that counted. The newspapers were all censored by the Germans and contained only good news about the Third Reich and how much better off France was under German control. No news of Allied attacks ever reached them by legitimate means.

She tucked her journal away and lay on the bed, curling

onto her side, hugging the pillow to her. Marie-Claire allowed herself the luxury of remembering the way it felt to have Benjamin climb into bed beside her, and wrap his arms around her waist. She pulled the pillow in tighter and remembered the weight of Antoine in her arms and spoke to him soothingly, as if helping him to go off to sleep. The dream-state that she could usually induce was becoming harder to attain, the longer it had been since she'd seen them both. It was nearly five months now and she hated the way she was forgetting the sounds of their voices.

Marie-Claire angrily snapped herself back upright, and pulled out her journal again. She needed to check the recipe and get it ready to deliver next Monday, if she did not hear from Jean-Baptiste.

\* \* \*

'*Bonjour, Mademoiselle Dubois*,' the priest said as he shook her hand on Sunday morning. She had chosen to remain as 'Miss', removing her wedding ring and hiding it, to make it simpler than having to explain to everyone whom and what she had lost. But one thing she hadn't counted on was that there were young men who might find her interesting. The old priest, of course, was not one of them, but Marie-Claire frequently found herself keeping her eyes dipped and avoiding the meaningful looks from a number of the young farmers and workers.

As she walked out of the church on this Sunday morning she saw that Charles, the priest's assistant and the man responsible for getting the newsletter printed, was in deep conversation in a quiet corner of the churchyard with someone she didn't at first recognise. It was not really her place to keep tabs on people, but she was finding more and more that Jean-Baptiste would rely on information she had of people who were coming and going through the town.

He still stayed based at the château, in Canon, the other side of Caen, but came to visit her around once a month. It had been five days since she'd heard that message via the two strangers in the café-bar. She was idly walking through the churchyard, wondering if she would get any news tomorrow, when Charles called out to her. She looked up and smiled and saw then the man he was with. She did recognise him after all, but was not used to seeing him dressed so finely in his Sunday clothes and had not seen him in church before. It was Louis Joubert, from the farm just outside the village.

'*Bonjour*, Charles, Louis!' she called brightly and waved. They both raised their hands to wave back, but she chose to walk off towards the woods for a stroll alone. She didn't know if Louis was someone to trust, though she knew Charles was a part of the undercover group. Perhaps he was testing Louis for information and wouldn't want her nearby.

As she crossed the square and went down the lane that went into the woods, Marie-Claire was glad as the noise of the town square became muffled behind her and she could hear her feet crunching on the twigs and leaf litter that lay in the gravel path. The trees overhead were in the full bloom of early summer green, and blossoms were everywhere. She marvelled again at the relentlessness with which nature just kept carrying on when lives like hers had ended so abruptly. The world was living under the threat of a terrible and dark, grey future, but the natural world knew nothing of this. Bulbs sprang up, leaves budded, birds lay eggs and nurtured their chicks, and the sun grew warmer by the day. Meanwhile, men like Jean-Baptiste were off risking their lives to fight the Nazi machine. She wondered if she would ever see him again.

Steps sounded from behind Marie-Claire and she fought the urge to run. Perhaps, she realised now, this had been an unwise path to take and for a moment she feared this might be one of the German soldiers, perhaps one who'd watched her walk in here alone. She fingered the little knife she kept in her pocket and wondered if she should click it open now or wait until he pounced. The hairs on her arms prickled and her breath quickened. She was trying to decide whether it was safer to keep walking deeper into the woods, or turn back and face whoever it was, just as he caught up to her and, calling her name, took her by the wrist and pulled her off the path and into the thicker undergrowth.

She would have screamed, except he held a hand over her mouth, and she cursed herself for her slow reaction. She'd dropped the knife on the ground.

'Shh, Marie-Claire, it is me,' said Jean-Baptiste softly, and she began to cry with relief.

'What are you doing? You scared me half to death!' she said as he released her, though she knew she must speak quietly. She bent to collect her knife and put it away again, and wiped the tears from her face.

'Yes, and quite deliberately so. You must not place yourself in such danger as this. I really must teach you some better skills. Do you see that you would have had no chance, then?' he asked, rubbing his chin which she now noticed had a longer growth of stubble than she was used to seeing. Marie-Claire was frustrated to have her weakness pointed out and explained she wished very much to have some better skills to help her in future.

'I take it all went well with you, as you're back again?' she asked, wanting to change the subject from her failure, and he grinned.

'All went so magnificently well; I cannot wait to tell you.

Come, let us walk on and I will tell you a story you will not believe,' he said, guiding her back out to the path and taking up step beside her.

He explained that their mission had been to infiltrate the Luftwaffe base that had been set up just outside Caen, simply to see what the security was like, perhaps take a look at some of the stores, and find out if there were any good spots where they could listen to conversations in secret. But, though they had expected a real danger in being caught and held captive, the reality had been entirely different.

On arrival, they had found the security system weak, the guards lazy, and a biplane left fuelled and unattended on the airstrip. Jean-Baptiste and his ally for the mission – both airmen by training – couldn't resist the opportunity. They climbed aboard, started the plane, and flew it right out of the airbase. Once airborne they had realised they needed to get out of French, or rather Nazi-occupied, airspace as soon as possible, and headed straight across the Channel, landing as soon as they could on the Dorset coast.

Flying a plane that was clearly painted with the Nazi swastika was a sure way to get shot out of the sky over England, but a quick-thinking Brit had noticed that the small biplane was not intended to travel as far as it had, and there must be something fishy. So they let it land, and surrounded it with armed soldiers who were relieved when two casually dressed Frenchmen had climbed out, unarmed and with their hands raised, explaining that they were part of a French resistance.

'Did they interrogate you?' asked Marie-Claire, stunned by both the bravado and stupidity of what Jean-Baptiste had done, but amazed by how he'd got away with it.

'It's not really what I'd call interrogation. They made us a cup of tea and allowed us to explain who we were, where we'd come from, why we'd stolen the plane—'

'And your reason for that, exactly?' she'd asked him, incredulous.

'Well, it was there, and they weren't guarding it and so... Look, it probably wasn't the wisest thing we've ever done, but wait until you hear where it got us!' he cried.

Officers representing the Free French in England were brought to the barracks – where the two men were being fed, bunked, and generally feted by the English RAF airmen on the base – and over the next couple of days they shared information and plans on what was occurring on both sides of the Channel.

'They already have a strong network here that I didn't know about, and now we're joining forces. With the backing of British intelligence, and some British spies who are already among us here, we will be so much stronger, and soon we will begin to cause real damage,' he explained, barely stopping to take breath.

'What kind of damage?' she asked.

'We aren't talking details yet, and even when we do, we will have to start working in small teams so that only the bare minimum of people know any details. It's safer that way. The less you know, the less you can accidentally share, hmm?' Marie-Claire nodded. She could see sense in that.

'So what happens from here?'

'For now, we all carry on as before. You work in the restaurant, write a little, look out for messages, and take note of any new people in town here. I will continue to work at the château, along with the other grounds staff and house staff there, and I will still make regular trips between Paris, Caen, here and perhaps Cherbourg. The agricultural produce from the château must be delivered far and wide, and I am a fine driver,' he said with a wink, and stopped on the track as he recognised the farm building they had reached.

'And is Adeline well?' Marie-Claire said, taking the chance to ask after her old friend at the château. 'I miss her. She was a great comfort to me.'

'Adeline is very well, and you should know she misses your company as well. She worries for you. I'll be happy to let her know how healthy you are looking,' he said with a warm smile, before continuing on the line of business he'd come here to talk to her about.

'Have you met Louis Joubert? He lives on this farm here,' he said, indicating a barn that could be seen the other side of a stile that led off from the woodland path.

'I know him, but barely. He sometimes comes in for a coffee. I saw him talking to Charles this morning, after church. Why do you ask?'

'Louis is already working with the British. We came back to France via this farm – his parents' farm. He lives and works here with them. He has no wife or family of his own yet, which keeps things very simple, and allows him to get out at all times of night and set up the airfields.' Marie-Claire was confused. She'd not heard of there being any airfield near here.

'Not a known airfield,' he explained. 'It is a simple farmer's field that is lit with three torches, and a signal given to the incoming plane. It was this British plane – a marvellous little thing called a Lysander – that brought us back and landed in a field not very far from where we are right now. With Louis at this farm, out of the way in the quiet here, and you in the café-bar in town, Charles managing the printing of the parish paper which the Germans are ignoring because it seems so simple they can't imagine how useful it is to us, we are becoming a formidable force, Marie-Claire.'

'But do you think we can really work to get back our country? The Nazi force is so huge and so determined,' she asked, feeling overwhelmed by the task ahead.

'We have no other choice. You are not going to give up, just lie down and let them take everything, are you?' She shook her head firmly in response, and he continued. 'No, exactly. You are already fighting back. We will keep going until we have won, or we die trying,' he said with an air of the victory he hoped for.

## 12

### SAINTE-MÈRE-ÉGLISE, MAY 1998

That night, Esther and Jules wandered home along the moon-bathed woodland path, hand in hand. They had kissed and talked, talked and kissed for several hours and now were beginning to turn their minds to the family at the farmhouse.

They'd begun to talk about what might happen next. But now, as they reached the stile – the spot where they'd kissed goodbye as kids, thirteen years earlier – the fact of the Joubert family loomed large. What would they all think of them, going off for an afternoon walk and coming home so late and suddenly intimately involved?

'We can't let them know, Jules. Let's just try and keep this under wraps for a while, hmm?' she said, as she rested her head on his chest between kisses. 'We'll give ourselves time to work it out privately before they all get any big ideas.'

'I think that's a good plan. I'll walk you to the door now, and sleep in the barn, as I did this afternoon,' he said.

'In the barn? Is there not a spare bed for you in the house?' she asked, puzzled.

'Not really, no. The house is full at the moment, but there's a good bed in there. Come on, I'll show you,' he said, crossing the stile and leading her by the hand into the barn, and up the hayloft ladder. The hens were muttering their roosting noises at the slight disturbance the couple made, and a newborn calf and mother in the corner of the barn raised their heads to see what was going on.

'There's a little room at the back here, see? It was a storeroom once, and then, during the war I think, it was used as a bedroom for visitors. Giselle and I used to come up and play houses in here. But *Grand-mère* didn't like it much. She said it was dangerous, but I think it might have been more than that.'

Esther peered into the tiny room and saw it was just big enough for a small bed, with a few shelves. The bed was old, and the bedding seemed very dated, but it was covered with an ultra-modern-looking sleeping bag which Jules must have brought with him.

'What's that in the corner?' Esther asked, seeing a pole with a handle leading straight up through the roof of the barn.

'I'm not certain, but I think it might have been a retractable radio aerial, left over from the war. Look at this old heap of junk,' he said, bending down and pulling out a primitive old wireless radio set-up that was stored under the bed.

'Wow! What went on here during the war, then?' Esther asked.

'I don't know. *Grand-mère* wouldn't ever tell us. She just said it was all a long time ago, and it doesn't matter now.'

'It's a very basic set-up, but it almost looks as though it was meant to be a secret hideout,' Esther said. 'I'd feel a bit nervous here on my own,' she said, shivering a little.

'I'm very comfortable up here – for a night or two.' He winked. 'But I'll take you across to the farmhouse door now,' he said as they climbed down the loft ladder and stepped across the farmyard. Jules risked one more kiss at the farmhouse door and hugged her tight.

'I feel like a very naughty schoolboy, sneaking around with you like this,' he laughed gently.

'Jules Joubert, for the way you dropped me all those years ago, you *are* a very naughty schoolboy!' she laughed. 'But I forgive you.'

'Thank you. But I'm going to need a lot more than your forgiveness, before many days are passed,' he added so quietly that she didn't even hear him as he stepped quietly across the farmyard.

\* \* \*

The next morning when Esther woke up, she stretched and was immediately aware of a great expectation – like it was Christmas morning. And then she remembered – Jules. She dressed quickly and went down for breakfast, pleased to find the whole family there.

'Good morning, Esther. Did you sleep well?' asked *Grand-mère,* who stood to warm some milk for breakfast.

'I did, thank you – very well. I had a lovely evening with Jules yesterday,' she said before she'd thought about it.

'I'm sure you did. He is very good company, you know. And he'll be here soon for his breakfast and our crêpe-making lesson, hmm?' the old lady said, and Esther realised she had completely forgotten the plan for the morning. But at least they had the perfect excuse to spend all morning in the same room together.

Jules, when he arrived in the family kitchen for breakfast, made a big show of going around to everyone and giving all his family a morning kiss and a cuddle, telling them it wasn't every day that he woke up in the same home as all his family. So, when he came to Esther, it seemed only natural to include her. But she knew, when their eyes met, that the whole round of affection had been meant entirely so he could get close to her and tell her with a hug and kiss that he'd meant everything he'd said the night before.

'Now then, you two,' began *Grand-mère*. 'Once we've cleaned away the breakfast things, shall we begin?' she said, and looked at them both with such joy, it made Esther determined to be the best crêpe-making student the old lady had ever taught.

'Do we need your recipe book, *Grand-mère*?' Jules asked, and looked around him as if to collect it.

'You can use it if you like, but I know the recipe without it,' she said as she turned her back and collected ingredients from the pantry cupboard. Esther noticed then that Jules had pulled an old, worn notebook from a kitchen drawer already, and was in the process of putting it away again. But as he did, she caught a glimpse of the curly cursive writing on the front. She didn't have time to read it, but did see the name written on the front before it disappeared back into the drawer.

Two hours later, they'd successfully made three batches of crêpes and had turned the last batch into crêpes Suzette which Esther had been reminded of during the cooking process. Jules was indeed a great cook, and *Grand-mère* was an even better teacher. They sat at the old wooden table licking the gloriously buttery and orangey sauce from their fingers, and laughing about the successes and failures of the lesson.

'All that this proves, *Grand-mère,* is that you are an excellent cook, and we will all be in your shadow forever,' laughed Jules who obviously adored the elderly woman.

'I think that being a good cook must run in the blood, Jules. You did a fine job too,' Esther said.

'Ah, well, our grandmother taught us all when we were children, just as she taught our father and aunt when they were young, isn't that right, *Grand-mère*?'

The older lady simply shrugged and muttered that it was nothing. 'I have always done whatever I can to help, and cooking is easy for me,' she said. 'Now then. What are you two going to do next? Jules, I think Esther would enjoy a drive out to see the beaches, perhaps? You could take us in that fine car of yours,' she said, sounding more and more as though she really was the oil that kept this family machine going. Jules looked to Esther with a question on his brow.

'I have no real plans, Jules. I had set aside this week to spend here on the farm with Giselle and the family. Perhaps she would like to bring the children along,' Esther suggested. And so, before long, there were two cars full of Jouberts, and Cartiers, and Esther heading for an afternoon on the beach, all packed up with a picnic, buckets, spades and beach towels. Jules made sure there was a seat beside him for Esther, but *Grand-mère* took the back seat.

'Which beach are we going to?' asked Esther as they settled in for the short journey.

'Ravenoville Plage,' replied Jules. 'It is nothing very special – especially when the tide is out as it is so shallow. But if the tide is in, we can have a swim, and Elodie will enjoy playing on the sand. It is a good beach for walking. Perhaps we can take a little stroll. Alone,' he said, looking to her with meaning and she smiled in return.

'Is this anywhere near the beaches that were used on D-Day?' she asked as an afterthought.

'Very close.' He nodded. 'Ravenoville Plage is just a little north of what you will know as Utah Beach.'

'Really? We didn't ever visit that when I came on my first trip with school, though we saw plenty of other memorials to the war. I expect it is a sad place to see,' she answered. 'Is there a memorial?'

'Oh yes, all kinds of things to mark what happened there. It is a long time ago, but history has its place, of course,' said Jules.

'Many good men died on that day. Many good men... and women,' said a quiet voice from the back seat. Both Jules and Esther had thought *Grand-mère* must have drifted off to sleep. Esther turned to face the older woman.

'Of course, *Grand-mère,* you were living here in Sainte-Mère-Église at that time, weren't you? It must have been a difficult time.'

'It was. Very difficult. But that was a long time ago, and look at us all now. A big, happy family going to enjoy an afternoon at the beach, watching the little babies playing happily on the sand. At one time, we would never have imagined this was our future.' She sighed deeply and grew quiet again, watching the scenery pass by the window for the rest of the journey.

At the beach, they unloaded chairs and umbrellas, and the tide was in, so everyone went for at least a paddle, if not a swim. Giselle and Hugo took Elodie for an ice cream, along with Madame and Monsieur Joubert, and *Grand-mère* stayed on the beach minding the sleeping Julien. Jules and Esther took the chance for a long stroll alone along the shoreline.

They talked of beaches they loved – Esther had holidayed in Spain, and many Greek islands, and Jules had a hankering to visit the great white sandy Australian beaches he'd heard of. She told him about Poole, and particularly Studland Beach with its strong connection to the D-Day invasion, with Fort Henry and all the troops who had left from that part of Dorset, headed for Normandy.

'It's strange to think that they came from my hometown and landed here, so close to yours,' she mused. Jules agreed and, looking behind him to check they were well out of sight by now, he held her hand, weaving their fingers together. She turned to him smiling.

'I can't believe how natural that feels,' she said. 'Do you realise, it was only twenty-four hours ago that we were in the café after the christening, both wondering exactly why the other was there?'

'Yes, it was only yesterday. But that was a lifetime ago. Now you are here, and I am here, and why shouldn't we be holding hands?' he laughed, but then turned a little more serious.

'I really do need to get back to Paris tomorrow, though,' he sighed. 'I was only coming up for the day on Sunday, and then everything changed,' he said with a frown and squeeze of her hand. 'I won't be back in the office until Wednesday now, by the time I get home tomorrow – because I absolutely want some more time with you here first in the morning. But work will be building up, and there are... other things I need to deal with. Did you say you were thinking of visiting Paris next week?' he asked hopefully.

'I did say that, and yes, I definitely plan to visit Paris now,' she said. 'Do you know anywhere I could stay?' she said, quite innocently thinking he'd suggest a small hotel.

'I think I could find you a spare bedroom in my apartment, and I'd love you to stay with me,' he said. 'It's very central and a great place to base yourself for sightseeing – you can even see the tip of the Eiffel Tower from my balcony. And then we can spend the evenings together – if you like?' he asked, suddenly seeming to doubt that she was as much into this new thing that had begun as he was.

She stopped walking and they turned to face each other, Esther drawing him in close and reaching up to kiss him.

'Jules Joubert, I like the sound of that very much.'

As they walked back again later, Esther found herself arguing with the little voice in her head that told her this couldn't end well. She didn't do relationships. She would never commit. The risk of heartache was just too great. But what if she was ready now? What if, after all this time, she'd finally healed from the hurt caused by her irresponsible father, and from watching her mother's pain? Jules had been immature and foolish, that was all. And now he was a mature man of thirty. He'd learned to be honest with himself and others. He seemed ready to commit to something outside of himself as well.

She could do this. She could dive in, and take the risk. What could go wrong?

# 13

SAINTE-MÈRE-ÉGLISE, OCTOBER 1941

Marie-Claire tried her best to laugh openly at the joke the German officer was making, but she was faking every twitch of muscle in her face. The hatred she felt for anyone wearing this steel-grey uniform, with its ostentatious braids and shining cross on the front of the jacket, only grew more profound as time went on, especially with the way she heard them speaking about the townspeople. The soldiers sat in the café-bar, drinking wine they never paid for, and laughing at the farmers going about their business. Today, Louis Joubert was the object of their scorn.

Louis had brought the haycart into town, laden with vegetables and milk to sell at the market. He had unloaded most of his wares at the stall set up with others in the central square beside the churchyard, where his mother was positioned to take sales for the day. He had returned to his cart and had been pouring off milk from a bigger churn into smaller containers that villagers brought to be filled with the fresh milk from his farm's dairy cows. Marie-Claire knew that they sold milk from the farm door as well, but the weekly market made it more convenient for a larger number of people.

'Oh, look at the pretty milkmaid out there!' one of the nastier soldiers said, laughing.

'Do you think she would come and sit on my knee if I asked nicely?' another asked in a terribly camp accent.

'What kind of work is that for a man?' scoffed a third.

'He should join us, and we could put him in a real man's uniform, and give him a real man's work to do,' said the highest ranking of them. 'But look at how dark his hair is, and have you seen his nose? I wouldn't be surprised to find he's a horrible little Jew!' he spat.

Marie-Claire was standing the other side of the counter in the café-bar with her back to the soldiers and was grateful for that. As it was, her face boiled red with rage and she gritted her teeth, pounding the pastry she was moulding with a lot more force than was necessary. She thought of the little pistol that Jean-Baptiste had acquired for her. She kept it upstairs in her room while she was working but she allowed her mind to take her through the motions of picking it up, turning around and aiming it at the brow of each of these four soldiers in turn. *Bang, bang, bang, bang.* She saw the horror on their faces and the blood that ran from their wounds as their heads fell back and they dropped lifeless, on the floor of the café-bar. She would walk over and kick them sharply, one by one, then walk out of the café-bar. The townspeople would be celebrating in the middle of the square and raising the French flag. The war had been won. The Germans flushed out, and there would be Benjamin and Antoine coming back to tell her what a wonderful job she had done.

'Hey, you stupid girl, did you hear me?' one of the soldiers snapped, so close to her that she jumped visibly. She wiped her hands on a damp cloth, and turned around to apologise.

'I'm so sorry, sir, I was miles away. What can I get you?' She smiled sweetly, noticing that Louis had just stepped inside, his work done for the day. She tried to will him to get out, sensing trouble ahead for him, but he had come to see Marie-Claire and would do so regardless of this danger.

She served the German soldiers their next bottle of wine and brought the bread and soup they had asked for, then took her notepad over to Louis who had sat down at table nine, with his back to the soldiers.

'*Bonjour,* Monsieur Joubert,' she greeted him and took his order for coffee, as he made what could have sounded like small talk with her, but she knew how to interpret it.

'The moon is bright this week, hey? I'll be working late on the harvest tonight,' Louis said. 'But it's hard work alone – would be good to get some more help,' he said, and shrugged as if to say this idea was impossible. Marie-Claire made sympathetic noises and told him she'd bring him his coffee right away, under-standing his message perfectly.

Tonight, there would be a Lysander landing – or touching down, at least – and, for some reason, he needed her to help set up the landing strip with torches, or to flash the signal to the pilot of the little British plane. Often Louis would do this alone, but he'd been asking for her help more and more lately. She would only find out later if there was someone being picked up or dropped off, or if instead it was simply a drop of supplies or a package pickup.

After Louis had finished his coffee, she was intrigued to see him light a cigarette and pull a deck of cards from his pocket and begin idly shuffling them, which caught the attention of one of the soldiers. The soldier spoke quietly to his friends.

'Let's show the stupid French Jew how a real man plays cards, hey?' And they'd all laughed and slapped their thighs.

Marie-Claire was disgusted by them. How dare they speak so

terribly offensively well within his hearing, although they obviously felt they were safe from her ears. She had become very good at lip-reading across the room. Part of her job here – the job according to Jean-Baptiste, that is – was to listen to conversations and report what was going on. She'd discovered quite early that if she watched people's lips she could work out what they were saying, even if she couldn't hear a thing, and her rudimentary German had come on in leaps and bounds in recent months.

'Hey, you!' called the German to Louis, who turned around looking like a scared little rabbit.

'Want to play cards? We can teach you how. Here – come to our table,' he said, and Louis looked as if he'd like to run out of the café-bar, but went across sheepishly to join them. Soon they'd made a big show of helpfully teaching him the rules of poker, and had called in a few extra friends to join them. They'd also sent Louis to find some of his local friends from out in the market square too, and Marie-Claire tried not to look surprised when he came in with Jean-Baptiste and one of the other young men who had been at the château when she was staying there – both of whom were protesting they didn't have time for cards, they had work to do. But the soldiers insisted. The expanded group of men ordered more wine and soon were deep into their play.

The sun had set and Marie-Claire had lit candles on the tables. She saw several regular customers turn and walk away rather than come inside. They weren't keen to come in for a meal when what looked like a regular Nazi party was going on in the local café-bar. The wine had been replaced by a bottle of brandy and the noise in the room made it seem that the French men were enjoying themselves after all.

Just as she started to wonder quite how Louis was going to extricate himself in time for the job ahead of him tonight, he stood up – none too steadily, which caused the Germans to break into great howls of hilarity – and signalled that he needed to go outside to relieve himself.

Marie-Claire saw her chance and ducked quietly out the back to go around the side of the building and meet him. She was prepared to berate him for his stupid drunkenness and found an entirely different kind of Louis to the one she was expecting. He was not drunk at all, and bent close to her, keenly whispering.

'This is a ruse. We are keeping them here tonight. Jean-Baptiste is bleeding them for information at the same time as we keep them safe out of the way here. You will go alone tonight, Marie-Claire. Set the flares at 23.15. The plane is due at 23.30. In the corner of the barn, underneath the haycart, you will find a small wooden box. It contains a package. Take it to the airfield and, as you've seen me do, run to meet the Lysander as it lands. An operative will be delivered, and you will hand over the package. Take care to remove the torches, and the code letter tonight is "J",' he said and, in the biggest shock of her night, squeezed her around the waist and gave her a quick kiss on the cheek before he left.

Marie-Claire gasped and held her palm to the cheek he had kissed, watching him rush to the front of the building and then set off slowly swaggering as if drunk again, back into the café-bar where he was greeted with loud cheers of welcome. She laughed quietly to herself and shook her head. She understood everything now. Everything except the kiss, and the way her skin had tingled all around her middle and down her legs when she'd felt his hand tighten on her waist.

It had been ten months since she had lost her beloved Benjamin and baby Antoine. She didn't think she would ever get used to sleeping alone, but she had begun to forget the sensations, the nerve endings that could be triggered by the touch of a man. What was Louis playing at? Did he mean anything by this or was it all part of the act in case they'd been seen? It must be that, she reasoned. Why else would a man be talking quietly to a woman down a dark lane, if he wasn't romantically involved with her? It must all be part of the ruse. But all the same, she was aware that his touch had ignited something in her that she'd forgotten had ever even had a life before.

At ten-thirty, her boss had signalled she could leave for the night. He'd locked the door to stop any other customers from coming in, but it was clear that the German soldiers were intending their little party to continue late into the night. Marie-Claire was grateful to him as she knew he was thinking of protecting her just as much as letting her get some sleep. Who knew what they'd become like in the early hours of the morning – if they were still standing. She snorted to herself as she thought about how in control Louis was, and presumably the other French men too, compared to the Germans who were fast on their way to becoming blind drunk.

She went to her room, pulled her curtains shut and lit her lamp. Then she changed from her waitressing and cooking clothes into the dark green men's trousers, big farmer's boots and a dark blue sweater that she kept in a box under her bed. She tucked her hair under a cap and looked in the mirror. On a dark night, and from a distance, no one would even recognise she was a woman, let alone which one, and the image helped her to discard the thoughts that perhaps Louis might see her as a woman, and not just a compatriot – a fellow freedom-fighter. She tucked her knife into her pocket, and her pistol into her belt, hiding it underneath the chunky woollen jumper. She took a deep breath and muttered the same phrase she'd been saying all year in this strange, new, dangerous life: 'For you, Benjamin; for you, Antoine.'

Marie-Claire quietly shut the door at the back of the café-bar, having snuck down the stairs from her room and past the internal entrance to the main restaurant. She could still hear the noise from the card game and knew nobody would be leaving anytime soon. But all the same, she checked carefully that nobody was following her as she jogged along the side of the square and down the lane that led into the woods. A year ago, she would have been terrified to be walking in the dark country-side alone at night, but not any more. For one thing, she really believed she had nothing to fear, and Jean-Baptiste had been quite correct in his assessment of how much she didn't have to lose any more. *What could they take from her? Her life? Pah! It was over.* She only lived now to bring down as many Nazi soldiers as possible and do everything in her power to fight back for what they'd taken from her. Fearlessness was a good thing, in her new line of work.

She trotted along the black path through the woodlands, but the moon was bright and shone through the leaves almost like dappled sunlight. Within a few minutes she had made it to Louis's farm. She climbed the stile and went straight to the barn. The old sheepdog stood up immediately and gave an inquisitive yap, but she quietly called his name, and soothingly told him what a good boy he was. He gave a friendly growl in acknowl-edgement that she was a known friend and he settled back down to sleep.

The farmhouse windows were all shuttered for the night, and the hens all abed in the henhouse, just making gentle roosting noises and shuffling a little on their perches. She found her way into the corner where the haycart stood and crawled underneath, looking for the box, and found it under a covering of hay. She took out the package – documents wrapped in brown paper and string – and shoved it into the shoulder bag she was carrying, then went to the storeroom behind the barn to find the torches, extra kerosene and matches, carrying these in another big canvas bag. Then she set off for the planned landing strip, three fields away to the north.

Once in the field, she followed the planned protocol and waited silently at the edge, watchful for any movement. An ambush by German soldiers was always a possibility, but so far here in Sainte-Mère-Église, the Germans seemed unaware of all that was going on under their noses. And right now, Marie-Claire thought ruefully, they were probably 'winning' card games and getting more drunk by the minute while Louis, Jean-Baptiste and the other Frenchmen had perfect control of the whole situation.

She checked her watch: 23.10. She heard her breath begin to come more quickly and worked to steady it. Taking one last look around the field, she decided it was clear and ran off to set the three torches, in the form of an 'L' shape, having checked the direction of the wind so she knew which way around to place them. She filled them with kerosene and lit each one, then waited by the last torch with a small board from the kit with which to hide and reveal the flame so she could signal the agreed letter to the pilot. She waited. Listening.

Marie-Claire's head shot up as she heard the familiar drone of the Lysander coming near. She checked her watch: 23.25. Perfect. She watched the sky and started signalling the letter 'J' – tonight's code letter. Dot-Dash-Dash-Dash. And again. Dot-Dash-Dash-Dash. She kept this up as the pilot flew over once, and back again and then she saw him make a final turn and come in to land.

She checked the edges of the field again for any movement or signs of light and then ran out to meet the landing plane, getting to it just as it stopped and a bag was thrown out, followed quickly after by the form of a man who ran past her, picked up the bag and kept running as Marie-Claire took a step up onto the ladder, threw the package inside and ran back to the edge of the field. She extinguished and collected each of the torches and by the time she'd collected them all and made it back to the safety of the trees around the edge, the Lysander had taken off and disappeared again.

Marie-Claire allowed herself a moment to shut her eyes and breathe. It was done. The first time she'd brought a Lysander in alone, and all had gone very much to plan. So far. She stopped herself from celebrating too early, just in case.

'*Bonsoir, Mademoiselle. Par où, s'il vous plaît?*' said a voice of a much higher pitch than Marie-Claire was expecting, and she found herself looking up into the face of a woman. A very beautiful woman, with blonde curly hair tucked under a cap. Marie-Claire smiled in welcome and led the way, at a trot, back to the farm.

Once inside the barn, Marie-Claire was about to introduce herself and remembered at the last moment that she needed to remain nameless. She simply smiled at the woman and showed her the ladder to the hayloft.

'Up there, at the back, there is a false wall. Behind it you'll find a bed, a jug of water, a bucket for a toilet and hopefully some food if it's been organised for you. Wait there until Lou— until someone comes to put you in touch with your next contact,' she said, and when the female agent smiled her thanks, Marie-Claire felt that she was part of something so great, so important, that she even experienced a little joy from her night's work. She was in a real army. And they could make a difference.

'Well done, you did a great job tonight. Perfect,' said the

agent, before turning to climb up the loft ladder, and then looking back to Marie-Claire again as if she'd just remembered something else. 'My name's Marguerite, by the way.'

Marie-Claire watched 'Marguerite' – almost certainly not her real name – disappear up the loft ladder. Then she turned and headed back into town, along the woodland path. She wondered if she'd ever see the woman again.

# 14

PARIS, JUNE 1998

Esther watched the Norman countryside fly past the train window as she sped her way towards Paris on Friday afternoon. She had always expected to make a trip into the capital for some of this holiday but now, she thought, the City of Lights held so much more delightful anticipation for her than the usual tourist round of city sights, restaurants, and art galleries.

By the evening of that Monday when they'd all gone to the beach, it was becoming obvious to all the family that Esther and Jules were getting along extremely well, and so nobody was at all surprised when they'd gone out for a long drive in the country-side on the Tuesday morning after breakfast.

Jules drove and they headed a little way north, where he parked in the stunning grounds of a château, and they walked through the woods in the morning sunshine.

'Are we allowed to be here in these grounds?' Esther asked. 'Is it not private property?'

'It is private property, but guests are able to park here and enjoy the grounds,' he answered.

'Guests?' she asked, puzzled.

'I booked a table for lunch – in case we are hungry by then. The food here is amazing, and it is quite an experience to take lunch in a thousand-year-old château, I think,' he said, and Esther's mouth dropped open in awe.

'Oh my word, that sounds amazing! I'll make sure I'm hungry,' she laughed, and they set off for a good long walk to work up an appetite fit for the count and countess of a château.

The château dining room proved to be as magnificent as Esther had imagined, complete with ancient stone walls and floors, the most enormous fireplace, and several full suits of armour standing guard in the halls. But even more recent battle history had been made in this place and, after a delectable lunch, the receptionist showed them the room where at the end of World War II, the surrender of Cherbourg had been signed by American and German officers.

Before they headed back to Sainte-Mère-Église, they had ambled around the grounds again and found themselves resting on a bench under the shade of an old beech tree. Jules wrapped his arm around her shoulders and she nestled into his chest, breathing in the scent of him.

'All that food has made me sleepy,' she said drowsily. He laughed gently, and bent to kiss her on her head. And then she turned her face up to him and, within moments, Esther was wide awake to his touch as they locked together, each hungry for the other's kisses.

'So,' he said gently, when they eventually pulled apart, 'I will drive back to Paris after I take you back to the farm this afternoon. And I will need to work all day tomorrow, Thursday and Friday. When are you thinking of coming down?' he asked.

'Perhaps I could travel Friday afternoon, to be there in time for dinner Friday night?'

'That's a date: Friday dinner in Paris,' he said, then smiled and kissed her again.

\* \* \*

For the rest of the week, after Jules had left, she'd spent every moment with Giselle, the children, and her new friend, *Grand-mère*, who shared her stories of her time as a cook, the manager of a crêperie, and as the farmer's wife here on the farm she called home. Esther had gathered that the old woman had lived in Paris, but had grown up in Fontainebleau, and spent holidays on the south coast, and yet it seemed impossible to entice her to share any details of her earlier life.

One evening, after being reminded of crêpes again, Esther made sure she found time to be alone in the kitchen. Giselle was busy putting the children to bed – always a hard task with the light summer evenings – and *Grand-mère* had gone to bed early. Monsieur and Madame Joubert were out after the late milking, doing some checks on the farm fences, and so she poured herself a glass of wine, and reached into the drawer in the old wooden dresser where she'd seen Jules put the recipe book.

It was well worn and well loved, looking at the state of the binding. The book was a journal, small in size and yet fat with handwritten pages, and several loose pages inserted at the end, which is what seemed to have caused the binding to break. And on the front, written in a curly cursive hand, it read, in French, 'The Recipes and Writings of Marie-Claire Dubois'. The 'Dubois' had been crossed through and underneath was written large, 'Madame Joubert'. At first the name confused her, as Esther thought of Giselle and Jules' mother as Madame Joubert. But of course, she was the daughter-in-law of *Grand-mère*, who was also Madame Joubert. But the old lady seemed to have had this journal since before she was even married.

Esther stopped to listen and check she would still be alone for a while, then she sat in the fireside chair, took a long draught of wine, and opened the journal. The first entry had been dated 1936 – so long ago – and was a simple recipe for coq au vin. The journal notes described the flavours, the best types of onions to use, and even a little history about an early dish – poulet au vin blanc – on which this recipe was probably based. Esther felt as though she was listening to a food documentary on the television as she read the beautiful descriptions.

She flicked over several more pages and saw that the entries became fewer in 1938, picked up for a while and then dropped off again for a year from late in 1940. But from 1941 onwards, there were several more recipes filling the pages.

Esther closed the book carefully and placed it back in the drawer. *Grand-mère* was certainly a very experienced cook and a marvellous writer. And Esther now knew for sure, having studied the writing style and become familiar with the hand, that the note she had found in that recipe book, the one with the French poem and the strange, minuscule message in English, had been written by *Grand-mère*. Now she just had to work out if she should ask the older lady about it, or just slip it into this journal, unnoticed. But it must be returned. For now, she slipped it into the back of the journal and left it there, where she believed it belonged.

She decided to wait until she'd had a chance to talk to Jules about it some more. He'd know.

By Friday afternoon, after many long phone calls with Jules and chats with the family around the old kitchen table, it had been agreed that the best option of travel for Esther was to catch the train direct from Carentan, just a few minutes' drive south from Sainte-Mère-Église. Giselle would drop her at the station, so that Esther's car could be kept secure at the farmyard. Although she felt quite confident driving into the city, there was nowhere to park her car without paying a king's ransom, and she wouldn't need it once there anyway. Besides, her route home to England was via the ferry from Cherbourg to Poole, so it made the best sense, as she would have to come back this way after her trip to Paris.

But when it came to book the train ticket, she chose to make it one way. Somehow, she didn't want to put a definitive end on the time she would spend with Jules.

'So you're repeating history a little and going to spend some time with my big brother in Paris, hey?' teased Giselle, as she drove Esther to the station after lunch on Friday.

'I hardly spent much time with him there when we were girls, Giselle – except for the coach ride to Paris, and a little while in the Notre-Dame,' said Esther with a laugh, remembering her first trip to Sainte-Mère-Église, when the school had organised an overnight trip to Paris. Somehow or other, Jules had managed to come along for the ride – saying he needed to meet someone at the university to talk about his study plans. She'd spent quite a while talking to him, and he'd met up with them when they visited the Notre-Dame Cathedral in Paris.

'Yes, that is true. It was the time in our own little Notre-Dame here in Sainte-Mère-Église, that was really special with him, hmm?' Giselle said with a wink and a laugh, making Esther gasp in shock.

'You knew about that? How did you find out?' she asked, aghast that anyone had seen them kissing when they were just kids.

'Oh, Esther, this is a very small town. There was a woman cleaning the church when you two were "saying your prayers", and she told her neighbour, who told the schoolteacher, who let my mother know,' she said, laughing loudly now. 'And then of course, you were writing to him, so we all suspected. But neither you nor Jules had ever mentioned it to me, so I didn't say anything.'

'Wow, so for all these years you knew that we had a bit of a thing back then,' said Esther, puffing out her cheeks and blowing the air away.

'We did. But we also never knew why it ended. And here you are again, and I have to say you already look like a well-matched couple,' Giselle said as she pulled into the train station car park.

'We do? In what way?' Esther asked, unfastening her seat belt and turning to look at Giselle, who simply shrugged.

'I don't know. You seem comfortable together. And the way you both smile when the other walks into the room? It shows a deep happiness. It is good. I never imagined I would say this about my irritating big brother, but I think he is good for you. He makes you happy, Esther. And he seems happy too – which I never thought I'd see. He's had so many girlfriends over the years, and I swear there's been a new one every time I've spoken to him in the last decade, but perhaps his days of flirting with every woman in Paris are over,' she said. Esther smiled a tight little smile, trying to ignore the seed of doubt that Giselle's words had sown. She kissed her friend on both cheeks in the French manner, and collected her suitcase from the boot.

And now it was early Friday evening, and the train was fast approaching the Gare Saint-Lazare in central Paris, not far from where Jules lived in his apartment. In some ways, she felt embarrassed that the whole Joubert family had been aware all these years that she and Jules had shared what they'd thought was a very secret kiss. But in another way, it was comforting; like a blessing, of sorts. It was just that little niggle of doubt planted by Giselle's offhand comment that troubled her.

When the train pulled into the station, she stepped off, hauling her suitcase behind her, and fumbled in her handbag to find her mobile and give Jules a call to find out if she should make her way to his apartment, or if she should meet him somewhere else. Just as she found the phone and pulled it out of her bag she jumped as someone reached around her waist. She spun to find herself wrapped in Jules' arms and to see his beaming face.

'Jules! I was just about to call,' she said, leaning in to return the cheek-kissing ritual he offered her.

'I couldn't wait for that,' he said with a laugh and then, searching her eyes to ask for consent, which she gave by joyfully reaching her face up to his, he kissed her fully and firmly in a long and luscious kiss. This, Esther thought to herself, was going to be a wonderful week, and she would not let her stupid doubting head spoil it for her.

They made their way to the metro platform and within minutes of Parisian bustle, they were stepping off and heading up into the light.

'My apartment is so close to this metro stop, I rarely use my car when I'm in town. It's parked in the basement for weekend trips to the countryside.' Jules laughed, lifting her heavy case with ease off the top of the escalator and showing her the way along the street towards his apartment building.

Esther was thrilled to be back in the thick of exciting Paris again. She'd visited a few times since her first trip all those years ago, and had often wondered where Jules was in the city. She took a glance at him now as he walked beside her, tall and lithe, with the same dark hair, still kept a little unfashionably long so that his habit of sweeping his hands through it made him look like that same young boy he was when they first met. But now he was a mature and confident businessman, and she was his equal.

The street was lined with trees and, though the traffic was busy, there was still that sense of classic charm everywhere she looked. Even the simplest of boutique stores looked glamorous, and each woman who passed by, even those tugging along their children or out walking their dogs, had an elegant panache to their outfits, the way they wore their hair, and they all left a trail of perfume in their wake. It was enough to inspire a shopping trip, she smiled to herself, partly planning some of the things she might do while Jules would be working some days in the following week.

Classically styled apartment blocks, some five or six storeys high, lined the street with shops, cafés, restaurants, and *boulangeries* all along at street level. Looking up, she saw that every French door had a little cast-iron Juliet balcony which made her remember Jules had said that part of the Eiffel Tower could be seen from his place.

'Yes, a little part. Just the very top of it,' he said laughing, and told her not to get her hopes up too much – the apartment was quite modest.

They stepped into the apartment block foyer and Jules held the lift door open for Esther. The apartment was on the top floor and when he opened the door, she couldn't help but gasp in surprise at the size of the place. The lounge room was vast, with a large separate dining room, and a separate kitchen. Jules went about the rooms opening doors and windows and telling her where everything was, then showed her the bedrooms.

'I have two spare rooms, but the smaller one is really my office, and it is such a mess,' he said, briefly opening the door to that one and sweeping his arm around a study that was lined with bookshelves and where boxes of files covered most of the floor space. 'But this one, I always keep clean, just in case of visitors. The view isn't too bad,' he said with a smile, as he went to draw back the sheer curtains, open the French doors and lead her out onto the tiny balcony.

Looking down, she saw a beautiful formal garden, dotted with benches and surrounded by a black iron railing. A child was playing with a little boat on the edge of a pond, while a woman who must have been her mother sat on a bench nearby, nursing a baby. And then Esther looked up and saw that even though the apartment building was not that tall, she could see for some distance, between the buildings. There was a glimpse of water, which Jules confirmed was the Seine, and then he stood behind her, wrapping one arm around her waist and, resting his chin on her shoulder, he pointed out through the buildings to where they could see the top third of the Eiffel Tower.

'Oh, wow! That is significantly more than just the tip, Jules! What a view,' she said with a sigh, and turned to see his face which was beaming.

'I do love it here. I love Sainte-Mère-Église of course, and the charm of our little village home is so different to this city. But Paris? It is a little like... perhaps I am married to Sainte-Mère-Église but Paris is my mistress?' he said with a guilty laugh that turned to the shadow of a frown on his brow.

'Jules, that is a terrible joke to make with the woman you have brought home to your apartment,' she said, laughing it off, but giving him a playful tap on the arm to show mock disapproval. 'But I do understand exactly what you mean. I felt a little like that with London, to be fair. I love my quiet harbour hometown, but the bright lights of London – the River Thames, the palaces, the theatres, the nightlife – it has an excitement all of its own,' she said.

'Talking of nightlife, we should get some dinner. It is early yet, but perhaps a stroll and a glass of wine before we find a restaurant?' he asked.

'That sounds perfect, Jules. But first, just let me take a quick shower and change, and then perhaps a cup of tea if that's allowed in such a ritzy French apartment as this?' she joked.

'I'm sure I can manage an English cup of tea for you,' he said, leaving her to unpack her bag while he headed out to the kitchen.

Esther enjoyed the luxury of the en-suite shower and wondered exactly how grand the master suite must be in this enormous apartment that Jules was determined to make sound like a humble flat. She glanced at the king-sized bed and was grateful that he had assumed she would want her own space, relieved to know they'd be taking this slowly. Because although they'd known each other for over a decade, this really was a very new thing.

Esther felt the warm evening breeze drifting in through the open French doors and chose a floaty summer dress with a pair of sparkly but comfortable sandals to wear as she was sure they'd be doing a fair bit of walking later. She brushed out her hair, and added a bit of make-up, before heading out to find Jules who was relaxing in the lounge with a coffee. There was a teapot, mug and milk jug on the coffee table.

'Look at you – so organised!' she said, and gratefully sank into the soft cushions of the settee to enjoy the brew she needed after an afternoon of travel. As she relaxed, she closed her eyes for a moment and, when she opened them again, she found that he'd folded his newspaper and was watching her, smiling.

'What?' she asked with a laugh. 'Have I mucked up my make-up or something? You're staring!'

He shook his head slowly.

'No, nothing is wrong. Everything is perfect. You look

wonderful. And I just can't believe that you're here, at my place. Esther, this is so strange, but wonderful. It is going to be a very good week,' he said, and came to join her on her settee.

* * *

Half an hour later Esther pulled herself away from where she'd been alternately nestling into, kissing, and talking with Jules. She went to check her make-up again – which was almost certainly smudged now, particularly around the lipstick – and they went out into the soft evening light where it seemed the characters on the stage of Paris had changed from the afternoon chorus into the evening players. Everyone was still dressed with elegance, but now there were a few more formal dresses and jackets, and the daytime cafés had transformed into restaurants for dinner. Jules showed her the quickest way to reach the path beside the Seine, and they found a bar overlooking the river where they ordered drinks.

'This is so special, Jules. I was planning on coming anyway, alone, to visit Paris, but now, with you – I feel like a kid again.' She beamed.

'And we have the whole weekend together, also. I will go to work for a few days next week, but I can make things work so we can spend plenty of time together as well. Perhaps we can even get a little out of the city as well, hmm?' he asked, and they talked of some of the sights she'd not seen yet: the Palace of Versailles, Château de Fontainebleau, and Monet's garden.

For dinner, they had wandered, hand in hand, up and down lanes and alleys until they found a tiny little place with just a few tables, and a deliciously indulgent Parisian menu, from which Jules recommended the *confit de canard*, and Esther wanted the ratatouille as a side, just to see how it was done properly in a place like this. In one corner of the impossibly small restaurant, a lone guitarist strummed and sang in French words which Esther could not translate but understood the meaning of perfectly. He was making love to his guitar as he sang so softly and must have been talking of love.

That night, when they reached the apartment again, Jules shut the door behind them and Esther pulled him into her arms to explore him with kisses and hands. They pulled apart several times and, unsuccessfully, tried each to part and go to their own rooms.

'You know,' Esther whispered softly to him, 'you haven't actually shown me where you sleep yet.'

He pulled back, just far enough to make sure he had her face in complete focus, and looked her directly in the eyes to find her meaning.

'You're right, Mademoiselle. How remiss of me. Would you like to see my room now?' he asked gently, teasingly.

She kissed him. His face, his eyes, his neck.

'I would, Monsieur. I would like to see your bed, particularly,' she said with a cheeky smile.

'I'm sure I can arrange a tour that will be to Mademoiselle's satisfaction,' he teased, and pulled her by the hand toward his room.

'Such confidence, Monsieur,' she laughed.

'Oh, I am quite sure the tour will satisfy you,' he said, laughing over his shoulder. 'I am very confident you will be nothing but satisfied.'

They laughed their way into his room. And Esther enjoyed the tour so much, that she stayed all night.

## 15

SAINTE-MÈRE-ÉGLISE, DECEMBER 1941

Winter in the country, where so much time was spent outside, was a different beast to winters she'd known in Paris. There, in the city, the wind could be bitter as it howled around buildings, but most of their lives had been spent inside, in the apartment, or in cafés, or the library, or theatres – back in the days when such freedoms had been so taken for granted.

Perhaps she only felt it so much here in Normandy because she was working alongside farmers, and her work with the resistance mainly happened out of doors. Even though her role was mainly to stay anchored at the café-bar where she could receive and pass on messages, or write the stories, anecdotes and recipes that were being printed into the parish newsletter, Marie-Clarie often found herself spending hours at a time, frozen, waiting in silence, on the edge of a darkened field.

Her first job of bringing in a Lysander back in October had not entailed much waiting at all, but as time wore on, the resistance realised they could no longer share such specific details as exact landing times for pilots. They would have a particular night earmarked, and might spend until almost dawn waiting to hear the plane overhead before racing around the field to mark out the landing strip.

Last night had been just such a night. She had returned to her bed by four in the morning and only had a couple of hours to sleep and get warmed through again before she had to get up and start work, opening the café. But she was due her afternoon off today, and planned to do nothing more than curl up in bed to recover. She was surprised when a note was delivered to her on table nine, asking her to go and light a candle for Uncle Jean at the church after lunch.

Marie-Claire hoped it was Louis she would be meeting in the church, as she was certain that once she'd lit a candle and sat in the third row from the front, on the left-hand side, as usual, somebody would come and sit just a little way along on the same pew as her.

Since that night in October when he'd given her the briefest of kisses, and touched her waist in a way that had sparked her womanly sensations back to life, she saw Louis through very different eyes. She noticed that when he smiled at her, his eyes shone, and when he asked her how she was feeling, she knew that he meant it. There was a concern for her, a gentleness that she'd not experienced from a man ever since she'd lost Benjamin.

Apart from Jean-Baptiste, her original saviour, the only person she'd met since that terrible night in Paris who had made her feel truly cared for, deeply loved, had been dear Adeline. The older woman had mothered her tenderly and helped her through her grief. Marie-Claire would never forget Adeline and knew she'd always be grateful to her.

Jean-Baptiste had taken care of her as well, but in a more distant and practical way. Whenever she saw him these days – which was rare – he was busy and focussed, and it was perfectly obvious that he had no time in his life for friendly affection. He was a machine, and a powerful one at that. Jean-Baptiste was the leader of the resistance force for a large part of Normandy and, as such, he had to keep moving and keep a very low profile.

The Germans in Sainte-Mère-Église still seemed to think he was no more than a farmer who came in to sell his produce from time to time. They'd thoroughly enjoyed smashing him at cards, and probably thought him an imbecile, he was so slow at the game. But they'd been played, well and truly, that night.

But something about Louis was different. He was focussed and driven, just like Jean-Baptiste, and he had still been able to remain at home, and was running a very successful safe house and drop-off point in the barn on his family's farm. And because he was local, it made sense that he would have relationships with people in the town. But there was something more, Marie-Claire knew. He often kissed her on the cheeks to say goodbye – a common thing for French acquaintances, sure, but perhaps not so often or as enthusiastically as he did it. He would squeeze her hand to say thank you, and she knew he watched her moving around the café-bar sometimes while he drank his coffee. If she glanced up and saw him watching, his face would break into a broad smile, making his eyes crinkle and shine.

At first, she'd been annoyed with herself that she was pleased by his attention. She felt guilty, as a married woman might, and often felt as though Benjamin had walked into the room and caught her in the act of betraying him. She loved her husband passionately still, and it confused her that she could feel even the slightest sense of pleasure from Louis's obvious affection for her. But every sight of the *Wehrmacht* uniform in town reminded her that she had no husband. And that realisation had led her to wondering if she could sense Benjamin's approval. He would have wanted her to be loved, and protected, and now that he wasn't here to do it, was it possible that Louis was here like an angel to step in for Benjamin?

Eventually, she'd started to return his smiles, squeeze his hand in return, rest a hand on his arm as they'd kissed cheek to cheek in greeting or farewell. And today, she suspected, she'd be meeting him in secret in the church.

She dipped her fingers into the holy water and touched them to her brow, crossing herself before collecting a candle and walking to the altar. After she'd taken her seat, she sat and said genuine prayers for those she'd lost, and for the protection of those she fought with. When she heard a shuffling nearby she turned her face and prepared to smile up at Louis from underneath her long, dark lashes.

'Marguerite!' she whispered, unable to hide her disappointment, but quickly recovered and looked to the front again, waiting for whatever instructions the agent had brought her.

'Louis needs your help at the farm,' whispered Marguerite. 'We are very busy at the château, with a large operation against the German airfield in Caen. Extra support came in by parachute last night, but one of the men broke an ankle on landing. We can't be sure how long the château will remain secure and are preparing to leave at any moment. The man with the broken ankle – George – could end up left behind and captured. So he is being brought here tonight, hidden in Jean-Baptiste's farm truck. Before the market, he will be taken to the hayloft. Louis is going to be away with us for the rest of the week, and needs you to visit George, take him food and water, and help him with anything he needs. When he is recovered enough to run across the airstrip, we will arrange to have him picked up and taken home.'

'Understood, thank you,' said Marie-Claire. 'Godspeed you all, *et bonne chance*,' she said as she crossed herself again, stood and walked out of the church without glancing any more at Marguerite.

The next afternoon, Marie-Claire packed up a basket of supplies that could have been for a picnic – except that the weather was far too cold for picnicking. She had a small loaf of bread, jam, a hunk of cheese, a small jar of pâté, several apples and a bottle of wine. As she set off for the farm, she thought through the story she would tell, if anybody inquisitive stopped her. *She had heard that Madame Joubert was unwell and was taking her a few things to cheer her up.* That would do. She strapped the basket to the bicycle she'd been using in recent weeks – sometimes she needed to get a great distance much faster than her legs could carry her.

She chose to ride out along the road towards the farm, rather than make this a secretive visit, but when she reached the farm gate, she was horrified to see a German army vehicle parked in the farmyard. She took the basket off the bike and hid it behind a milk churn at the side of the farmhouse before letting them see her walk past the farmhouse window. She braced herself and went in to visit Madame.

There were two officers who had made themselves very comfortable at the old woman's kitchen table and she did indeed have a cough, which made things much easier for Marie-Claire.

'Oh, Madame, I heard that you were unwell and came to see if I could help you,' she said, going straight to the kitchen sink and beginning to clear some dishes, ignoring the German officers as if it was the most natural thing in the world that they should be here. Thankfully, it didn't seem that they were prowling around the farm at this stage.

'Mademoiselle, you are a friend of this family? We have come to find the young farmer, Monsieur Louis Joubert, but it seems he is away from home,' the older of the two men said.

'Oh, yes? I expect he has deliveries to make, is that right, Madame?' she asked, and the older lady nodded.

'I have told them, I don't know where he's gone or when he'll be back. All I know was that he had something to deliver to a farmer in Coutances. Perhaps he is going to stay overnight before he returns,' she said with a shrug. Marie-Claire was still unsure whether Louis's mother knew that he played a role in the resistance or whether he kept her completely in the dark to protect her. Either way, she was doing a great job of protecting her son right now, let alone the English agent who was hiding up in her hayloft. Marie-Claire knew that there was a small spyhole in one end of the barn wall that those in hiding could use to find out what was happening in the farmyard below. She wondered what he must be going through right now.

The next hour dragged by as Marie-Claire found one job after another that she could do for Madame Joubert, and eventually the soldiers grew tired of waiting for Louis to appear and set off back to town. Alone in the farmhouse kitchen, both women breathed freely again.

'*Ma chérie*, do you think you could go and collect the eggs for me, please? I'm rather worn out after all that,' she said, waving her hands around the room with an expression of disgust. 'I think some of the hens have been laying up in the hayloft. You might need to take a basket up the ladder to collect their eggs, hmm?' she said, with a wink so tiny, Marie-Claire couldn't be sure she hadn't imagined it. But she was certain now that, at the very least, this old lady knew she had a silent house guest.

Marie-Claire collected the basket from around the side of the farmhouse and went into the barn, carefully taking the ladder up to the loft. She'd never actually been into the little safe room at the back, but had guided several people to it. She saw now how well hidden it was. There was hay stacked up several bays high and deep and over in the far corner a small gap was left between the side wall of the barn and the hay. She slid through the gap and found the panel in the back wall which could be lifted out, making a small door. She knocked on it with the code she knew: three short raps and two longer. In moments, the door panel was removed, and an inquisitive face appeared.

'Come in, my dear – I was told to expect you, and I see you've brought gifts!' he said with a voice much cheerier than Marie-Claire had been expecting. He held out a hand in greeting. 'George Baker. And this is my rather troublesome left foot,' he said with a snort, and hopped his way back to the narrow bed. She looked around the room, if it could be called that, though it was no bigger than a cupboard. A small bed, a bucket with a lid, and a large jug of water was all the furnishing she could see, just as she'd been told. Somehow it seemed even more rudimentary than she imagined. She placed the basket down on the bed.

'I'm sorry, I didn't bring a plate or cutlery, have you—' she began to ask, and George whisked a tray out from underneath the bed.

'I'm ready for a feast, but I'm afraid there is only one of everything. I feel very rude that I can't ask you to join me,' he apologised, as Marie-Claire took the supplies from the basket for him. 'I also hadn't expected them to send someone quite so lovely,' he said, shocking her into looking directly at him with her mouth agape.

'Quite lovely,' he said with a deep smile, and she felt her face warm with a blush. She coughed and tried to think how to turn his attention away from her.

'How is your ankle feeling? Do you need anything?' she asked, and he just waved the idea off, dismissively.

'It is very painful, but I have it strapped tightly. In a few days' time I'm going to start trying to get up and down the ladder to see how I get on. Hopefully I won't be stuck here too long, being a burden to you all,' he said.

'It's no bother. It's nice to have someone to talk to, quite honestly,' she said, without thinking.

'You don't have anyone at home to talk to?' he asked, and she was suddenly overwhelmed by the idea of home and family and someone to talk to each night to share the trials of the day, and the hopes for tomorrow and all the other little nothings that made up the whole feeling of family and home. The tears had begun before she understood why and she never really knew how she'd come to be leaning into his shoulder, his arms wrapped tightly around her, as she sobbed. He held her for what felt like hours, gently stroking her hair and kissing her head, making soothing sounds as she told him her story, and shared her pain and her hatred for the Nazi machine that had taken everything from her.

The night had grown dark outside, which they could tell because the cracks in the barn wall no longer let in light, and yet it was not safe to light a candle. The safe room had to remain utterly secret.

'How will you get home safely now, in the dark?' George asked her with so much concern, it melted her.

'Don't worry about me. I'm used to it – always out here in the middle of nowhere quite alone at night. Though, admittedly, I'm not usually dressed like this,' she said, glancing down at her calf-length dress and stockinged legs. It was only then, when she heard the hens below squabbling for spots on the perch, that she remembered Madame Joubert had asked her to collect the eggs. She quickly gathered up her empty basket, pulled her coat on and hurriedly said goodbye to George. She had been with him for well over an hour, and Madame Joubert would be wondering exactly what was going on.

As she turned to say a quick farewell, she was surprised to see that George had stood again and reached out to take her hand, inviting her to step in close to him. He cupped her face in his free hand. She froze and looked into his eyes to ask him without words what was happening, why were their faces so close, and why could she not turn and walk away, when he bent down and kissed her on the lips, lightly, but with a transmission of emotion that felt like electricity. She pulled away and looked to him for answers again but all she could do was answer the magnetic pull and she kissed him back, reaching up her hands to pull his head closer to her. She heard him groan softly with pleasure and she pushed her body close to his. In the end it was George who pulled away, gasping and whispering to her hoarsely.

'I think you'd better go now, Marie-Claire, before I do something I would not want to have held against me.'

She turned and left him then, hurrying down the ladder and quickly running around the barn and into the henhouse to collect as many eggs as she could find.

She rushed across the dusky farmyard and into the farmhouse kitchen where Madame Joubert was asleep in the chair beside the fire. Marie-Claire quietly placed the eggs in the waiting dish in the table, and let herself out, back to her bicycle.

That night, she lay in bed and dreamed of Louis. She saw Louis's face up close to hers, and felt Louis's lips on her own, and imagined Louis kissing the soft skin on the side of her neck. But the next night, she went back to the farm to visit George again.

# 16

PARIS, JUNE 1998

On Monday morning, after a wonderfully satisfying weekend of long sleeps, lazy dinners, and languorous sex, Jules dragged himself away from Esther and headed into his office for a few hours.

'I'll try to get home as soon as I can. There are some things that just can't wait, but once I set things up for the week, I should be able to get home soon after lunch. And then I should only need to make a few phone calls, which I can do from anywhere,' he explained, giving her a long kiss before he left.

Esther fell back to sleep again, making up for the hours she'd lost during the middle of the night. Wonderful as the midnight distraction had been, she still needed to get plenty of sleep. This holiday was supposed to be a rest, after all.

After she dressed and showered, Esther found fruit and yoghurt in the fridge, and a container with fresh bread to eat with some of Madame Joubert's jam that Jules had brought home with him from the farm. She made a cup of coffee and sat out on the balcony to eat, and to decide how to spend the morning.

They were planning all kinds of trips and outings for the week, including the Palace of Versailles, and Monet's home and garden, so she didn't need to go far, but Esther was hungry to get out into the city. So she dressed in her good walking shoes, a cool dress, and threw a bottle of water, her map of Paris, and a couple of apples into her little backpack. She took the key Jules had left her and went out to walk along the river.

A couple of hours later, Esther was feeling very pleased with herself that she had managed to walk to Shakespeare and Company, with barely a look at her map. The bookshop was not nearly so crowded as it would have been on a weekend, and she allowed herself a good hour to browse the shelves and came out with a package that she knew she'd enjoy reading when her bedtimes were not quite so occupied as they had been the last three nights.

Back at the apartment she made a cup of tea and then decided to rearrange her things into Jules' bedroom. Since Friday, all her belongings had remained in the guest room, but she'd not slept in there once. It seemed silly to move between the two rooms now. So she gathered up all her clothes and popped them into the expansive walk-in wardrobe in the master suite.

Esther sat on the edge of the bed, untangling her underwear from some jewellery, and decided to put these small things in the drawers in the bedside cabinet. But when she opened the top drawer on what had become her side of the bed, she was surprised to find things there already.

She left the drawer open and tried to take in what she was seeing. Slowly, she took the first few items out. The drawer contained a silky pink and cream negligée, some very skimpy ladies' underwear and a packet of condoms.

Shocked to her core, Esther threw the items back into the

drawer and slammed it shut. She sat, staring at it for some minutes, almost as if she might will the contents to go away.

Perhaps these were just a few things that a previous girl-friend had left behind, and Jules had no idea they were still here, she reasoned.

Esther chose to believe that story. Later, Esther realised that if she'd been honest with herself, she knew that this was the moment when she'd seriously started to doubt him. But she hadn't been ready for the honeymoon period to be over and so she'd chosen to ignore it.

Even when Jules came home that afternoon and it was on the tip of her tongue to mention what she'd found, and get it cleared up and out in the open at once, something stopped her.

Instead, she stayed quiet, and pushed the doubts aside. Surely if Jules went looking around her place, he'd find evidence of past boyfriends too, wouldn't he? Not underwear, perhaps, but maybe something.

* * *

'What shall we do tonight, Esther?' Jules called to her from the shower on the Friday night. Their week together had been filled with outings and dinners, and long nights and lazy mornings. And now this was her last night in Paris before she was to head back to Sainte-Mère-Église the next day, pick up her car and make her way back to Cherbourg for the ferry on Sunday morning.

'Shall we just stay home? Perhaps cook something here?' she suggested, looking in the fridge and realising they didn't really have the supplies to make a good meal.

Jules appeared out of the shower wrapped in nothing but a white towel, worn tight and low on his trim waist. *I could just eat you*, Esther heard herself thinking then laughed as she turned back to the fridge.

'There's not much here though. Perhaps we do need to go out to eat?' she said.

'*Non, non.* Eating at home is a good idea. I will get dressed and go to the *supermarché*,' he said and, waving his arm in the general direction of the pantry, added, 'just let me know what you feel like eating, hmm?'

They agreed on prawns and pasta, so Jules set off for supplies.

Esther was just laying the table, and opening a bottle of wine, when she heard the apartment doorbell ring. She was sure it must be Jules, and he'd forgotten his keys and perhaps his wallet, as he'd only been gone a few minutes, so when she opened the door to be met by the most beautiful woman she'd ever seen, Esther was speechless with shock.

'Oh, hello – are you sure you have the right apartment?' Esther said, looking around the hallway to see if anyone else seemed to be expecting a guest.

'Yes, this is definitely Jules' place,' the woman said curtly. 'Is he here?' she asked, looking into the apartment.

'Um, no. He's just gone to the shops,' replied Esther, feeling very uncertain about exactly who this woman might be. 'Can I give him a message for you?' she asked.

'Sure. You can tell him he's a dirty, cheating pig,' spat the woman, who folded her arms and seemed ready to anchor herself in for a fight.

## 17

In the week leading up to Christmas, the people of Sainte-Mère-Église had done their best to rally around and create some semblance of Christmases past. There was a tree in the town square which had been decorated with candles, and gold and red ribbons. Inside the church there were wreaths of holly, orange and cinnamon. But there would be no great feasts this year. No real fun or frivolity.

Marie-Claire had been out in the lanes collecting holly that she wanted to use to decorate the café-bar when she first met the children of the Epstein family, Jacob and Golda.

'Jacob, help me, I can't reach as high as you,' the little girl had called pleadingly to her big brother who was collecting the best sprigs with the most berries.

'I can't help it if you're a pathetic, weak girl, Golda,' he'd called back meanly, and Marie-Claire had stepped in at once.

'Excuse me, young sir, but that is no way to speak to a lady,' she said sharply, and the little boy looked horrified to be caught out by an adult.

'I don't believe it is Golda's fault that she was born a few years after you. And being younger and shorter has nothing to do with weakness, or being a girl, wouldn't you agree?' The little boy had shrugged and nodded.

'Come with me, Golda, I'll help you get the best berries,' Marie-Claire offered, lifting her higher up the bank.

They walked back into the square together, where the Epsteins were waiting for their children at the market.

'*Bonjour*, Madame Epstein, *et* Monsieur,' Marie-Claire said, and introduced herself. 'Jacob has been learning a lesson about how to treat young ladies, haven't you?' she asked, and saw his father's face darken.

'Jacob, son, come for a little walk with me,' he said sternly, and took Jacob to the other side of the square for a talk.

'Was he causing trouble?' his mother asked.

'Just being unkind to Golda, and disrespectful, simply because she is a girl,' Marie-Claire explained. Their mother tutted and frowned.

'He doesn't understand how important it is for us to stick together, and to quietly fit in with the Christmas traditions. We are trying to teach him that everyone in our family is equal.'

'But look at the gorgeous holly she has collected! Would you ladies like to come into the warmth of the café and help me tie some of these up?' Marie-Claire asked, knowing that decorating for Christmas was not a normal activity for Jewish families but understanding perfectly Madame Epstein's concern.

By the time they'd finished adding the decorations, Marie-Claire was on first-name terms with Rachel Epstein, who now knew that Marie-Claire's husband had been Jewish too, and how he had died.

'You poor woman. I can't imagine your pain.' She winced,

and reached a hand to touch Marie-Claire. 'How can you stand the sight of them?' she spat as a couple of German soldiers walked past the window. Marie-Claire just shrugged in response.

'Let's just be thankful that we are here and not in Paris, where they seem to have a higher degree of hatred for anyone Jewish,' she said.

The café-bar was busy on Christmas Eve with plenty of people who had come in for the last market of the year, to buy what supplies could be had. The soldiers seemed to be in a holiday spirit and Marie-Claire was glad the café-bar would be closed tomorrow for Christmas Day. She was looking forward to going to church and then planned to walk secretly out to the farm, and spend the rest of the day with George.

His ankle was improving greatly, and the resting and the strapping had helped him heal fast. He was able to get up and down the ladder quite quickly now and had been trying short runs across the floor of the barn. He felt sure he'd be able to make the fifty yards or so he would need to run across an airfield to then clamber aboard a Lysander and make it home. But, he'd told Marie-Claire, he was not in as much of a hurry to leave France as England was to get him back. And she was loath to let him go.

She'd spent hours with him over the last eight days while Louis had been away, talking about her old life – an indiscretion which she knew he might come to regret later, especially if he was ever picked up by the Germans and interrogated about her. But George had probably had much more formal training for undercover work than she did, and so he didn't tell her anything about who he was and where he was from, except his name, which she presumed was false anyway.

Louis had been gone longer than she'd expected, and something inside her had shut her heart to him, as if in self-preservation, so she wouldn't have to face losing him. If she convinced her heart that she didn't care for him, then the shock couldn't hurt her, when it came.

Meanwhile, George and Marie-Claire had become so used to one another that they would lie side by side, sleeping, enjoying the warmth of each other's body, listening to the other's heartbeat and waking to begin kissing all over again. But she'd not spent all night with him. And they had never dared allow themselves the freedom to undress, to become fully intimate together.

But Marie-Claire had decided that after church on Christmas Day she would go to visit and not return home until the next morning. She hadn't told George her plan as she knew he would object, wanting to protect her reputation.

At first Marie-Claire had been confused by who exactly it was who excited her when she kissed George. She was always fully in the moment with him, but then later she would often find that she could only think of Louis. But as the time had drawn on, and she'd still heard nothing from anyone at the château, she became more certain that they'd all perished. Perhaps she would never see Louis, or Jean-Baptiste, again. She wondered too if Marguerite had been with them. No news at all for eight days was a very long time. And she was determined not to be hurt again like she had with the loss of Benjamin.

She had published Christmas recipe ideas, and written a menu for a festive feast that was achievable under the current restricted rations, but none of these had needed to be infused with code. The parish newsletter was now being read out on the local radio station which the Germans in town had allowed to be reinstated – an incredible boon to the local resistance as they knew their frequency could be picked up across the Channel. The Germans had obviously decided there was no risk at all to a few recipes and idle writings of a woman, or news about a farmer's cow being stuck in a ditch.

The bells rang out for midnight Mass on Christmas Eve and Marie-Claire put on her warmest coat, scarf, hat and gloves to head out across the square and take her place inside the church with most of the other townsfolk. She looked around to see who she knew, and was surprised to see that the mother of Louis, Madame Joubert, was there.

'*Bonsoir,* Madame,' Marie-Claire greeted her, with a friendly kiss. 'I didn't expect to see you out so late tonight.'

'We are all alone at the farm,' she said, indicating herself and her husband and obviously intimating that Louis had still not returned. There seemed to be a question in her face that Marie-Claire could not answer. She didn't know if they would ever hear from Louis again, but could not say too much. Not here, not now.

'And what are your plans for Christmas Day?' Marie-Claire asked the older woman.

'We are going to stay here in town tonight with my brother, and spend the day with him tomorrow,' she explained, just as the priest began the service and everyone bowed their heads to pray.

The sounds of the *In Splendoribus Sanctorum* began and Marie-Claire allowed herself to drift away on the movement of the music. *In splendoribus sanctorum, ex utero, ante luciferum, genui te*; 'In the brightness of the saints: from the womb before the day star, I begot you.' When Marie-Claire had been married to Benjamin she had grown used to the Jewish customs and rituals that he taught her, though he tried to play them down, and accepted her basic Christian faith simply as a part of who she was. But this was the script from the church of her youth and her home, and it was what felt the most familiar and comfortable at Christmas.

Holly, pine, citrus and cinnamon scents filled the church

and, when the incense was lit, she could smell myrrh too. She kept her eyes closed and prayed. And then her mind turned to George, alone now until the morning after tomorrow unless she went to him, not that he ever had any contact with the Jouberts – who still had not openly admitted that they were aware of the safe room in the hayloft. George wasn't expecting her to visit until sometime on Christmas Day but now she thought of changing her plans.

When the service ended, the townspeople filed out of the church, each quietly wishing one another a *'Joyeux Noël'*, though they did so with gritted teeth and a silent wish for this occupation to be over before they could possibly enjoy a fully happy Christmas again. She went across to her room above the café-bar and sat on the bed in silent contemplation for some minutes. Then she changed into her warm, practical resistance-work clothing, gathered the few items of food she'd set by for her Christmas meal, slung them into her shoulder bag along with a bottle of wine, and set off on the little path through the woods leading to the farm.

It was only when she got to the barn that she realised she might frighten George, who would undoubtedly be sound asleep and would suspect a raid. She climbed the ladder quietly and then decided noise was a better option, and marched across the hayloft floor, gently calling his name before she gave the knock on the door.

There was no sound. No movement. For a terrible moment she thought he must already have left, or worse, been discovered and taken. But there was no sign of disturbance around. She knocked again.

'George, it's me, Marie-Claire. Are you awake?' She heard the small door being unlocked and opened from the inside and found herself staring up at the baffled face of a very sleepy man. His golden-blond hair, usually so carefully combed into place, was growing long and stuck up at odd angles now. A shaggy growth of stubble was growing longer. His deep blue eyes were wide open in surprise but they still anchored her in security and comfort, as they always did. He was taller than her by several inches and his strong broad shoulders hunched now as he leant in towards her.

'Marie-Claire! Why are you here so late? Come in. Is everything alright?' he asked, holding her close once she'd stepped through the little gap and stood up straight before him.

'Everything is fine. I came to wish you a Happy Christmas,' she said, leaning up to give him a kiss. He gladly kissed her back and pulled her into a tighter hug, whispering into her hair.

'But it is so late, and you're cold. I thought you weren't coming until tomorrow.'

'I couldn't wait until then. I wanted to see you tonight. And I want to stay with you, all night,' she said, and his eyes widened as he read her face for her full meaning.

'You're staying? All night?' he asked, and she nodded.

'And all day tomorrow as well. I brought food,' she said, holding up the bag, and they both laughed.

'Then let's have a glass of wine together. Happy Christmas,' he said, and pulled her back to kiss her so long and hard that they soon forgot about the wine.

When Marie-Claire awoke in the morning she took a moment to remember why or how she could be staring at a rough-hewn timber wall, just inches from her face, and then she felt the warmth of the naked body that was wrapped around hers from behind. He was gently stroking the skin of her hip, his fingers lightly travelling down her thigh as he kissed the nape of her neck. She moaned with joy and remembered the power of their lovemaking through the night.

For a moment when she had first lain down, naked beside him, she had suddenly feared that she would have forgotten what to do. But he had kissed her face and her neck and her breasts and her tummy until she was burning for him and soon she pulled him towards her, so hungry for his body.

They had whispered each other's names and dared to groan out loud, knowing there was nobody at home in the farmhouse below. And now as she lay in his arms as the dawn light played in the tiny rays it made through the pinholes in the wall, and dust motes danced above them, she felt her need for him rising again. She turned to face him and kissed him, gently at first and then with a hunger, biting at his lips and begging him for more.

They lay panting, legs woven together and holding hands afterwards, waiting until each had recovered.

'Merry Christmas, my lovely,' George said at last as he leant up on one elbow, stroking her hair away from her face. She watched him for a while and then remembered why they were both here. What had brought them together, and would ultimately take them apart, and soon.

'How is your ankle feeling now?' she asked him, and he laughed a little.

'I think the exercise has done me good. I have much less pain now. I ran back and forth across the barn floor yesterday ten times in quick succession, and there was barely any swelling afterwards.'

'They'll be taking you home soon, then. And I'll never see you again,' she said.

'Don't say that. We don't know that. The war could be over in a couple of years more, and then I'll come and find you. You'll find me. You can come and live in England, or I'll come here and we'll live on a farm together. We can dream of that,' he said.

'I think we would be better not to dream, George. People die. Things end. It's the way that it is,' she said, images of Benjamin, Antoine and Louis flashing before her, and she realised that she'd fully prepared herself for news of Louis's demise. And with Benjamin gone, Louis almost certainly gone, and George about to be gone from her life forever, she wondered if she'd ever know security again.

They shared the Christmas food together, and drifted in and out of sleep, talking, kissing and making love throughout the day. When the dark of night fell again, Marie-Claire was just falling into a deep and delicious sleep when she heard the sound of footsteps in the hayloft outside.

She shook George awake but placed a finger firmly over his lips so he would remain silent and listen. Soon the secret knock came on the door, and George scrabbled to pull on his clothes, and Marie-Claire hid under the blanket, eyes wide with fear. Was this Louis? Or one of the others? Or had the safe room finally been discovered by the enemy? She realised she was trembling with fear.

'Who is it?' asked George in a whisper at the door.

'It's Marguerite, George, open up. I've news for you,' she said. He turned back to Marie-Claire and she saw from the look on his face that he knew as well as she did what this news would be. He stepped outside into the hayloft and Marie-Claire strained her ears to hear what news Marguerite had brought.

'There's a Lysander flying in tonight. The mission in Caen was successful, and we managed to steal plans which we think will interest British High Command. There is a package to be picked up and they're taking you home to get your ankle properly looked at. Do you think you'll make it? The field is two miles away.'

'I can make it if I have plenty of time to rest on the way. And I've been practising running. I should be fine,' he said. 'What time are we aiming for?'

'You should be there by midnight, but we don't know when the flyover will be. I wanted to send Marie-Claire to set the torches, but she's not at home, so I'll have to do it myself. I just hope she's okay. It's so unlike her to be out of touch. But anyway, you go on ahead soon, and meet me there, to give you plenty of time. And if I don't get to talk to you later, all the very best, George. I'll bring the package and run it out to the plane myself, in case you don't make it there in time. I'll see you around, perhaps here again, or there,' she said, and then she was gone.

He shut the door tightly and then stood running his hands through his hair. Marie-Clarie could see he was fighting emotion. They both waited in silence until they were sure that Marguerite had reached the base of the ladder and headed out of the barn, and then he sat on the bed beside her, taking her hand in his.

'You see? Everything ends. You are leaving,' she said, and realised she was in much better control of her emotions than George was of his.

'You're right,' he said with a sniff, and wiped his face on his sleeve. 'And anything could happen, to either one of us, once we leave this room tonight. But at least it sounds as though the others have survived their mission, and it was successful,' he said a little more brightly. 'Louis will be back here to run things again soon, so you won't be lumbered with caring for any clumsy injured men.'

She smiled and stroked his hand.

'You've really been the most charming patient, George. And

I'm so glad I came to see you last night. No regrets?' she said, still trying to filter through the information that Louis was still alive, after all.

'No regrets at all,' he answered, and continued to dress and pack his meagre bag of belongings.

'Would you do me one favour, Marie-Claire?' he asked, and she nodded.

'Stay here, in my bed, until I've left. And then I'll always remember you here as if I've just left for work and I'm coming home to you later. I'd like to take that memory with me. That dream.'

An hour later, George had disappeared through the little secret door and Marie-Claire lay in the dark, listening to his steps as he crossed the hayloft, went down the ladder and left the barn. She imagined him walking – limping along the wood-land path deeper into the country to the field that Marguerite had named.

But she started to worry about the great distance he had to go. He hadn't left the barn in a long time, and while he'd been practising on the ladder and running across the barn floor, that was nothing like trying to get two miles across open country, with dips and hills and rabbit holes to avoid. What if he didn't make it in time?

Marie-Claire dressed quickly and slipped down the ladder, running out of the barn and along the woodland path as fast as she could. Within minutes she'd caught up to George who she found leaning against a tree, sweat soaking his shirt and his breath coming in fast pants.

'Marie-Claire! What are you doing out here?' he managed to gasp.

'I knew you wouldn't make it on your own. You're not nearly healed enough for this, are you?' she asked, and he grimaced.

'I thought I might make it – but it was probably wishful thinking,' he said as she leant into him, wrapped his arm over her shoulder and took his weight.

'Come on, I've got you,' she said as he hopped and she led him on in a fast three-legged trot. 'I know a shortcut up here too, and that will make it faster.'

Within twenty minutes she'd helped him reach the edge of the field where the Lysander would come in. George fell into the grass and breathed heavily while he recovered, wincing as he felt over his ankle which was now terribly swollen.

'You have to rest here and get up the energy for your run out to the plane, George. I'll wait here to see you make it, but I can't let Marguerite see me,' she said, and stroked his hair, kissing his temples as he lay back and rested.

Marie-Claire saw Marguerite arrive on the opposite side of the field and begin setting out the flares. They heard the Lysander come in and, after a short but deep and intense kiss, George left her and ran at a limp across the field, dragging his injured ankle behind him. She held her breath, hoping he would make it in time as the Lysander was not going to stop. Marguerite ran from the darkness towards the plane from the opposite direction, but she must have hit a rock or a hole and she suddenly fell forward, landing with a thud, the bundled package rolling away from her. George was never going to have time to reach both the dropped package and the plane so Marie-Claire called out to him, risking breaking cover for all of them, to tell him to keep going.

She pelted at a full sprint towards where Marguerite had fallen, grabbed the package and pivoted at high speed, running for the plane as it came towards her.

George had grabbed a hold on the step and was almost up as she reached the side of the plane, threw the package in through the small door and watched as the plane left the ground, and George disappeared inside.

Marie-Claire fell to her knees and felt the flood of adrenaline through her body, her chest heaving with pain from the exertion. She turned back to where Marguerite had fallen and saw her slowly rise to her feet, holding her left arm close to her body. Marie-Claire came to her senses and ran around the outside of the field, extinguishing the torches and collecting them up as she went.

When the two women met in the middle of the dark, quiet, empty field, Marie-Claire lent her arm to Marguerite and they walked together back to the safety of cover.

'Thank God for you, my dear. I don't understand how or why you are here, but thank you. That was very nearly a disaster. But both George and the package are on their way back to England now.'

'I, well, I... You see,' Marie-Claire began, unsure how to explain anything.

'Shhh. It doesn't matter. I think I may have dislocated my shoulder,' Marguerite said, and taking it in one hand, gritted her teeth and heaved, moaning in pain as she set it right again, and wriggled it to check.

The two women parted, after Marie-Claire had offered to take the landing equipment back to the farm and Marguerite had headed off on her bicycle.

Back at the farm, Marie-Claire stowed the equipment then went up to the hayloft. She tidied the little room and made it ready for the next incoming agent. She presumed Louis must come and replace the sheets at some point, but she mustn't do anything that might signal she had ever been here. She packed away the food remnants and wine bottle and washed out the plate and glass and mug with water from the jug and left them on the tray underneath the bed. She straightened the blanket and then shut the tiny door behind her, creeping carefully down the ladder and out through the back of the farmyard to the path through the woods. She thanked God that all had gone to plan – reasonably to plan – and that the important package of information was on its way to people who could help them make a real difference, and that George was safely on his way home. And she knew that she would never see him again.

# 18

## PARIS, JUNE 1998

Esther realised that her mouth was hanging open in a most unattractive way, and she suddenly felt self-conscious in the presence of this beauty, who must surely be a model. She was perfect. Perfect bone structure, the most amazing figure, fabulous clothes, impeccable make-up and hair, and dazzling eyes. But she was also very, very angry.

Esther came to her senses, closed her mouth and decided to invite the woman inside. Whatever she had to say to Jules, Esther wanted to be here to hear it as well, so she was certainly not going to send her away.

'Jules will be back in a few minutes. Please, do come in and you can tell him yourself,' she said, warming to the fight she could feel was about to start.

'I'm Esther, by the way. And you are?' she asked.

'My name is Adèle. I am the girlfriend of Jules,' she said, and Esther saw by the look on her face that she was pleased by Esther's shock.

'Um, I'm having a glass of wine. Would you like one?' she

asked. Soon the two women were sitting awkwardly on opposite sofas in the living area.

'So, how long have you known Jules?' Adèle asked Esther.

'Thirteen years. You?' she said without missing a beat and saw the other woman raise one eyebrow in surprise.

'Just two years. We've been dating on and off all that time. So how long has he been keeping you here secretly during the week while I usually stay at the weekend?' Adèle asked.

'Oh, well, actually, we only just got together as a couple last week and I've been here since last Friday night,' Esther explained.

'Hmm. That makes sense. He left me a message last Wednesday telling me not to come around. I guessed he would be busy last weekend. But he didn't mention anything about this weekend. Perhaps he was keeping all his options open, hey?' she asked, and Esther felt the delicate part of her heart that she'd been about to give to Jules crumple like a ball of paper and burst into flames.

'I have to ask,' Esther said quietly, almost stammering. 'The underwear in the drawer, beside the bed – is that yours?'

Adèle nodded in response. 'I'll collect it now, if you don't mind. I won't be back here again after I've finished with that pig tonight,' she said, and disappeared into the main bedroom just as Jules turned his key in the lock and walked into the room, beaming.

'Have I got a delicious meal for you, my lovely!' he cried, unaware that his fragile veneer of helpful, kind and caring boyfriend was about to implode on him.

# 19

The weeks following Christmas were cold, dark, dismal and still. Marie-Claire knew that whatever it was that she'd shared with George was over, and she would never see him again. She had heard from Marguerite that the mission in Caen had been successful, but still had seen no sign of Louis.

The town was near dead, after the brief warmth of community that Christmas had brought. And Marie-Claire fell into a dark space of gloom that she hadn't known for over a year now. Perhaps it was the very fact that she'd gone past the first anniversary of losing Benjamin and Antoine. Or maybe it was all to do with finding and then losing George. Or it could have more to do with longing for the company of Louis and not knowing when he might return. But in the end, she decided that if only all these filthy German soldiers would get out of her sight, her café-bar, her life in general, everything could at least have the chance of brightness again.

The war had gone on for over two years now, the complete occupation of Paris a full eighteen months ago. The British had been trying to infiltrate the occupation with their undercover agents, and small attack groups coming across the borderlines at times, but no major progress was being made. Not that any of them would really know what was going on elsewhere: the Nazi propaganda machine told them that all was going superbly for the Third Reich. They lost no battles, their wealth was expanding, and all the people in their occupied territories were very happy to be saved from their lot – and to be getting rid of their Jews. She hated them most of all for this determination to destroy the race of her husband's family. There was talk of more restrictions for Jewish people to come, even out here in the provinces. She shivered at the thought.

She longed to hear from Louis about the success of their mission into the airfield at Caen to help lift her spirits. At least to see him again, to feel his comforting hand on hers, to see the kindness in his face, which might help her come back to her senses again.

She was busy in the café-bar, preparing bread rolls for the lunchtime rush, and didn't turn around when she heard the doorbell tinkle.

'I'll be with you in just a minute,' she called politely, setting aside the latest batch of perfectly rounded bread dough balls to rise. She wiped her hands clean on her apron and turned back to the counter, fully expecting to see the grey tones of a *Wehrmacht* uniform and a rigidly serious face.

'Adeline! Oh, my dear friend, my Adeline!' she cried, running out from behind the counter to take the older woman in a firm embrace.

'I'm so pleased to see you too, my darling,' crooned Adeline, returning the affection.

'Why are you here? How are you here?' asked Marie-Claire,

looking out to the pavement and noticing that Jean-Baptiste's truck was parked up across the road.

'I have come for a little rest. Jean-Baptiste and Louis felt it would be best if we all, let me say, took a little holiday from the château for a week or two,' she whispered into the softness of Marie-Claire's hair.

Marie-Claire guided Adeline over to a quiet table and brought them each a cup of coffee.

'Are Louis or Jean-Baptiste going to come in?' Marie-Claire asked quietly.

'No, I don't think so. Jean-Baptiste wanted to meet with Charles at the church office, to talk about plans for him to move out to one of the beaches. Apparently, he needs a base very near the beach for a mission that is in the early planning stages. And Louis is going home to his parents. I think he is preparing the way for me to stay with them for a short while. He said I should come in here and spend some time with you. So, *ma chérie*, tell me how you are. How you really are,' she said with a look that Marie-Claire knew to be asking her for everything.

Two hours later, when the lunch rush was over, and the two women had shared a conversation in small bite-sized chunks, it was time for Marie-Claire's afternoon off and they went out into the cold for a walk together.

'To be perfectly honest, Marie-Clarie, I am surprised that you are doing as well as you are. You have made such enormous life adjustments over this last year, and you've settled into this new work with the resistance very easily. The difficulty is that we are all living in limbo. This cannot go on, and yet we can see no end,' Adeline said.

'I think that is the real problem. We are hoping for a world that we don't know we will ever see. I certainly will never see my

Benjamin or Antoine again, and I will never have another family,' said Marie-Claire with a shrug.

'Why do you say that? You are still young. You don't know what will happen to you, who you will meet. It might seem impossible to move on now, but one day, perhaps?' Adeline said gently.

Marie-Claire walked on in silence, feeling guilty for the way she had spent that time with George, so recklessly, without a care for Benjamin or even Louis who she knew cared for her. She didn't know what had overtaken her, to make her behave so. But even with the guilt she felt now, she couldn't feel regret. It had been good for her, and just what she needed at the time. Perhaps now she felt so low partly because of the loss of George. But she was not about to share such an intimate detail, even with Adeline. She shrugged and pulled a face.

'Perhaps I will settle down again. But I cannot believe I will ever love a man with the same depth that I did my husband. He has left a great wound in my heart, Adeline, a space that cannot be filled by another man.'

'No, I'm sure it cannot. But I think you will find that in time, the space left behind by Benjamin might be able to move aside a little and there will be another space, in another shape, for another man. It won't be the same, but there will be love, and happiness, and satisfaction in life again, Marie-Claire.'

Marie-Claire wondered now about the space that George had taken up and started to see that it might be possible for another kind of love, a different one, to form again. Perhaps, if this wretched German occupation would come to an end, there was hope for a brighter future. One day.

The afternoon had grown dark, and the women had walked around the town square and through the churchyard twice, just as Louis came into the square on his bike and stopped outside the café-bar to greet them as they walked back again. He waved and smiled to Marie-Claire, then came closer to speak to her quietly, unwilling to shout to the listening ears around that he had even been away.

'It's so good to see you again! Are you well? You look tired. Are you sleeping? Adeline, do you think she is too cold out here?' he fired off rapidly, taking her hands into his and drawing her in for a kiss on both cheeks.

'It's good to see you too, Louis, and you need not worry. I am quite well. But yes, it is terribly cold out here,' Marie-Claire assured him, feeling warmed and heartened that he cared so much for her.

'I have the perfect answer. Come and join us all at the farm-house tonight – stay with us there until tomorrow. We have plenty of room, and it will be good to be together with friends, yes?' he asked her, and she soon found herself swept along with the small family crowd that was gathering out at the farm.

\* \* \*

Later that night, after Madame Joubert had done a magnificent job of feeding so many extra mouths with the same small piece of lamb she had planned to cook for three people, aided by the addition of many, many vegetables, in a delicious and huge pot of ratatouille, the friends remained around the old kitchen table late into the night. Louis produced a bottle of Calvados and Marie-Claire was rolling it slowly around her glass, staring into the rich gold depth of the brandy, her mind many miles away.

'Where did you go, Marie-Claire?' Louis asked gently when she finally raised her head and met his gaze across the table. She glanced around the room and wondered what the hilarity was about at the other end of the table. Jean-Baptiste had challenged old Monsieur Joubert to an arm-wrestle and Adeline, Marguerite and Charles were busy clearing the table of dirty dishes and glasses so they could begin.

'I... I can't really say where I was. I was just thinking about other times. Happy times like this. When there was a future. Before there was a war. Before any of us knew what the rise of Hitler was going to bring us to,' she said.

'But look at us here,' he said, waving a hand around the company. 'We are friends. We are family. We can still have fun. And we are achieving great things. There is hope, you know, for us all,' he said, and reached across, gently squeezing her arm. She smiled and placed a hand upon his in response.

'I heard all about what you did for George,' he said, and Marie-Claire's heart stopped for several beats before picking up at a racing pace. He did? What did he know?

'Marguerite told me that you did a wonderful job in our absence, taking him food, and keeping his whereabouts secret,' he said with a happy smile. 'You are becoming quite the experienced undercover agent, hey?' he said with an innocence that caused Marie-Claire a sting of pain. She fought to hide her embarrassment and changed the subject.

'And the mission at the airfield all went well, then? No casualties?'

'They didn't even know we'd been there, as far as we can tell. But we've vacated the château as a precaution just in case any of us were followed back there. Jean-Baptiste and Adeline will return in a few days and see what is happening. We can't believe they haven't come to take over the whole place by now. All over the country these great houses are being requisitioned by the *Wehrmacht* as command bases.'

'Perhaps they will make a move once the airfield is attacked?' Marie-Claire asked.

'More than likely. They'll certainly need another base then.'

'And the attack is scheduled soon?'

Louis glanced at his watch. 'We should hear the bombers come overhead tonight.'

'So soon? How will they have organised themselves so quickly?' she asked, amazed at the speed of turnaround.

'We have been feeding the British intelligence information about the airfield for months now, ever since Jean-Baptiste first stole that plane last year. The last few pieces of the puzzle were sent over in the package that left the same night as George Baker,' Louis said. Marie-Claire dropped her eyes to the floor, her nerve endings wringing with renewed sensations at the mention of George's name on Louis's tongue.

'Thank you for taking care of him while I was away, Marie-Claire. I heard from Marguerite that he was in good shape to make it out to the airfield on his own that night. I imagine he is resting up in hospital now with his ankle in plaster.'

Marie-Claire wondered why Marguerite had left off the detail that she'd been there, and that the package – and George – would never have made it without her. But she was grateful for the discretion, all the same. She waved her hand dismissively. 'It was nothing. He was very easy to care for,' she said and, against her better judgement, asked about him.

'Will George be sent back here once he is recovered, do you think?' Louis shook his head firmly.

'No. Almost certainly not. He was a face who was here for a while and then he left. If he were to return, and anybody recognised him, his story might not be believed. If they send him back into action, I am sure he will be sent somewhere completely different now,' explained Louis, and Marie-Claire chastised herself inwardly for having even had hope enough to ask. She would never see him again. She knew that. She must simply put him behind her and move on. She didn't realise that she had been looking out of the window of the farmhouse kitchen, up towards the back wall of the barn while she'd been thinking of George.

'There's no one out there now, of course. But the safe room is ready for the next time it's needed. I'm still amazed we've managed to keep things secret here all this time,' said Louis.

'Yes, your mother did a great job of staying quiet and innocent that afternoon the German soldiers came to look around the barn. And they didn't find the safe room then.'

'I don't know if she was keeping quiet – she simply doesn't know it exists. She thinks these are all farming friends of mine,' he said, glancing towards his mother who was busy making custard for a dessert.

'I'm not so sure, Louis. I think she understands more than you realise. But it is probably best to keep as much detail from her and your father as possible,' she said quietly.

Louis watched his mother working in the kitchen and Marie-Claire saw him go through a variety of emotions, from incredulity to a high respect. Everyone was doing their bit, even those who had not been formally taken under the wing of the resistance.

Just after midnight, as Marie-Claire was settling into a room that she was to share with Adeline that night, where Madame Joubert had made a bed on the floor with cushions and eiderdowns, she heard the drone of planes flying a distance overhead.

She caught Adeline's eye, and knew that she had heard it too. They heard the sirens start up in the town and raced to the window, looking out to see searchlight beams ripping through the sky. Soon the planes had passed over, and the all-clear was sounded. But the women went to bed knowing that the German airfield in Caen was about five minutes away from total destruction. It scared Marie-Claire a little, the level of satisfaction that it brought her to know that people were dying at the hands of the British bombers at this very moment. What had the war done to her?

## 20

PARIS, JUNE 1998

'And which one of your "lovelies" might you be addressing, Jules?' asked Adèle as she appeared from the bedroom, holding a collection of skimpy underwear items.

Jules looked as though he was mid-heart attack. His face went ashen, he seemed to be trying to speak but could utter nothing coherent, and he stumbled, almost dropping the bags of food.

Esther took the supplies from him and set them on the kitchen counter. Both women waited for him to respond.

'Adèle, what are you doing here? How did you get in?' he asked at last, looking around the room and seeing two glasses of wine on the coffee table.

'I let her in, Jules. She wasn't expecting me to be here. And it seems that until very recently, you were expecting to spend this weekend with Adèle. When were you going to tell me that I'm just one of the women you keep hanging on for entertainment?' she spat, folding her arms and working hard to control her breathing, squashing the anger down.

'Esther, what has she told you? Adèle – this is ridiculous.

Why are you here? Why now?' he demanded. 'Esther, I know it seems impossible, but please trust me. Please listen,' he begged her, waiting.

Esther took three deep breaths, and looked from Jules to Adèle then back again. She believed that she knew Jules and she wanted to trust him. This other woman was a stranger, and Esther needed to hear both sides of this story.

'Okay, I'm listening,' Esther said quietly.

'Adèle and I have had a casual relationship, now and then, for the last couple of years. She has a child – whom I've never been allowed to meet – and other partners who keep her entertained when she grows tired of me,' he said with a wry sideways look to Adèle. 'I don't mean anything to her, and she has always made it perfectly clear to me that this is not a relationship. It's just physical. Isn't that right, Adèle?'

Esther watched him as he spoke and though the mention of these two together physically was horrible to her, she saw how vulnerable he was making himself – how he had been used by Adèle. Perhaps Jules wasn't the cad – the philanderer – here. Adèle was. Esther tried to breathe through her anger as she processed the idea. For millennia men had been treating women as objects and abandoning them when a better offer came along. But in this case, the roles were reversed. Times had changed. Adèle had visited Jules whenever it suited her – when she needed him – had locked him out of her personal life, and wasn't prepared to give him any more than that. But was he in love with her? She needed to know that. Esther looked back to Jules who was watching her face intently. Then she turned to Adèle.

'Adèle? Is this true?' Esther asked.

Adèle shrugged and scowled. 'We had an agreement,' was her only rebuttal. 'But it is clear that this is the last time we will ever see each other, Jules,' she said as she stormed out of the apartment and slammed the door behind her.

Jules looked as if he'd been slapped hard in the face. He took a few ragged breaths and then looked up to Esther.

'Please, Esther, let me explain properly. I need you to understand. The last time Adèle was here, I confronted her and told her that if this was never going to develop into a real relationship, then I wanted to end it. She became very angry and hit me. I told her to leave. I honestly never thought I'd see her again. That was over a month ago,' he said, holding his hands up in confusion. 'Last week, when I got back to Paris, I called her to tell her that I'd met someone else – someone important – and I made it very clear that this was serious. I never wanted to see her again. She didn't answer the phone but I left a long message on her answerphone. I honestly don't know what she was expecting to happen by turning up again like this now.' He rubbed his face in his hands.

Esther walked to the fridge and pulled out the bottle of wine, pouring a glass for Jules.

'I think we should sit down and have a long talk,' she said, going to the settee to take a seat. Jules followed. They looked at each other across the wide, open space that had deepened between them. After a minute of silence that felt like a year, Esther spoke.

'Do you love her?' she asked and watched his eyes. He took a deep breath and frowned before answering.

'I thought I did, at the beginning. It was just like the start of a normal love affair. I wanted to see more of her, and when I learned about her son, I asked when I could meet him. I told her I loved her and wanted to be with her. But then I didn't see her for a while, and when I did, she explained that she didn't want a relationship. She didn't need one – she didn't love me and never would. It was that blunt. I should have just ended it then, but I was weak, Esther. I loved being with her, and I hoped, I suppose, that she would change her mind. So I stupidly went along with the arrangement the way she wanted it. Sometimes she would come for a weekend. I had someone to eat dinner with, and share the night with, but I was nothing to her.

'A month ago, I realised it had to end – that's when she slapped me and left. And last week, I rang her to make certain she knew I never wanted to see her again. And yet, despite that, tonight, she obviously came back thinking she could just pick me up again – like an old toy,' he said, leaning back and resting his head on the back of the settee.

'So if I hadn't been here this weekend, if she'd arrived and you'd never been to Sainte-Mère-Église for the christening, or met me again, what would have happened, Jules? Would you have just slipped back into bed with her? Because you do still love her?' Esther asked.

He lifted his head and looked directly at her while he thought his answer through.

'*Non*. I had decided it was over. I knew I needed to move on else I would be stuck in this strange place – seeing someone but not in a real relationship – forever. No, Esther, I don't love her any more, and it was over before I met you.'

They ate dinner quietly, and for the first time since she'd arrived in Paris, they spent the night side by side without making love. Instead, they talked, and cried, into the early hours, about commitment, abandonment, and all the terrible emotions brought on by love.

By the time Esther left Jules in Paris the next day, they had made no firm plans for seeing each other again.

## 21

### SAINTE-MÈRE-ÉGLISE, SPRING 1942

Spring in Sainte-Mère-Église was beautiful again, full of blossom, and warmth and long daylight hours. And it was all the more so for the beautiful friends that Marie-Claire had around her now. She had become quite close with Rachel Epstein, and had often eaten with the family. The familiarity of Jewish customs and foods had been a real comfort to her.

She'd seen so much more of her friends from the château in Canon too. Ever since the attack on the airfield, it had become impossible for the resistance crew to return to the château, which had been taken over completely as a German command centre, just as they'd expected it would be.

Sainte-Mère-Église now became the central base for the group headed by Jean-Baptiste, but he stationed himself near the coast at Vierville-sur-Mer, where he was gathering information for the British on the coastline of this part of Normandy.

And in the summer, news reached Sainte-Mère-Église of the most horrific aggression towards the Jewish community in Paris. Marie-Claire was serving in the café-bar and overheard the conversation between two middle-aged women.

'My brother arrived from Paris just yesterday, and I would not believe it could be true if I hadn't heard it from his own lips. He said there were thousands upon thousands, rounded up like criminals. Men, women, children, elderly – all the same – dragged from their homes and marched to the sports arena. Kept there for days they were, and then buses started to take them away – who knows where.'

Marie-Claire started again to clean the table next to theirs, which was already spotless. She felt sick to the core but needed to hear more.

'And these were all Jews, you say?' asked the second woman.

'All Jews, every one of them. My brother said his bank manager was one of those taken. It didn't matter if they were rich or poor, influential or not. The only criteria was being Jewish.'

'Oh, this is too much! What reason can they possibly have?' The other woman simply shrugged in response.

'I don't know. But it is getting worse and worse. All Jews now have to wear a yellow star to show their religion – even those who claim to not ever have visited a synagogue. They are making their decision based on who the parents were, or grandparents even. It is so wrong.'

Marie-Claire's thoughts flew first to the Epstein family. She must warn them to try harder to stay invisible to the German soldiers here in Sainte-Mère-Église.

That night, Marie-Claire raced out to the farm on her bicycle and as soon as she found Louis, working in the barn, she fell into his arms, sobbing.

'My sweet girl, what is it?' he crooned, stroking her gently as she cried. 'Are you hurt? Has someone been asking questions about us? Our work?' he asked.

'No. Not hurt, and no. We are safe. But I've heard the most terrible news from Paris,' she said and began to cry again. Later, once she had explained all that she knew, and gone over again the way that Benjamin had been killed, simply for being found carrying Jewish books, Louis bent to kiss her head, still holding her tightly in his arms as she shook with fear and rage.

'But you are safe, Marie-Claire. You are not even Jewish yourself, are you?' he asked.

'I know, but there are Jewish families here in Sainte-Mère-Église. Some of them are my friends now. We must warn them. We must get them to safety before they are forced to wear this yellow star, and taken away too.'

Louis looked around the barn, and up to the hayloft above. There was a milking shed in one of the other cow fields as well, and an older barn that was no longer in use.

'We could house families here for a short while, and then make contact with other groups further west, in Brittany, where the occupation is less dense, though much further south into the free zone would be best,' he muttered his half-formed ideas out loud.

'Yes, and perhaps even help them get as far as the south coast, or perhaps into Spain?' Marie-Claire asked.

'It is a long way to travel, undercover, but we do have compatriots in the south. Jean-Baptiste would know what to do.'

'If we can just save one family, Louis, we must do something,' she said, desperate to help.

'We will do everything we can, my dear,' he said.

She turned to hug him tightly and gave him a heartfelt kiss on the cheek in thanks.

'What is this? I offer to help and suddenly the beautiful Marie-Claire is kissing me?' He laughed, lightly mocking her, but she saw that he had been thrilled to be touched this way by her. 'What would I have to do for you to kiss me, really, Marie-Claire? If I save the whole world, could you love me then?' he asked, and she saw he was serious. Very serious. His breathing had become ragged, and she realised she'd aroused him.

She'd been leaning on Louis for support for many months, and had allowed him to become so close to her, but had never yet returned his faithful love with the affection she knew he desired. And, if she was honest with herself, she'd desired it too. She had known that since before she'd ever become involved with George, and even afterwards too. It was Louis who had awakened her to the idea of being touched by any man other than Benjamin.

'You've already saved me, Louis. You don't need to do anything else for me,' she said and reached up her hand, slowly stroking his face. He closed his eyes and leant into her hand, kissing her fingers.

She raised her lips to his and kissed him softly, once, twice, and as she was pulling away, he leant in and kissed her back, fully, firmly and with a passion that made her groan in delight. She pulled him down into the softness of the hay on the floor around them and at last allowed herself to feel free with Louis, pulling him close to her as they tumbled and rolled together.

Later in the afternoon, when Marie-Claire had pulled bits of hay from Louis's hair and he'd done the same for her, they brushed themselves down and walked hand in hand into the farmhouse kitchen. Madame Joubert missed nothing and, the corners of her mouth twitching ever so slightly as she regarded the pair, she asked simply if neither of them had any work to do.

'Actually, *Maman*, that is something we've come to talk to you about. How would you feel about feeding a number of guests who might come to stay at the barn – a large number of guests?' he asked, and then they sat at the table and proceeded to lay out their plan.

Louis sent a message to Jean-Baptiste, asking for his help

with contacts in the free zone to the south. Marie-Claire met with Rachel Epstein and together they drew up a list of families in town that she knew to be Jewish.

'Marie-Claire, are you sure you want to be involved with this? It is so dangerous for you,' Rachel said.

'I would do anything to help you and the other Jewish families here get away from those monsters, Rachel. I could not live with myself if I did not help you,' Marie-Claire explained.

The next day, Marie-Claire saw one of the women shopping in the market. She found a way to get beside her, where nobody could hear them.

'Madame Mandel, I want to help you,' Marie-Claire began quietly, as she studied the contents of her shopping basket. Madame Mandel looked about her and frowned back at Marie-Claire.

'You work at the café, yes?' she asked. 'How would you like to help me, my dear?'

'Have you heard of the crimes against Jewish people taking place in Paris?' Marie-Claire could see by the terror on the woman's face, and the way her eyes darted around the crowd in the market, that she was very aware of what had been happening.

'It is not just in Paris, my dear. My son has been beaten several times on his way home from the farm – for no reason that we know of other than they say he looks like a dirty Jew,' she said, and Marie-Claire could not hide her shock.

'I heard from Mrs Epstein that one of the Abram girls was attacked too. The bastards seem to think they can treat everyone worse than animals!' Marie-Claire said, and went on to explain her plan.

'I work here in Sainte-Mère-Église with some others who are fighting against the German occupation. You should know,

Madame, that my husband was half Jewish and he was shot by a German soldier in Paris.' Marie-Claire watched as the blood seemed to drain away from Madame Mandel's face.

'I have a husband and three children here. What are we to do? Where can we go?' she asked desperately.

'That is my reason for talking to you. We believe we can help you get out to the free zone, and travel south. You will stand a much better chance of escape, the further you go from Paris,' she explained. 'Do you know the Joubert farm?'

Within days, with no great fuss or attention, the family of Madame Mandel had moved into the barn to await instructions on where they might be taken next. And over the next few weeks, nine families were moved out of Sainte-Mère-Église, right beneath the noses of the German soldiers who had not an idea that these families existed. There were just two more families to move – the Epsteins and old Madame and Monsieur Oppenheimer who were still very reluctant to leave.

'We've lived here our whole lives, my dear child. What would we do in the south? We've done no wrong, I'm sure they won't cause us any trouble,' they'd said to her just days before when she'd gone again to plead with them to come to the barn with her. The notices had now begun to be plastered around the town, with an image of a yellow star, and the command that all Jews over the age of six years must wear the star on their outer clothing. And very soon the German soldiers began investigations as to which families in town this applied to. Marie-Claire helped to lead them off the scent and was warmed by the number of people who backed her up.

'No, I don't think we have any Jewish families living in Sainte-Mère-Église, Monsieur,' she said, sounding all innocence, when she was asked directly one day. 'It is a small town, and everyone knows each other. I'm sure we would know if there were any

Jews living here.' She shrugged and continued to clear the table where the soldiers were seated.

An hour later, Marie-Claire heard female shrieks and male shouting coming from the other side of the square. She ran out into the middle of the square to see what was happening and her heart fell into the core of the earth as she tried to take it in. Two German soldiers were dragging Madame and Monsieur Oppenheimer by the hair. Marie-Claire's blood turned to ice water. She knew it was too late for this lovely old couple now. There was nothing she could do. Just like Benjamin, they were doomed as soon as the bastards had decided it was their turn.

That night, Marie-Claire went to Rachel, taking a wandering route to get there from the café-bar, and checking she wasn't followed. They'd seen the Oppenheimers removed in a truck and now knew beyond any doubt that it was no longer safe to stay. The two women were certain that all the known Jewish families had left, and now it was time they made a plan for the Epsteins to get out too. Marie-Claire helped them to pack up a couple of small bags, and remembered her own sadness at leaving her apartment in Paris on the evening that her world had been about to end.

She waited quietly while Rachel said farewell to her husband, as they'd agreed that when the family moved into the barn, first Rachel and Golda would go, and then David and Jacob were to follow some hours later, to avoid raising suspicion. The truth was that, by this stage, under Marie-Claire and Louis's direction, not only had nine families left town already, and all were well on their way to compatriots in the south, but other families had spread out and moved into the homes they left behind, so that there were no obviously empty houses to create any suspicion. But now that the Epsteins were moving out, she hadn't had time to make a plan for their home. She was just grateful they didn't have any animals to leave behind, as these were such a giveaway, just as Minette would have been for her and Benjamin.

Marie-Claire took the back lanes with the Epstein girls, carefully watching over her shoulder in case they should be followed.

'I think the drama with the Oppenheimers has helped, if anything,' Marie-Claire said, surprised that they'd met nobody along the route. 'The soldiers think they've found their one Jewish family left in the town.'

Once at the farm, Marie-Claire settled them into the barn and then rushed them up to the hideout in the hayloft when she heard angry voices coming from the farmhouse kitchen.

She wandered into the kitchen nonchalantly and was immediately confronted by two soldiers. They were young. Very young. No more than eighteen or nineteen years old. They'd been sent here to find out if Madame Joubert knew of any Jewish families in town, as she sold milk to most people around here.

'I sell them milk. I don't ask where they go to church,' she was saying, probably for the tenth time, looking at the annoyance on her face.

'*Bonsoir,* Messieurs,' Marie-Claire said with a gentle smile. 'Can I help you?' She then managed to get them into a relaxed state by the fire, drinking several glasses of Calvados, where she regaled them with stories of how much the old mayor had hated the Jews and had cleared the town out, long before the Germans had arrived.

'So you see? Your job has been done for you. Old Monsieur *et* Madame Oppenheimer were the only ones he couldn't get out, because they threatened to spank him like they had when he was a boy,' she laughed, slapping her leg along with them as they hooted. She helped them back into their car, and saw them drive

in a haphazard fashion down the road and away to town. She
turned then and stormed back into the kitchen to see if Madame
Joubert was alright.

'You, my dear, are a wonder! You should really get on to the
stage, you know.' She smiled, and then turned grim. 'But that
poor old couple.'

'I know, I know. I tried to warn them and help them, but they
wouldn't listen. But at least the Epsteins are safe – half of them,
at least,' Marie-Claire said, turning back towards the barn, a
worried expression on her face.

'Oh no, they are all here now. Louis brought David and Jacob
in while you were talking to those idiot young boys here in the
kitchen,' Madame Joubert said. 'I watched them through the
window while you were keeping them busy with your stories.'

'Oh, thank God!' cried Marie-Claire as she ran out to the
barn to see the family who were all now settled into the hayloft.

They decided not to wait until morning. Louis took the
Epsteins on their way into the night within a few hours. And
Marie-Claire was never to see or hear from her friend Rachel
again, but from all they could gather, the family was safe some-
where in the south. Perhaps they had even made it away to
America via the south coast.

The plan had worked so well that Jean-Baptiste shared the
information down the chains of communication so that others
might try the same plan too. As far as Marie-Claire was
concerned, every single family that was saved was worth the risk.

She didn't know how long the families would remain safe
where they had ended up, but the satisfaction of having beaten
the Germans at their game made her feel invincible – danger-
ously so, Louis told her.

'Marie-Claire, you must remember that as fast as we are
working to undermine the German occupation, they have their

own agents out trying to hunt us down. Please be careful. Stay on your guard, hmm?' he said as he walked her slowly home late one night.

'We shouldn't even be out this late, you know. If they caught us now, they might take me – or both of us – on grounds of breaking curfew and who knows what they would do to try and get information out of us,' he said, looking over his shoulder to check they weren't being followed.

'Well, then, you'd better come inside so we don't get caught,' she said, with a mischievous grin, and pulled him in through the door at the back of the café-bar.

## 22

POOLE, SEPTEMBER 1998

Esther checked the clock on the office wall for the fifteenth time in the last hour. Still twenty minutes to go until she was due to leave. She had arranged to go at four o'clock on this Friday afternoon, so she could hop on the train and head up to London in time. The plan was that she'd check into the hotel, then walk back to Waterloo International station where she would meet Jules as he got off the Eurostar as a foot passenger direct from Paris.

The last time Esther had seen Jules, they'd parted with a tearful hug and a simple kiss on the cheeks, in the French style. The joy that Esther had found in trusting him had been shattered by the discovery of his relationship with Adèle. And so, she'd explained to Jules, she didn't think she could carry on.

But he had written to her, explaining how genuinely sorry he was that he'd been so stupid to have not told her about Adèle, and how it had all ended before he'd even seen Esther at the christening. He missed her terribly, knew that he was falling in love with her, and needed to see her again.

Esther had written back and told him that she missed him too, and she opened her heart completely through a letter that ran for pages. She wrote about how her father had abandoned her and her mum when she was just a tiny girl, and how the pain from being abandoned had changed her forever. When she'd first met Adèle that night, she had of course jumped to the conclusion that it was Jules who'd left Adèle hanging, and that he was likely going to do the same to her. And although she now knew the truth, the whole incident had left her reeling with relived pain and the sense that she had to protect herself from hurt.

Esther turned to her best friend, Kelly, to talk it all through and they'd met up for a country walk in Worth Matravers, and a pie lunch at the Square and Compass. As they'd walked from the pub down through the village and past the duck pond, Kelly asked, innocently, how Esther's latest trip to France had gone.

'Oh, Kelly. I have so much to tell you and no idea where to start,' Esther replied. 'But you remember the school trip to Sainte-Mère-Église?' she asked, and Kelly nodded, knowing the close friendship that Esther kept up with her pen pal, Giselle. Esther told her everything as they walked – seeing Jules at the christening, the spark between them, the exciting week in Paris and then the devastation of learning about Adèle.

'But he insists it is definitely over – it was over before he met you again?' Kelly asked, as they sat on a rock at the Winspit Quarry, looking out to sea.

'Yes, it is over, and I believe him, I do. But it scared me, Kelly. I had started to let go and trust him. And then there was this avalanche that hit me and knocked me off my feet. I just don't want to be in a position where I could be the one left behind again.'

As they walked up the hill towards the village, Kelly soothed Esther's anguish and reminded her that not every man was destined to leave her. In fact, in all Esther's relationships through her twenties, it was Esther who had ended things. Plenty of men were solid stayers.

'Take my Jordan, for example. He is an absolute rock, and always has been. He'll be with me forever. You don't have any reason to believe Jules won't be the same. It wasn't him who abandoned Adèle really, was it? She was using him – as strange as it seems – and, when he eventually realised that, he got out,' Kelly reasoned.

Back at the pub, they bought their pies and a pint of cider each, and sat on the picnic table out the front, watching the sun play its game in and out of the clouds over the sea ahead.

'So you think I should give it another chance?' asked Esther, and her friend nodded, her mouth too full of pie to answer. Eventually Kelly wiped the crumbs from her lips, took a big drink of cider and replied.

'Esther, you fell for him. You had something real. He hasn't done anything wrong, and he wants you. He loves you. Just give it a chance. And if I'm wrong,' she said with a wink and a nudge, 'you can come and live with me and Jordan and we'll make a threesome,' she said, and the two friends laughed like children.

The letters had continued between Esther and Jules, and now he was coming to see her. This weekend in London was being kept quiet from both her family and his, so they were staying in London until he went back to Paris for work late on Sunday night, and she was to take the last train home to Poole. He didn't want his family interfering, for one thing, as he knew they would if they thought he was in a serious relationship with Esther. And as for Esther's mum, well, it was probably going to come as something of a shock that she'd fallen for a man – after all this time of being single – and, as far as Lucy Holt knew, Esther'd simply gone to France to visit Giselle. Esther was going to look for just the right time to let her mum know she had this tentative but potentially life-changing relationship with Jules – which she hoped would go well, but this one weekend could equally be the end of it all.

And now, as Esther was packing up her desk, a little earlier than usual on this Friday afternoon, she was terrified.

She popped home and made a fuss of Archie, writing a quick note for her neighbour to thank her for dropping in and checking on him over the weekend. She finished packing her small weekend bag, then walked up the High Street and on to Poole railway station, which was closer to her little townhouse than her workplace was at Upton House. She smiled to herself as she compared her humble terraced home at Baiter, near the harbour's edge, with the grand opulence of Jules' magnificent Paris apartment. But both served their purpose – and both had been a perfectly adequate home to each of the single people, for many years.

On the train ride from Poole to Waterloo, Esther read over the many letters she had received from Jules in the last month. Jules had a home computer, and had been trying to convince Esther she should get one too, so they could communicate faster, via email, but she still preferred to handwrite a real letter. They'd each written about twice each week, and she felt she knew him more and more intimately with each new missive. And then there were all the phone calls, too, and yet, this face-to-face meeting was daunting.

And so, when she saw him walking towards her that night on the platform of the station at Waterloo International, Esther wasn't sure how to greet him. Her heart melted when she saw his face, his smile, his uncertain expression. He was hoping she still wanted him – really wanted him – she could see. She was ready to give this a chance, and so when he kissed her on both cheeks she pulled back and looked at him for a moment before leaning in to kiss him on the lips. He tasted divine, and the groan of release and relief that she heard him utter told her how much he had missed her. She wrapped her arms around him and allowed herself to let go.

The next morning, when they had finally managed to get out of bed and take showers, just in time to enjoy the hotel buffet breakfast before it closed, she'd taken Jules on a walking tour of London. They'd walked around the Houses of Parliament and visited the Churchill War Rooms to see the control centre and map room, and then taken a stroll through St James's Park where they looked though the railings at Buckingham Palace. A Tube trip took them on to the Tower of London and Tower Bridge, and then from there back to Covent Garden where they'd had a long and late lunch, a stroll around the market and then a quiet cocktail before seeing the newly opened musical, *West Side Story*.

'So, what did you think?' Esther asked Jules, who laughed.

'I think you know that it was very hard for me to translate, yes? But I could understand that this was a very sad story. But the best part was to watch your face. You were enjoying each moment so much, Esther,' he said, and squeezed her hand as they walked side by side along the river, across Waterloo Bridge and back towards their hotel.

As they approached the underside of the next bridge they could smell the delicious aromas of a late-night burger bar, and stopped to eat a sticky and satisfying meal.

'Not quite up to the standards of Parisian cuisine,' Esther laughed as she licked her fingers of the juicy sauces from her burger. Jules laughed and shook his head as he finished an enormous mouthful.

'No, but this is London. And here, when I'm this hungry, this is better!'

The next day, they left their bags at the hotel reception and headed for Trafalgar Square and a long stroll through the National Gallery, where Esther showed Jules some of the paintings by Monet, and especially the *Water Lily Pond*, which meant so much more to them both after their visit to his house and gardens back during her time with him in Paris. They walked on through Piccadilly and up to the Ritz, which Esther told Jules was a place she'd always dreamed of staying – or at least having high tea there. She watched people coming and going and looked up at the glorious building, before she tugged him away and on to Hyde Park Corner.

'I'll go and hire us some deckchairs, Jules. You fetch the tea,' she said as they reached the lawn beside the boating lake – a perfect spot to rest in the warm sunshine for a while.

'I could get used to living like this,' Esther said as she watched a couple almost falling in the water while they stepped into their little boat. 'Being here with you, I mean,' she said, turning to look at Jules who smiled back at her.

'Me too. And I'm looking forward to seeing your home, meeting your family,' he said, hinting at the commitment he was prepared for. All day, in between the sightseeing, the walking, and the noisy, windy Tube platforms, they'd been talking through what they both wanted from a relationship, and they were in one mind: solid commitment, no secrets, and promises they would keep. And, more practically, they talked over ways they could make this relationship work – without it having to cost them a pricey city break each time.

They drank their tea, talked and people-watched for an hour before Jules looked at his watch and told her it was time they should get going. It was still hours before his train was due to

leave, she knew, but perhaps he was tired of sitting in the sun –
something that Esther was happy to do anytime.

'Let's just catch the Tube back, to save our legs,' she said, but
Jules preferred to walk down Piccadilly. There was something he
wanted to see.

By the time they passed the Ritz again, it was four in the
afternoon, and Jules tugged her towards the stairs, but Esther,
confused, told him they probably shouldn't go inside without a
booking.

'But what if we do have a booking?' he asked, and Esther's
jaw dropped a little more than was elegant, as she looked to
Jules, into the flashy foyer of the Ritz and back to him again.

'You didn't?' she asked, incredulous.

'I did, actually, if that is okay with you? Tea at half past four.
Shall we?' he asked, holding his arm out to the open door and
picking up her hand to hold it.

Inside, the elegant tea room hummed with the sophisticated
sound of light chatter, cutlery and glasses chinking, and the
tinkling of a piano from the corner of the vast room. Almost all
the tables were full, and several parties had bottles of champagne to go with their delectable plates of sweet treats and tiny
sandwiches. As a waiter took them to their table, and Esther saw
how beautifully dressed everyone was, she felt very glad for her
choice of a long and flowery sundress for the day, when she
might have been in shorts and T-shirt on any other summer
Sunday. She looked up at the great high ceiling and crystal light
fittings overhead.

'It's so beautiful in here,' she whispered to Jules as they sat
down.

'Why haven't you been before?' he asked. 'I've been to eat at
the Ritz in Paris many times.'

'But it's so expensive, and when I lived here for university, I never had any money. And now that I'm working, I live so far away. I rarely come to London, to be honest. It's probably different when you live right in the city, like you do,' she said, as the waiter flipped open the linen napkin and laid it on her lap.

'Champagne?' Jules asked, as he saw her looking through the drinks menu. 'Let's celebrate,' he said.

'And what are we celebrating?' she asked him with a small smile.

'A new beginning, and a future we can trust in, together,' he whispered hoarsely. Together. With Jules. She liked the sound of that.

'Champagne, then. On a Sunday afternoon at the Ritz. Perfect. When did you book this, by the way?' she asked, suddenly wondering quite how he had managed to organise it.

'I memorised the phone number when we looked in earlier, and then when I went to buy our cup of tea at the park, I made a phone call. We were lucky to get in, apparently – they had a late cancellation,' he said, happy to share the secret he'd been keeping for a couple of hours now.

'You're good at surprises, Jules,' she said and then regretted it instantly as she thought of Adèle.

'Yes. I'm sorry for all the surprises. I think you would prefer it if I was a little more – how do you say – predictable?' he asked.

Esther thought for a moment before responding.

'Yes and no. I like the good surprises – the happy ones,' she said, lowering her chin. He reached across the table and took her hands in his.

'I'm so very sorry, Esther. I was stupid. I promise to try and make all my surprises happy ones from now on,' he said, with a hoarse croak in his voice that told her all she needed to know about how much he meant it.

* * *

Three weeks later, Esther pulled her car into a space in the car park at Hamworthy, just beside the Channel ferry loading area. Jules had managed to take a couple of days off work and she was meeting him as he arrived early in the morning, having come across on the *Barfleur* as a foot passenger. The arrangement had been that he would drive from Paris to Sainte-Mère-Église, from where Hugo would drive him to Cherbourg and drop him at the ferry terminal. And he'd taken the overnight crossing, hiring a cabin to get some sleep.

Esther had arrived far earlier than was needed. The drive was only ten minutes from her home, but she'd been awake half the night thinking of Jules, and bubbling with excitement to see him again. She had been trying to rationalise the way she couldn't seem to think about anything else. Jules had become the centre of her world. And she was very aware that not one single other man had ever managed to capture her heart this way.

Esther noticed the cars were beginning to roll off the ferry now and she tried to see where the foot passengers would alight. This was a new one for Esther. She'd travelled on the ferry with a car dozens of times before, but never on foot. It was certainly a much more economical way to do the trip, and made sense when both she and the Joubert family lived so close to the ferry on either side of the Channel. But Sainte-Mère-Église was quite a distance from Jules' home in Paris. Just as she was mulling over the details, the ins and outs, and wondering what their next weekend together might look like and where it could be, she saw him, striding off the boat. The sight of his tall, lean figure, and that shock of gorgeously shiny and long dark hair, caused a sharp intake of breath, as it always did when she hadn't seen him for a while. She got out of the car and waved with two arms, hoping he would see her, but he didn't know which direction to look.

Esther left the car and walked over to the crowd of hikers, cyclists, and this one very smart Parisian businessman, dressed for a summer weekend in Poole. He still hadn't seen her until, unable to hold back her excitement any more, she'd broken into a run to greet him.

'Esther, *mon amour!*' he cried, dropping his bag and throwing open his arms wide to catch her in a big hug and swing her off the ground. They walked hand in hand back to her car, and then she drove him home via Poole Quay, giving him a guided tour on the way, without realising it.

'Esther, are you trying to sell Poole to me as a place to live?' he asked with a grin and very twinkly-eyed wink. 'Because in a very short time, you've already made it sound wonderful.' He laughed and she joined in.

'Poole is a beautiful place – so different to Paris, and Sainte-Mère-Église too. But it's twinned with Cherbourg, of course, and I'm sure you will see some similarities, though the docks and ferry port are the main things. We have this beautiful harbour too,' she said, pulling the car into a parking spot on the quay to give them the chance to view the whole glorious vista, before heading home and unlocking the front door.

'I know this is going to be tough – but I'm determined to make the best possible impression on your family,' Jules said gravely and with a face set like steel, making her wonder exactly what he could be talking about. He knew she didn't live with her mum so what could he be saying? As soon as she unlocked the door and led Jules through to the lounge, she realised what he meant, and laughed.

Jules dropped his bag, scoured the room with his eyes, and went straight to the window where Archie had draped himself over the sill to keep one sleepy eye on the world outside. Jules knelt beside the cat and took one limp paw in his hand.

'Monsieur Archie, it is a pleasure to meet you. I have a very important question to ask you. May I have the honour of sharing your beautiful Esther with you?'

## 23

### SAINTE-MÈRE-ÉGLISE, MAY 1944

The fact that Marie-Claire had managed to maintain her role, and her cover, at the café-bar in the middle of Sainte-Mère-Église was an absolute miracle, according to Jean-Baptiste. She had been there for over three years now, and everybody in town loved her. But Louis Joubert loved her best of all. She spent all her free time at the farm with him, and he would drop in to visit her whenever he came into town. Whenever he was away, his return felt like a victory to Marie-Claire, as she never knew quite what he was doing, or how dangerous it was. She did know though, that as the war went on, and the Allies grew closer to an invasion to take France back from German occupation, that the work would become more dangerous.

The people of France, and Sainte-Mère-Église in particular, were growing ever hopeful of an end to the occupation. The situation for Jewish people around the country had become absolutely dire, and the free zone in the south no longer existed. The German weapon of Gestapo was everywhere, and people were beginning to find it hard to trust even their oldest and closest friends and neighbours. The need for survival had driven some to collaborate and become informants, but others were accused of collaboration when they had no choice but to do as ordered by the Germans.

And yet, despite the dismally dark backdrop to their lives, the weather had turned distinctly from spring to early summer. Marie-Claire noticed now as she cycled out to the farm on this Sunday afternoon that the hedgerows were abuzz with bees, crops were growing in the fields, and the sun was warm on her back.

The evenings were growing longer and this made for greater difficulty for Lysander visits, as it reduced the amount of time they could use cover of darkness. But just two nights ago, Marie-Claire had been surprised by an old friend.

The plane had finally come in to the area at three in the morning, and she'd been waiting since before midnight. The moon was bright and there was no wind at all as she'd run out to light the torches. She had a packet to deliver to the plane but, first, two operatives arrived. Once under the cover of the woodland trees, she was thrilled to see that one was Marguerite, whom she hadn't seen for over a year and had wondered if she would ever see again.

This afternoon she was hoping to hear news of the upcoming invasion, but she knew any details shared with her would be scant, as she was so often around the soldiers. Though everyone on the resistance team knew they could trust her implicitly, nobody ever knew anything that they didn't need to know. Just in case.

When she walked into the farmhouse kitchen, Louis jumped up to greet her with a kiss and held her hand as she sat in a chair he had saved for her beside him. Madame Joubert had made coffee and was pouring freshly heated frothy milk into the cups and handing them around the table.

'Marguerite is just about to update us on what has been happening in England, and what we are to expect here,' said Jean-Baptiste, who had made a rare visit into Sainte-Mère-Église from the coast where he had been mainly based for the last couple of years.

'The south coast of England has been preparing a major force for the attack, by sea and air,' Marguerite began. 'In a place called Dorset, just across the Channel from Cherbourg, there are thousands of troops from America, and they have been practising landing on the beaches there. Winston Churchill, King George and the Allied generals Eisenhower, Montgomery, and Admiral Louis Mountbatten have all been to watch the exercises from a concrete fort positioned along the beach. But there have also been several mock practices all along the Dorset coast, aimed at misleading the Germans. They have been firing rockets with rope ladders up against the cliffs and false information has been leaked to known German spies that the Allies intend to land at the cliffs in the Pas-de-Calais region to the far east,' Marguerite began.

'From what I can see, they are being well and truly deceived,' Jean-Baptiste continued. 'German defences along the coastline here in Normandy are being dropped back and many troops have been moving out to the east to bolster defences along that part of the coast.'

'Many Allied troops will arrive directly in landing craft, which are being built in Poole – the town on the coast directly opposite to Cherbourg. They are producing the landing craft at the pace of one every single day and there will be hundreds ready very soon,' Marguerite said.

'You've seen them?' asked Marie-Claire.

'I work in the harbour there, on boats, and yes, I've found a way to get a good look around the harbour and the shipyards, which have all been extremely industrious. There will also be thousands of soldiers with parachutes dropped in by air. There are airfields stacked as far as the eye can see with planes and gliders. In fact, this is how we will see our first action,' Marguerite added. 'There will be parachutists dropped quietly into the countryside surrounding here and their job will be to sneak in and take the town from this side, just as the beach landings are taking place.'

'And how will we know when this will occur?' Louis asked.

'This is where we have to thank Marie-Claire for her input.' Jean-Baptiste smiled in her direction. She didn't know what he was referring to.

'The recipes and little anecdotes and stories that she has been creating, which have been broadcast on local radio for some time now, they've paved the way for some lines of code taken from a poem. It's by Paul Verlaine – "Chanson d'automne",' he said.

'Oh, I know it! It is beautiful,' said Marie-Claire. 'Terribly short and full of emotion: *The long sobs of autumn's violins, wound my heart with a monotonous languor,*' she began.

'Yes, that is the one. This is the message we will hear on the radio when we know the invasion is imminent, just the first three lines. And then, when we hear the final lines, that is our signal to go into full-scale sabotage mode,' said Jean-Baptiste.

'Sabotage? What exactly are we sabotaging?' asked Madame Joubert.

'As you know, I can't tell you all the details. But operatives around the country are poised to go into all-out war with the occupant Germans. There will be railways destroyed, roads and bridges blown up, army bases razed to the ground. All is falling into place to bring them to their knees, just at the point that the

Allies arrive. Here in Sainte-Mère-Église, I will let you know what you each must do,' he finished.

Each one around the table remained silent, taking it all in, fearfully, hopefully.

'So this is really going to happen? The Allies are coming back, and we will overthrow the Germans?' asked Marie-Claire.

'That is certainly the plan, my friend,' said Marguerite.

'I think this calls for something stronger than coffee, excuse my impertinence, Madame Joubert,' Marie-Claire said to the response of very loud laughter from all her friends, and Louis went for a fresh bottle of the apple brandy they all loved, giving her a luscious kiss as he left the room.

\* \* \*

For the next three weeks, Marie-Claire barely saw Louis. He disappeared with Jean-Baptiste and returned once, briefly, and she managed to sneak him into her room above the café-bar where he let her know a few details about what he'd been doing. She had been desperate to see him as she had something important to tell him. But after their fierce and passionate reunion, when they lay together in her twisted sheets, both glowing from the exertion of their lovemaking, she found it hard to bring up such a gentle and sensitive topic.

Marie-Claire kissed him and stroked his hair and held her hand to her tummy, secretly thankful that the father of her second child was alive, still. At least for now. She would tell him once this was all over. He didn't need news like that to get in the way of the important work he was doing. She had mentioned it to Madame Joubert though, the woman who she hoped would be her mother-in-law someday soon. The older woman had held her close and cried silent tears of joy mixed with fear.

'Let us all hope we can make France safe for this little one, hmm?' she had said, gently kissing Marie-Claire's face.

There were cells to the north, east and south of them which were all working together ahead of the upcoming invasion. Marguerite had gone south toward Caen where she was going to take part in the destruction of an army base there. Louis had been rallying teams to come and help with the battle for Sainte-Mère-Église which would take place once the paratroopers arrived on the outskirts of the town.

Louis checked the store of weapons and ammunition that he'd hidden in Marie-Claire's room. Several other homes around the square also had supplies which had been brought in, hidden in laundry baskets, shopping bags and potato sacks. Charles had even managed to hide machine guns in a storeroom inside the church. Marie-Claire felt that the whole of France must be abuzz with the expectation of this invasion, but had to keep reminding herself how secret it all was and go about her business each day as if nothing had changed.

Once Louis had checked and counted the guns in her wardrobe, he shut it quietly and came back to join her in the bed. The night was still bright at gone nine o'clock, and they lay together in the unlighted room, the curtains blowing gently in the soft summer breeze that came in through the open window. Later, they lay on top of the eiderdown, naked and glowing with the heat of the night and their lovemaking.

Marie-Claire's long hair spread across the pillow and Louis ran his fingers through it, stroking her skin with his other hand.

'Louis, if something should happen to one of us during the battle,' she began, wondering if now was her chance to tell him about their baby she believed she was carrying, but he shushed her at once.

'*Non, ma chérie*, do not talk this way. All will be well,' he crooned, kissing her.

'But no, Louis, it might not. Guns will be fired, people will fall. We both might not make it. But if I fall, you must know this. I have loved you, deeply, and I think of you as my husband.'

Louis leant up on his elbow to look into her face while she continued.

'It has not been easy for me to reach this place, and the journey has been long. But, although Benjamin remains my husband in my heart, I know I have made room for you too. I love you, Louis,' she said, caressing his face with her fingers.

'Marie-Claire, I waited a long time to know that you were ready for me. And loving you has been the best thing that could have happened to me in this war. This is not the way I would have chosen to ask this but, after the battle, when we are free, will you marry me? Will you be my Madame Joubert?' he asked, taking her hand and kissing her fingers.

A single tear escaped her eye and ran down the side of her face. She swiped at it quickly, but noticed that Louis had begun to cry too.

'Look at us: two fierce resistance fighters, weeping like babies.' He laughed and kissed her on the lips. 'But you haven't answered me yet. I'm waiting.'

'Yes, Louis. After the battle. After we are free. I will marry you. And you are going to be a perfect father to our baby,' she said, and grinned as she held his hand to her belly.

\* \* \*

Each night, the members of the resistance all across Northern France would stay close to their radios, listening for the code they were expecting. On the night of 1 June, Louis and Marie-

Claire were together at the farmhouse when they heard the first three lines of the poem included as part of a news broadcast: *The long sobs of autumn's violins*, said the newsreader. Marie-Claire and Louis locked eyes and held their breath. Yes, they had both heard it. The signal had come that the invasion would begin within two weeks from now. Louis shot out of his chair and immediately went to the radio he now kept in the safe room in the hayloft up in the barn. He extended the aerial through the small hole he had made in the roof, so it could be lifted up and retracted fast – the Germans were constantly on the lookout for new aerials, ever since they had banned the town radio station, but this one would be very difficult to see even if they caught him while it was up. He started to relay the latest town newsletter and, just before he read Marie-Claire's latest recipe, he made mention of the lovely summer weather, and said, '*The long sobs of autumn's violins won't be with us for many months yet.*' And then he continued with reminders for market day and other parish news. He hoped enough of his cell would have heard it, if they hadn't heard the BBC announcement earlier. There was nothing else to do but be ready at action stations.

Four nights later, at a quarter past eleven at night on 5 June, the next three lines of the poem were spoken over the radio waves – *wound my heart with a monotonous languor*. Marie-Claire had been waiting by the receiving radio in the farmhouse and raced out to the hayloft and relayed the message to the local cells, in the midst of a story about a bull that had escaped a local farm, and then retracted the aerial. She took a half minute to pray – for the mission, for the men who were coming to save them, for herself and for Louis. This had to work. The world was depending on it.

Her head shot up in shock as she heard distant gunfire, and she flew down the ladder into the farmyard below. Some of the others had been stationed to wait for paratroopers in fields to the north, but now she could see searchlights ranging over the town, and there, falling right in the midst of the light and gunfire, were white parachutes. Something had gone awry, and they seemed to have been dropped directly above the town centre by mistake.

Her heart nearly choked her as she grabbed the bicycle and rode as fast as she could, directly into the battle she could hear ahead. Louis had already left to go who knows where and begin the destruction of the railway. Jean-Baptiste was away near the beaches with another branch who were clearing the roads and bridges that way. All over Northern France, the resistance had sprung into action to do everything possible to keep the Germans back, but right here in Sainte-Mère-Église, something had gone terribly wrong.

She reached the back of the café-bar, flung the bicycle down and raced up to her room where she pulled out a gun and knelt at her bedroom window. There were dozens of parachutes but some of the men landed with such a thud that they must have been shot on the way down. She saw German uniforms below and shot them from above. One. Two. Three.

It was just the way that Jean-Baptiste had trained her, all that time ago when she was first brought here to Sainte-Mère-Église. Even back at the château, he had taken her out to the walled garden and lined up tin cans for her to take aim at. He'd been amazed at how good a shot she was even then, and her steady hand had him wondering if she'd be better in the field working as a sniper than hidden away in the café-bar. But he needed a woman there in the café-bar, and knew she'd be perfect for that role.

She'd barely ever had time to practise, but in recent weeks she'd taken the rifle out on the farm and had a few shots at rabbits, just to check she still had a good aim.

Marie-Claire had been amazed at the number of guns they'd managed to get for this mission and learned that they'd been dribbled in by agents coming across from England, plus lots had been stolen from the Caen airbase back when the team had infiltrated it. Where they'd been hidden all this time was still a mystery to her, but now they seemed to have plenty of weapons to fight this final battle.

Gunfire began to burst from bedroom windows all around the square and then she saw more fighters coming in from the other side, helping the Allies to clear parachutes and get to safety. Soon the battle was raging in the square, just as Louis had said that it would, and there did seem to be more French fighters than German. And then she saw a parachute stop dead in the air and she realised it had snagged on the church steeple.

The poor man was a sitting duck. Marie-Claire kept shooting and four, five, six German uniforms fell. The man on the steeple still hung there but he'd stopped moving. Was he shot? There was no way to find out, and the battle had moved on around the square when she heard an almighty explosion.

Monsieur le Maire's house was blown up, the flames lit the whole night sky, and hopefully, she thought, it had taken the officers from the *Wehrmacht* division based there with it. She grabbed four rifles and slung them over her shoulders, then ran down the stairs and through the back lane to reach one of the houses on the opposite side of the square. Marie-Claire barged in through the open door and thrust the spare guns into the arms of the waiting residents. *Stay low, and don't rest*, Louis had said. The battle would likely go all night, and they were to stay alert until the arrival of soldiers on foot.

Two hours later she could still see the paratrooper hanging from the church steeple, lifelessly. He must have been shot. But they must all keep going. They must do everything possible to give the landed paratroopers the chance to do their job, while everyone waited for the arrival of the troops coming inland from the coast. It was the longest night Marie-Claire felt she had ever lived through. And, somewhere out there, was all she had left in the world to call family: Louis, Adeline, Marguerite, Jean-Baptiste, Charles, Madame *et* Monsieur Joubert. *God, help me if I lose them all*, she prayed.

By dawn, the Americans had arrived on foot. The way had been cleared for them and Sainte-Mère-Église was quickly liberated from the occupying Germans, though the battle was bloody and intense. Those from the German side who were still alive had regrouped at a base outside of town, where they'd taken the few prisoners they'd captured during the night.

Marie-Claire saw through the smoke that the man who'd been hanging from the steeple was gone. His parachute still hung there but he'd been cut free. Perhaps his friends had cut him down so they could give him a decent burial.

She wandered through the quiet and smoking town square, alive as it was with activity and some semblance of celebration. But she could not celebrate yet. Not until she'd heard if Louis and the others had made it through the night.

At the café-bar the enormity of the battle hit her, and she began to weep, wiping her face with smoke-blackened hands. The front windows were all shot out, chairs and tables all upturned, and everything covered in glass. She pushed open the front door and stood aside as more glass crashed to the floor from the front window. She found a broom and started to sweep up the mess, slowly picking up chairs and tables, trying to make sense of this battlefield. She heard someone crunch across the glass-strewn floor towards her and she spun around, hoping to see Louis. It was Adeline – looking just as exhausted as Marie-Claire felt. But she now knew she had one friend alive, at least, and fell sobbing into Adeline's arms.

'Well done, my dear, you did such a good job last night. I heard you on the radio,' Adeline said. 'Everyone has done so well.'

'Is it over yet?' Marie-Claire asked.

'I think it is just beginning,' Adeline said, gravely. 'But Sainte-Mère-Église is liberated, and so are many other towns in Normandy. The Allies are pushing eastwards towards Paris even now.'

'And Louis? Jean-Baptiste?'

Adeline's face crumpled and she looked away, taking big breaths to steady herself before breaking the news.

'I'm afraid that Jean-Baptiste didn't make it. He put himself in the position of the greatest danger and he was caught by a bullet. The message came to me just an hour ago.'

Marie-Claire tried to take it in, the idea that the man who had first rescued her on that dreadful night when she had lost Benjamin could possibly be dead. It couldn't be so.

'And Louis?' she dared to ask.

'I don't know, Marie-Claire. I just don't know. I am trying to find out. Nobody has seen him for hours.'

'We don't know if he made it?' asked Marie-Claire desperately.

Adeline shook her head and Marie-Claire heard herself wail like an animal caught in a trap.

# 24

PARIS, JANUARY 1999

For the first time in the last four months, the grey clouds of doubt and gloom had begun to creep into the bright and sunny world of Esther's world with Jules. As she sat on the Eurostar, speeding her way towards Paris, she was glad of the darkness when the train went underground. It matched the sense of fear and anxiety that had replaced the joy in her soul.

She sighed and read over her last letter from Jules, when they'd been planning this weekend trip. She'd begun to expect something was wrong but was in complete denial about the reality – so much so that she didn't dare talk to Jules about it. It had seemed strange, keeping this thing from him, when they had begun to share everything and anything about their daily lives now. But, after she'd taken the test, and then visited her doctor just to make sure, she knew that the only way to give him this news was face to face. The idea of that conversation now filled her with dread.

As her train arrived at the Paris Gare du Nord station, she began to feel sick again, unsure this time if it was the general nausea she'd started to recognise or if it had more to do with

anxiety. She and Jules had become so much a part of each other's
lives that they'd talked seriously about where they might best
live together, to be able to each continue their careers and enjoy
the best that both Dorset and Paris had to offer, as well as
Normandy which they both loved and thought of as home too.
The work that Jules did was very much centred in Paris, but with
Esther's skills as a translator, she knew she could find work on
either side of the Channel. But now, with the possibility of a
baby coming into the picture, would she want to live in France
while her mum and grandad were back in Poole? As an only
child in their compact and close family, would it really be fair on
them to move away and take their little grandbaby away too?

Esther remembered again the meeting between Jules and her
family, back on that weekend visit in October. Archie, the cat
who had held the place of the main male in her life for the last
five years, had accepted Jules with the cool, austere and non-
committal attitude that he gave everyone and everything. But
over Sunday lunch at her mum's place, Jules received such a
warm welcome that Esther knew he would fit right in. He'd
admired Lucy's amazing roast beef and Yorkshire puddings, and
taken a stroll around the garden with Grandad, whom Jules was
happily addressing by his first name. He had shown Jules the
apple tree he planted for Esther when she was born, now almost
bare of the apples that had ripened a few weeks earlier. Esther
had been watching from the kitchen where she was making a
cup of tea to take outside to the patio chairs and wondered what
the two men had found to talk about. When she placed the tea
tray on the table and walked to where they were standing, now
admiring the late roses, she could hardly believe what she'd
heard Grandad say.

'Oh yes, I spent a fair while in Normandy during the war,
son. Not that I like to talk about it much – terrible time, really.

But it was worth it, in the end, I suppose. So many were lost,' he said with a quaver in his voice, 'but we got the Germans out, and here we are – all living in freedom after all. There was a time when that seemed impossible.'

'Grandad, wait a minute – did you just say you went to Normandy during the war? Where Jules is from?' asked Esther, completely aghast that she'd never heard this fact before.

'I did, yes, love. I was injured there, and then I came home, and that was that. Never really saw the place, to be honest,' he said, suddenly clamming up as he always did when talk of the war began. Esther never really knew if it was PTSD or if there was something else. She knew that everyone in the services had been told they were not allowed to talk about the war, and even all these years on, perhaps something of that order still remained with him. Still, she wondered. How had he ended up in Normandy and what was his injury? But she knew better than to press on, and left it there. Jules and Grandad had already moved on to talking about the tricks with roses, and the problems with aphids, and she was amused to see how much Jules was interested until she remembered that he was, at heart, a farmer's boy.

Grandad and Mum loved Jules from the very beginning and told her in the days and weeks to come that they were so happy to see her with someone who obviously made her happy too. And he did make her happy. In these last two months Esther had been happier than she could remember. And now there was this shock coming into their joy, frightening her with its intrusion. She had never imagined herself as a parent, not after watching her mum cope – and sometimes not cope – with parenthood. But that was because she was single, and Esther's dad had left them. If Esther knew Jules would always be by her side, could it be different? Better? Having a baby had never been her plan and she'd never imagined it could come like this. She was scared.

Esther stepped off the train and looked around for Jules. When she heard him call her name, that same bubble of excitement and anticipation welled up and she hurried to hold him in a tight hug.

'How is my beautiful English rose today?' he asked, after kissing her hungrily. She hesitated for a second or two, wondering how much of her turmoil to reveal, and when.

'I'm all the better for seeing you,' she said in the end, grasping his hand firmly as they walked out to the metro station.

'What would you like to do for dinner tonight, *chérie*? Are you feeling quiet or would you like some of the excitement of Paris?' he asked with a gentle smile, knowing as he did now that her introverted nature meant that, sometimes, she just wanted to be at home quietly with him, but at others she craved the bright lights and noise of the city.

Staying at home was the perfect option for Esther tonight, where she felt most comfortable with Jules in his apartment, and could spend time quietly talking with him. The news was going to be a big shock, she knew, and she didn't want him to have to deal with it in public any more than she would have wanted to.

After an initial cup of tea, Jules made a move to the kitchen and started to pull together a pizza dinner, and Esther sat up at the bar to help and chat with him. He opened a bottle of Pinot Noir and pulled two glasses from the cupboard. When he handed one to Esther, she brought the glass right to her lips before remembering that she ought not to be drinking. She hesitated and from the look on Jules' face, knew that he saw something was wrong.

'It's a good bottle. Three years old,' he said, taking his first sip and smiling. Esther tasted the tiniest sip of wine on her tongue, before she rested the glass on the tabletop again. She took a deep breath and searched out for the depth of Jules' eyes. He was ready. He knew something was wrong. He put down his glass and took her hand in his.

'Is everything alright, *chérie*?' he asked gently. She had rehearsed about ten different options of how to say this, but in the end, none of them fit.

'I shouldn't really be drinking,' she started, and watched his face change to show his confusion. 'They say it's not healthy for the baby,' she said, and waited. His eyes widened, his mouth dropped open, and he leant closer to her, taking both her hands in his now.

'What?' he asked, with a tiny shake of his head. Esther nodded. He came around to her side of the bench and, standing in front of her, he rested his hands gently on her shoulders.

'Yes, Jules. Although it was completely not our plan, we seem to have made a baby,' she said, and unconsciously moved her hand to cover her tummy gently. She waited for his response.

He looked down to where her hand was resting on her impossibly flat tummy, concealing as it did the hope of a new life that neither of them had imagined was likely. He took a deep breath and lifted his hands to cup her face, kissing her gently on the lips.

'Esther, this is... unexpected, I must say the truth,' he said with a small smile and lift of his brow. 'But you know, I am here for you. With you. Wherever this takes us on our journey, I'm not going anywhere. I want you in my life forever and we will make this work. Whatever happens.'

She nodded and wiped away the lone tear that had surprised her. She supposed it must be relief that he was going to take as much responsibility as her. But it was also fear. Because while she couldn't begin to think of the alternative, she still didn't know if she was able to change her life so fast and become a parent right now.

Jules left both their glasses of wine on the bench and, taking her hand, led Esther back to the settee, where they cuddled together.

'When is the baby due?' he asked, after they'd stayed wrapped in silent thought together for some time.

'Around the middle of August, the doctor thinks. I'm about ten weeks pregnant now.'

'Ten weeks? You've known this long, and didn't tell me? Esther, this is too much to keep inside, alone. Please, tell me everything,' he encouraged.

And so, they talked, well into the evening, and eventually Jules finished making the pizza and they ate. They talked about all the different options, and places to live and raise a child, and what life would be like if they made another choice now, and didn't raise a child at all. But they kept coming back to family, and home, and life, and the joy that a child could bring.

'Have you told your mother?' he asked later, as they lay in bed, face to face.

'Not yet,' she said with a tiny shake of her head. 'I feel guilty for that. I've shared so much with my mum, but this was your news to hear first,' she said, stroking his face. 'And I think I felt that, because I didn't know what would happen, if in the end there wasn't going to be a baby, I didn't want Mum to have to deal with that as well.'

He kissed her.

'Esther, what do you want? I mean, what do you really want? This is happening to both of us, and we need to stay together on it, of course, but it is your body. It is, ultimately, your life that will be most disrupted, I think. What do you want to do?'

Her tears began to fall again as the enormity of this change in their lives began to settle in. Would they ever enjoy a simple, romantic weekend again, without the weight of parenthood on their shoulders?

'I want to be with you. Forever. And this baby is partly made of you, too. So it is *ours*. He or she is always going to be part of our story, Jules. I think I want us to become parents. But I'm scared.'

Four weeks later, Jules drove to Cherbourg and met Esther when she disembarked as a foot passenger on the ferry. She arrived in the afternoon, and had stayed inside the ship for most of the journey, as the February weather now made for bitter winds at sea. She'd braved the cold, wrapped up in a coat and scarf with gloves and a warm woollen hat, so she could watch the harbour go by as the ferry left Poole. There were very few pleasure craft about, and the trees on Brownsea Island were now stripped bare of the rich reds and browns they'd worn in autumn, naked and making space for the spring growth to come. The beaches of Sandbanks and Studland were empty and windswept, but as the ferry passed Old Harry Rocks she saw some keen ramblers out enjoying the bracing weather because, though it was cold, the skies were clear and blue, and that made for a rarely perfect winter's day for a hike.

When she met Jules, she was as thrilled as ever by his welcoming, beaming face. His car was still warm from his long drive up from Paris, thankfully, and within less than an hour from docking at Cherbourg, she was sitting at the old farmhouse kitchen table with the loud and chattery Joubert family bustling around them both with coffee, cakes and cuddles.

'We haven't seen you two since November!' Giselle cried in

mock admonishment as she gave them both powerfully big hugs of welcome.

'Are you well, Esther?' she asked quietly. 'You look very tired. Are you working too hard?'

Jules caught Esther's eye and they shared a momentary conversation of souls. They would wait until everyone was seated, and quiet, to make sure that everyone heard the news at once.

'A little tired, yes, but that ferry crossing was a touch rough in the wind today,' Esther said.

When all the coffee was made and everyone was seated calmly around the table, licking their fingers after the sticky, buttery cakes were all eaten, Jules found a moment of calm, and nodded to Esther, who smiled back.

'Now you're all here, and you're quiet for five minutes – which is quite rare in this noisy family – I have to say something.' Jules laughed as he lifted little Elodie up onto his lap. 'Esther and I have an announcement to make,' he carried on, and the table erupted in joy before he could finish. He held up his hands and hushed them.

'You don't even know what I'm going to say yet!' He laughed and batted away all the comments and questions they threw at him.

'Esther and I have decided that we want to become a family,' he began, and noticed the sharp and eager looks on the faces of the three women, who had picked up on his implication much faster than the men. 'And yes, there will be a wedding,' he said directly to Elodie who must have been picturing a fairy tale in her little mind as she clapped her hands together.

Now the family cheered, and the sounds of happy congratulations were accompanied by many more hugs, kisses and claps on the back. Jules waited until they hushed again before he continued, to answer their most demanding question: when?

'We aren't sure yet whether to get married in the summer, or later, in autumn...' he said obliquely, and then continued after a brief and quiet pause.

'Because it has to be either before, or well after the baby is born.'

And then Esther felt sure that the happy noise of the Joubert family must have been heard all over Normandy.

\* \* \*

Later that evening, when Giselle and Hugo were putting the children to bed, and Jules went to the barn to help his parents meet the vet who was here to help with a sick cow, Esther found herself alone beside the crackling fireplace with *Grand-mère*.

'So, my dear, you are bringing me another beautiful baby to bounce on my knees, *oui*? And we all wondered if Jules would ever settle down,' she said. 'I am very happy that you have chosen him, Esther. I know that he will care for you well.'

'He is a good man, *Grand-mère,* and I love him. He promises to stay beside me, and what more could I want?' she said. 'But, I am a little frightened,' she continued, after a pause. 'Having a baby was not in our plans for anytime soon. It would have been much better if we'd been able to wait until we were more settled, more used to living together,' Esther mused as she watched the flames flicker in the grate.

The old grandmother was silent for a few moments, but then drew breath and sat up a little straighter.

'Esther, I'm going to tell you something that not even all my family know. My grandchildren – Giselle and Jules – don't know this story, but it is probably time they heard. And you need to hear it,' she began.

'When I was a young woman in Paris, long before I met Jules' grandfather, Louis Joubert, I met a beautiful man. His name was Benjamin Dubois, and he changed my world. We were crazy in love for each other, and we married, and lived in a tiny apartment in Paris, with no money. And then, I had a baby boy,' she said, and Esther's mind did all the mental leaps and bounds. Who was this baby, and where did he fit into the Joubert story? She knew that Monsieur Joubert had a sister, but she hadn't heard about a brother.

'My baby boy, called Antoine,' she said, her voice cracking with emotion when she said the name aloud again after all these years, 'he died, in the war. In an accident. He was only two years old. And his father, Benjamin, died too – though that was not an accident but a Nazi bullet,' she said, and Esther's heart jolted with the pain that she saw in the old woman's face.

'There is almost never a good time to bring a baby into the world, but 1938 in Paris was probably about the worst time and place ever. You and Jules have nothing to worry about, my dear. Your little family will be safe, and happy, and all will be well. You'll see,' she said with a warm smile and with eyes that glistened. 'And every little child is precious, and worth holding on to with all of your strength.'

And Esther knew, then, with a deep and comforting warmth in her soul, that *Grand-mère* was right. All would be well.

The pair of women sat in contented silence for several minutes until Esther remembered that she had still never talked with *Grand-mère* about the note she had found and returned to the back of the recipe journal. She wondered now, with this newly revealed story from the old woman's past, if this was a good time to raise it.

'*Grand-mère*, some years ago, I found something that I think might date back to the time when your little boy was born,' she said, and watched as the old lady's eyes opened wide. Esther got up and went over to the dresser, took out the recipe journal she had seen used several times since last summer, and flicked to the back page.

'I found this page years ago, on one of my earlier visits. I thought it was just a scrap with an interesting poem on it, and that's why I kept it. But later, I saw it had a personal note – a memory perhaps, and I think that you wrote it, *Grand-mère*,' said Esther as she passed the page over. *Grand-mère* reached for her reading glasses to better see it.

The old lady read the words slowly and Esther watched as her expression changed from happy to cloudy.

'I knew this poem very well, during the war. It was important to know it in both English and French, for some work that I was doing,' she explained. 'So I would practise writing it out. Perhaps I did this while a dish was baking in the oven and I had some time to spare,' she added.

'And there's a tiny note at the bottom, you see?' said Esther and *Grand-mère* peered more closely to read it.

'That is too small for my eyes now, *ma chérie*. What does it say?' she asked. Esther read the line to her as it was written, in English, and was surprised when *Grand-mère* held a hand to her mouth and started to cry.

'Oh, my dear, that is a memory from a long time ago. A very long time ago now. The memories of war are difficult when they come, yes?' she said, and Esther knew that she'd learned all she would know. This note was personal, and definitely written by old *Grand-mère* Joubert. But there was something else she wanted to raise.

'You have obviously been a very skilled cook – and writer –

for most of your life, *Grand-mère*. Apart from feeding your family and teaching them so well, have you done anything with this knowledge, or writing?' Esther asked. The old lady shook her head gently.

'*Non*. I always meant to, but just knowing how to cook well has been enough, in the end,' she said. Esther thought *Grand-mère* might slip the note into the old recipe journal again, but saw that she folded it and tucked it into her apron pocket instead. And Esther knew that she was never likely to discover the identity of 'G' – if he had even existed.

## 25

DORSET, ENGLAND, JUNE 1944

George Baker checked his pack and his parachute again, and
again. He had arrived at the airfield from Swanage by train and
then bus and had tried to stay a little separated from the American paratroopers who were due to be dropped into Normandy
along with him. As an undercover agent, it was unusual for him
to travel to France this way, and in the past he'd been landed
alone by a Lysander, but mission control needed someone to get
right into the middle of the action in Sainte-Mère-Église, and the
fact he had already been there before gave him some advantage,
even though the risk of being recognised was a danger. The invasion was due to drop them all just outside the town, and his
remit was to break away from the main attack group and get into
the German base there, disable their radio transmission equipment, and get out alive. After that, he was to regroup with some
of the resistance team he had become familiar with two years
earlier, and get to Paris ahead of the invading Allies. He
stretched out his leg and rolled his ankle again, still concerned
about the landing. His ankle was quite well healed after his

injury over three years earlier but it still gave him trouble in cold or rainy weather. The marrow of his bone liked to remind him of the memory of pain. Dropping from the sky was probably not the best thing to do.

He had caught up with Marguerite just a few days earlier, on a trip to Poole. The pair had known each other on sight when they met in France, but their training kicked in immediately and they'd not shown any outward signs of recognition: never let anyone else know that they knew each other back home, that George had once been a schoolteacher in her hometown and he had been approached to train as a spy when someone in the know heard about his photographic memory. George had been a familiar face in the local pubs, and they'd known each other as distant acquaintances. So, when he'd been tasked with meeting her in Poole to learn of the preparations for invasion occurring there, he'd slipped right into agent mode and spoke to her as if she were a complete stranger.

'I hear there's a bit going on in the harbour,' he'd said, and slowed his pace to hers as they walked the length of the quay together. He learned from her the extent of the shipbuilding that was occurring in terms of landing craft ahead of the invasion, and he told her how successful the landing practices had been over on the beaches at Studland. George had been one of the few agents who had been there at Fort Henry to watch it all from the background, along with Churchill and the King.

'Terribly sad about those American chaps who died though when the floating tanks sank – and I still can't believe they were wasting live ammunition in a practice,' he'd said, shaking his head sadly for the dreadful waste of life the accident on the beach had caused.

'But it's nothing to what the invasion will bring, George. I hear you're going over again?' she'd asked, and he told her all he knew, which was very little, but that he expected to be meeting up with old friends in Sainte-Mère-Église again.

There was a long pause while Marguerite seemed to be organising her thoughts before she spoke again.

'Things have changed there you know, George. People have moved on,' she said.

'But surely the Joubert family is still at the farm? Is Louis alright, and Jean-Baptiste – he's still in control?' he'd asked, and his mouth opened and closed again as he was about to ask about Marie-Claire, but stopped himself.

'They're all well, George, and Marie-Claire spends most of her spare time with Louis, when she can manage it between work and operations,' she said. 'They've become quite a couple, I think,' she added, determined to help him adjust his ideas before he landed.

The shock to George was sickening, though he knew he had never been sure he would even see her again, let alone have any hopes of a future with her. It had just been a few of the most blissful days and nights of his life, with the most beautiful girl he'd ever seen. That was all, he thought wryly. Nothing really, he told himself, and tried to shake the jealousy and sadness that threatened him. He shook himself back to the job in hand.

'I understand you have a map for me?' George asked.

'I do, but not on me. Go on into the Swan Inn for a drink, and I'll meet you in there in half an hour. I'll hand it to you wrapped in a packet with some fresh fish,' she said.

'How delightful! I'll think of Poole Harbour every time I open the map and smell it,' he laughed.

That had been four days ago, and now he was waiting to be loaded onto a plane, wearing the American uniform as a disguise from his real job as a British secret agent, and with the fishy-smelling map tucked inside his shirt.

* * *

As the C-47 flew over the Channel and grew close to the Normandy shore, every man on board hooked up to the static line, ready for the drop, and said their prayers, thinking of the ones they loved and hoped to get home to. They were all suddenly flung to one side, as the plane roared and one of the engines burst into flames.

'We're hit!' yelled a voice from near the cockpit, and George knew it must have been a lucky shot from a ground-based German anti-aircraft gun. They were surely only minutes away from where they were due to be dropped, just outside Sainte-Mère-Église, but the plane began to lose altitude too early. Within a few moments the barked orders over the din of the roaring engine told them they were being dropped before the plane lost control and the pilot would have to make a crash landing. The rear door was opened and the men jumped into the black night, one after the other, much closer together and nearer to the ground, and very much closer to town than they were meant to be.

George felt his heart in his throat as he jumped, then began to count as he'd been trained to do, but as the night air rushed past him and the few lights from the town shone out, he knew there was no time to lose and pulled the cord on his chute. Gunshots rang all around, and he heard as one then another and then more of the men falling through the sky with him were hit and hung there dead in their harnesses, waiting to strike the ground.

There were buildings everywhere, but the town square

beside the church was the best spot to aim for. He swore under his breath repeatedly at how this mission was going completely awry before it had begun. They were in town too early – the landing craft would probably have only just made it to the beaches, and then those men would have to secure the land between the beaches and here, running for a good couple of hours to get here.

Just as George was holding his breath and doing his best to aim for the open square, he felt an explosion in his chest as the jolt from his harness broke several ribs and left him unable to breathe. His chute had caught on the spire of the church. Gunfire still raged all around him and he saw *Wehrmacht* uniforms running across the street below. *Dead. I must act dead*, he thought quickly, knowing that they were training their sights on any Allied bodies they could see. George dropped his arms to his sides and his chin onto his chest and, despite the roaring pain from his broken ribs, did his best to remain absolutely still.

Two hours later, Louis arrived on the outskirts of town, from near the beaches where he'd been helping clear the way for the landing Allies. He knew that George was supposed to have landed out at the German base, but that was before their transport had been hit and offloaded all the men right over the town. It was a disaster. And George was here somewhere – but dead or alive, he didn't yet know.

The battle had raged on but when the onslaught of the Allies finally arrived from the beaches, they ended it fast. The few enemy soldiers left had run to their base, but there was still work to do. Louis was sheltering in the porch of the church when he heard an old familiar voice calling him.

'Joubert! I'm up here – you've got to get me down,' called the voice from somewhere above. Louis crept out and couldn't believe what he could see. A parachute was caught on the steeple, and hanging from it – alive and reasonably well – was George Baker.

'What the hell are you doing up there, George? There's work to do!' cried Louis with mock anger. 'Hang on, I'm coming up,' he called, and ducked into the church before he could hear George's reply.

'Yes, sir. No plans to go anywhere, anyway,' George said, and laughed to himself before wincing from the pain.

Within moments a small hatch door opened in the church tower and out climbed Louis, together with Charles, who had been using the church tower as an excellent sniper hideout. The two French men worked to haul George up onto the little ledge around the steeple, trying to keep their movements smooth once they understood the pain he was in from his cracked ribs.

'Thought help was never coming,' George said, and then smiled his thanks through gritted teeth to both men. 'Are either of you coming with me? I've got the map of the base here,' he said, tapping his chest very lightly.

'Charles will stay here and help in town. Many of those fighting here are the women and they're going to need help, but I'm coming with you. I've got bicycles waiting,' he said, then turned to Charles as they were making their way down the steep tower staircase.

'Find Marie-Claire, will you? I see the café is wrecked, but she'll be here somewhere,' he said, scanning the town square as they reached the open door of the church.

As they rode off on bicycles side by side, George took his chance to ask after Marie-Claire.

'So, I take it that you and the lovely Marie-Claire are an item now, Joubert?' he asked, struggling to breathe, stay balanced and ride at the same time he spoke with his broken ribs throbbing.

'We are very much together, George, my friend, and she is wonderful. I waited, and she came to me – eventually. And now – you have to keep this secret and take it to your grave – do you swear?' Louis asked.

'I'm not planning on going to my grave anytime soon, Joubert, but whatever it is, your secret is safe with me. What is it?'

Louis grinned and laughed a little. 'I'm going to be a father! Marie-Claire is pregnant with our baby, so now she'll *have* to marry me,' he called with glee.

George acted his most delighted and happy self while on the inside the part of his heart that Marie-Claire had inhabited shattered into a million pieces as though he'd just trodden on a mine. She had been his, very briefly, and then the war had taken him away, and now she belonged to Joubert. He'd lost her. And she would have Louis's baby too. She'd probably already even forgotten she met a man named George, he thought and winced, more from the pain in his soul than the jarring potholes along the road.

Louis and George made it out to the German base, hid the bicycles under some shrubs, and snuck around to the hole in the fence that had been prepared for their arrival. The men hunkered down, hidden, and George took out the map and showed Louis, whispering.

'I just have to get into this room, here, and destroy the radio equipment. I was supposed to arrive while this lot was all busy in town, but it looks like there are at least a dozen or so men hiding here, which makes it a bit more tricky,' he said under his breath as a guard passed by not far from them, though he wasn't doing much guarding and looked extremely panicked by what he must know was coming for him soon.

George headed off while Louis stayed behind to cover him. But as George reached the main building easily, he heard Louis following behind fast, unhindered.

'Stay here, Louis – it's only a few turns down this corridor and then I'll need to get back out this way,' George said as he darted off down the dark corridor.

Louis waited, watching the darkness that George had disappeared into, and crouched in the dark, pistol cocked. And then he heard the tiniest sound behind him. Before he could turn around, the cold barrel of a German pistol was held to his head.

'Drop your weapon!' ordered the soldier.

Louis blinked slowly and took a long, deep breath as he gradually lowered his gun toward the floor and raised his hands in surrender. He shut his eyes and waited to hear the shot he knew must follow soon, but the explosions, when he heard them, came from much further away. He opened his eyes and saw flames coming from the corridor where George had gone toward the radio room.

German voices were shouting from every direction and soldiers came running, guns drawn, heading to where Louis had last seen George disappear. The soldier who'd been holding a gun to his head just moments ago now ran off to join the crowd too. Louis stood, picked up his gun and backed away to the fence.

'Come on, George, get out of there!' he whispered through gritted teeth. Louis looked around him and saw there was nobody out here behind him – his way was clear to escape – and then he heard George's voice and saw him rushing through the flames and towards the drawn guns of the German soldiers who were lined up waiting for him. The whole base was now aflame and it seemed George had brought utter destruction on the place. But as he ran out, screaming, he cried a message to Louis.

'Get out, Joubert! Go to Marie-Claire!'

There was at least a dozen shots fired, all hitting George at quite close range, and he was forced back, flying into the flames.

For a moment in time, Louis was frozen to the spot, watching the space where he'd last seen George, and then he ran, silently, before the Germans remembered he was there.

## 26

POOLE, JULY 1999

Esther woke to the aroma of coffee and the pretty sound of a blackbird singing outside the window, in her tiny garden. She yawned and stretched, and when she rolled over, she saw her gorgeous floral dress hanging from the curtain rail to keep it uncreased. She smiled.

Today was the day they'd been planning for months now. Not *the* big day – that was to come some weeks later in August, the day on which their baby would be born. But this was the day of their official marriage ceremony.

In the end they'd decided on two weddings – one in Poole and another in Sainte-Mère-Église. Today, the civil ceremony in the beautiful rooms at Upton House, overlooking the park, down the lawn and out towards the backwaters of Poole Harbour, would mark their official wedding day. And then later, in October, well after the baby was born, they would have a blessing ceremony in the Notre-Dame de-l'Assomption church in Sainte-Mère-Église. Her mum and grandad were planning on coming to France for that ceremony, but mostly it would be the Joubert family celebration and little Elodie was excited to be a flower girl. For that blessing ceremony, she was planning a more traditional ivory gown, but would wait until nearer the time to find out what size she would need after the baby. For today, Esther would be wearing this flowing pink delight that hung in her room.

Esther had fallen in love with the dress as soon as she'd tried it on. It was long and light, and it flowed to the floor in waves of delicate pink chiffon, printed all over in cerise petals that were strewn across the fabric as if blown there by a breeze. The full skirt was cinched in just above her beautiful baby bump with a chiffon sash that tied in a big, loose bow at the back. The opaque butterfly sleeves draped elegantly to her wrists.

'Ah, my beauty awakes,' said Jules as he came into the room holding a cup of coffee. 'You take this one, and I'll go and pour myself another,' he said, resting the coffee cup on Esther's bedside table and kissing her on the forehead. She thanked him with a smile and sat up.

'What time is your mum coming?' he asked, when he stepped back into the room moments later. He sat on the bed beside her and Esther reminded him of the plan. Lucy Holt was arriving around ten o'clock and would curl Esther's hair and help her to get dressed. Then they would all travel together to Upton House where their closest English family and a few friends would be meeting them – and, of course, all of Esther's colleagues from the Chamber of Commerce who worked in the upstairs rooms of the Country House where their ceremony was taking place.

'The cake is being delivered straight to Upton House this morning, and don't forget you need to pop up to the High Street to collect my bouquet and the buttonholes,' she'd added, grimacing slightly as the baby chose that moment to have a good wriggle and kick. Jules saw the baby move and bent down to plant a kiss on Esther's tummy.

'Big day for you today, little one. I hope you are planning on behaving well and sleeping all day, hmm?' he said with a grin.

When Lucy arrived later that morning, after Esther and Jules had eaten a lovely big breakfast of French pastries and tropical fruit, Jules headed out to fetch the flowers and left the ladies to do Esther's hair, which was to be curled with tongs, and tied back gently, pinned in place with two diamante clips.

Jules drove Esther, Mum and Grandad to Upton House and the grounds were all looking gorgeous in the spring sunshine. The gravel road up to the main house was lined with daffodils, tulips and a few early roses. When they walked up the steps and into the grand entrance hall of the old Country House, they were met by cheers from all Esther's colleagues who lined the railings of the circular gallery above them, and watched as a few photographs were taken. The dining room was decorated with white linens and spring flowers and after the brief ceremony, everyone gathered to cheer as the bride and groom cut the cake, which they all shared with a glass of champagne each – and Esther allowed herself a small glass too.

'Mmmm, I've missed these bubbles,' she said with a sigh, after chinking glasses with Kelly.

'Only a few weeks now, and you can enjoy a bit more freedom again,' Kelly said, sympathetically.

'Yes, only about six weeks until we meet the baby now,' Esther said, rubbing her bump. 'But if I end up breastfeeding then I still have to be careful about drinking,' she added.

'Do you think you will? Breastfeed, I mean? I think I'll want to with mine, but I know some people never could manage it,' said Kelly, rubbing her own little baby bump. 'But whatever you end up doing, make sure it's what you want to do. I've heard that some of those nurses can be a tad bossy about what's best for the baby,' she said and both women laughed.

'It's not your standard wedding breakfast chat, is it?' asked Esther. 'Shouldn't we be talking about the flowers or the dress, or something?'

'Esther, you're not a standard sort of a woman and you never have been. You're amazing, and super-talented, and living an incredibly interesting life with your gorgeous Frenchman,' Kelly said with a big and heartfelt smile. 'I'm so happy for you. And I'm so grateful that you gave him a chance, Esther. He really was worth taking the risk, wasn't he?' she asked, and Esther leant in to give her friend a kiss on the cheek.

'Thank you for being there for me, Kelly. You were so right. Jules is wonderful.'

'And this little chap – or chapette – is very blessed to have you two as parents,' said Kelly.

'I hope we do a good job. It's all a bit daunting really, but Jules is amazing. Anything I can't work out, I'm sure he'll be brilliant at it!' They laughed again just as Jules came over to kiss his new wife.

'Who will be brilliant, at what?' he asked.

Esther turned to face him and give him a luscious kiss and a squeeze.

'You. Everything,' she said, just as they were called to pose for a big group photo out underneath the sparkling chandelier in the grand entrance hall.

The small family dinner that night was held in Esther's favourite French restaurant, Isabel's, a place where she and Jules had shared many cosy dinner dates together. The gorgeous and intimate restaurant was decorated in rich, dark colours, and the wide, curved bay windows looked out onto the central green, which always reminded Esther a little of the town square in

Sainte-Mère-Église – though this English square was made up of a wide lawn, complete with park benches and budding spring trees.

The dinner was divinely rich and French, and after everyone had eaten, Jules and Esther danced, swaying gently to the traditional sound of French café music that the owners played for them on this special day. Jules held Esther's hand as they danced, lightly stroking her fingers with his thumb, and she rested her cheek against his.

'Are you happy, *ma chérie*? Have you enjoyed the day?' he whispered into her ear.

'I am happier than I've ever been before, Jules,' she said, turning to kiss him. 'Here's to us, and our baby, and our life together. Whatever that looks like,' she said, and he kissed her.

\* \* \*

Four weeks later, Esther woke in the middle of night and, after trying to get comfortable, realised that perhaps she should try getting up to go to the toilet. She didn't seem to be getting any sleep, whatever she tried. And it was there, in the bathroom, that she felt it. A pain, a twisting, a tightness unlike anything she had felt before. Something like a cramp but it came with a strange tightening across her now very large belly. And then it was gone.

An hour later, Esther was lying in bed on her side, watching the minutes tick by on her alarm clock. About every ten minutes she felt this strange feeling and wondered if this could be it, but it wasn't really a pain, just a kind of tightening. But more and more with each wave, she realised that it made her hold her breath. Perhaps this was it, after all.

After the clock eventually ticked over to 5 a.m. she felt it might be time to wake Jules. Esther made the enormous effort it took to roll over and stroked him lightly on the shoulder and down his side until he eventually sighed and lifted his hand to hold hers, patting her gently.

'Jules,' she whispered and waited.

'Jules, my love, I think it's time,' she said.

'What time?' He yawned, and then she saw him draw breath and hold it. He turned over quickly then and leant up on one elbow and opened his eyes wide.

'Time? For the baby?' he asked, and she had to smile at the look of utter shock on his face, as if this was the last thing he was expecting a few days before her due date.

'I don't know, to be honest. I've never done this before,' she said with a wry smile. 'But something is going on in my belly, quite regularly, and it is beginning to feel like pain,' she explained. And then Jules jumped up and pulled on his clothes, checking the last few things off the list of what they needed and adding them to their hospital bag.

The sun was rising and shining onto the harbour waters outside when they locked the front door and got into the car.

'This is the last time we'll do this,' Esther said, as they drove away and Jules looked at her, puzzled.

'The last time we will drive to a hospital to deliver a baby? I hope not! I'm sure we'll be having six children, yes?' He laughed, and she laughed with him in a moment between contractions.

'That's not what I mean. I'm saying this is the last time that just two of us hop into a car. When we come home again, we'll have a third member of our family with us,' she said, and Jules reached across the car and held her hand in his.

'I like the sound of that – our family. I love you, Esther Holt-Joubert,' he said, and blew her a kiss, squeezing her hand tightly.

\* \* \*

That evening, Esther sat up in her hospital bed cradling the unbelievably beautiful baby boy in her arms, just watching him breathe. She tucked the blanket under his chin and stroked his face, and lifted him to her lips so she could kiss him again, and she knew she would never stop kissing these beautiful cheeks.

Jules was napping in the big armchair and he stirred when the baby sneezed, coming over to first kiss Esther and then take his son in his arms to kiss him too.

'So, are we going to make a decision before long, do you think?' Esther asked Jules. 'Mum and Grandad are coming in at seven o'clock and they are going to want to know what to call him.'

They went over all the choices again and the last one seemed to sound just right, so Jules decided to ask the baby.

'What do you say, Fabien? Do you think that will suit you? Fabien Joubert? We like it, but it's your decision, of course,' he crooned gently, and the baby yawned.

At the end of September, Jules and Esther packed everything they thought they might need for a few months in France. The car had not an inch of spare space, what with all the baby equipment and extra clothes and a few pieces of kitchen equipment that Esther wanted to add to the Paris apartment from her home in Poole.

Jules strapped Fabien into the car seat in the back, and they made the very quick trip to the ferry terminal. They wanted to have Esther's car with them, so had chosen to go across the Channel on the water rather than under it for this trip. And besides that, the first stop was going to be Sainte-Mère-Église, where the whole family was desperate to meet baby Fabien.

Jules had taken the last six weeks more or less off work, to adjust to fatherhood. He had only gone across to Paris a few times to catch up on some business appointments. The rest of the time, he had been in Poole with Esther and Fabien, enjoying the cocoon of new parenthood and all of its rollercoaster ride of emotions.

Esther had fallen madly in love with her baby from the very start, but never quite anticipated the strong effect that hormones would have on her emotions. The ups and downs of the baby blues, the lack of sleep, the problems with breastfeeding, and the ultimate decision to give up and simply put the baby on to the bottle – which made the whole little family much happier – had all taken their toll. But a genuine and deep joy in parenthood, and the determined nature of both parents to make the best of everything, all helped to hold it all together.

And now they were ready for the next stage of their adventure: the trip to France to set up home in Paris, and to plan the French blessing ceremony.

When Jules drove Esther's car in through the farmyard gates that afternoon he honked the horn loudly, and people came running like children to an ice-cream van from all corners of the farmyard. Monsieur *et* Madame Joubert had been in the barn together, and Giselle ran out of the farmhouse with Julien in her arms and Elodie holding her hand. *Grand-mère* came, leaning on her stick, from the little table outside the kitchen window, where she'd been sitting in the sun enjoying a peaceful cup of coffee.

The oohs and aahs and cries of adoration for baby Fabien might have been heard all the way into town, Jules joked, as the family was so thrilled to finally get their hands on this precious little bundle. When they were all sat around the big kitchen table, and the rich, creamy coffee they all loved was being served, Fabien slept soundly amidst the hubbub as he was passed from one adoring relative to another.

'How long are you staying with us, *mes chéris*?' asked Jules' mother, as she held the baby tight and gently rocked him.

'We'll just stay on the farm for the weekend, *Maman*, then head off to Paris on Monday. We need to meet with the priest at church here and see what we can arrange for the blessing, but then I need to get back to work and we're keen to get the apartment sorted and settle Esther and Fabien in,' Jules explained.

'I still think you would be better off staying here, on the farm,' said Giselle. 'What is Esther going to do in the city, with no friends or family around?' she asked, looking at Esther with concern.

'It's not ideal, but my work is there – at least for now. There is a chance that more flexibility is coming. Our company is working more and more on the internet now, so perhaps working outside of the city might be possible one day,' he said.

'Surely there are other businesses outside of Paris who need skills like yours too, Jules?' asked Hugo, and the two old school-friends went for a walk around the farmyard with their coffee to catch up together.

On Sunday morning the whole family went to church where Jules and Esther stayed back for a meeting with the priest before coming home to the farm for a gloriously luscious long lunch in the garden behind the farmhouse.

Esther remembered the lunch she'd had here, in this spot of this garden, with these same beautiful people, at the end of her exchange trip holiday all those years earlier and, looking down at Fabien, asleep now in a carrycot beside her, she smiled. Jules nuzzled into her side and kissed her on her cheek.

'You are happy, my darling?' he said, and she nodded.

'I love it here so much, Jules. I've always felt so relaxed on the farm, and your family always made me feel that I was included, right from the start. This farm feels like home to me,' she said, and Jules nodded softly. He was about to say something else when they were interrupted by *Grand-mère*, from across the table.

'What did the priest say, Jules? When will we be celebrating your marriage?' she asked, and Jules and Esther explained the plans for the blessing.

'The date has been set for 30 October. And the priest mentioned something special about Fabien's birthday, on 25 August, *Grand-mère*. Apparently that is the feast day of Saint Louis. He said he thought you would like to know that,' Jules said, and went across to hug his grandmother when he saw her eyes glisten and lip begin to tremble.

'Oh Jules, that is so special. Your grandfather would be so very proud of you all, you know,' she said, wiping her eyes.

'He wouldn't have been even more proud if Jules had wanted to stay on the farm?' Monsieur Joubert added as a joke, but they all knew he still felt that Jules was letting the family down by moving away from farming. *Grand-mère* surprised them all then, by speaking up loudly.

'Your grandfather, Louis Joubert, was the last person who would ever have insisted anyone stay somewhere and do something against their will,' she said boldly. 'He was a real adventurer – a courageous fighter for the cause of the resistance, and he went wherever his work needed him to go. Just like Jules,' she said, and gave him a firm pat on the hand.

'You must always do exactly what you need to do, my boy, never what anyone else expects of you. I think it is a wonderful coincidence that Fabien was born on the saint day of Louis. I think it means he is looking over your family,' she added, and Jules thanked her.

'And the priest also suggested we should combine our blessing with a christening for Fabien,' he said, to cries of delight from all the family.

'And I can be *la marraine*!' called Elodie. Esther picked her up and cuddled the little girl into her lap.

'Do you think you are grown-up enough to be a godmother, Elodie? It means you might have to look after Fabien all on your own one day, you know?' she asked with mock severity.

'Would I have to change his nappies?' Elodie asked, screwing up her nose.

'Absolutely!' said Jules. 'And they are pretty stinky, let me say,' he added.

'Hmm. Perhaps I will just be the flower girl at the wedding instead,' she said, and the table erupted in happy laughter.

* * *

A week before the blessing and christening ceremony, Kelly and Lucy arrived on the Eurostar to stay with Esther and Jules in Paris. They'd come to help with babysitting in those last busy days, spend some time with Esther as she made her final decisions on her outfit, and to take Esther out for a quiet little hen's night.

'Well, this is a beautiful big apartment, Esther, love,' called Lucy as she walked through the enormous living area and looked out onto all the balconies. 'And so central too. I see there are some nice little parks not far from here. You'll appreciate those when this little man starts to walk and needs his running space outside. Best way to tire them out for a good afternoon nap it is, a morning running around in a park,' she said, and Esther joined her on the balcony.

'Yes, the parks really are lovely, and it's a fantastic city to see on foot. I've already walked him around the Louvre more than once – Fabien's become quite appreciative of the *Mona Lisa*,' Esther added with a laugh. 'But seriously, we have begun to wonder if apartment life is the best thing for him as he grows. I mean, thousands of other people in Paris do it this way, but it's just not what I'm used to – nor is Jules, having grown up on the farm like he did,' she said thoughtfully.

'Yes, perhaps in time you could move further out of town to a little house with a garden,' suggested Lucy, sitting down on the floor to play with Fabien as he batted the toys hanging above his play gym mat.

Esther thought about the ideas she and Jules had been talking through with Hugo, but decided to keep them to herself for now. Best not to get anyone excited about their possible changes just yet, in case it all came to nothing. She decided to change the subject.

'Are you sure Grandad will be okay getting across on the ferry on his own, Mum?' she asked.

'Don't worry about him, Esther, he spends his life walking all over Poole and the Purbecks and can organise anything. I never knew a fitter, more intellectually agile eighty-two-year-old man than him,' she laughed. 'He says he's not even getting a cab to the ferry. He's going to walk across to Hamworthy from his flat, as he's only bringing a small wheelie case that he can manage quite easily. And you or Jules are going to pick him up from the ferry, aren't you?'

'That's right, two days before the ceremony, once we've all moved up to Sainte-Mère-Église together at the weekend,' Esther replied.

'Right then, Mum, we'd better get Fabien ready for this shopping trip. Time to pick up my dress and find some shoes,' she said, starting to pack the baby bag full of never-endingly needed supplies.

'Why don't you and Kelly go out and leave Fabien home with me, Esther? You've got some milk in the fridge, I see?' she suggested.

'If you don't mind, Mum, that would be fabulous! It can get a bit tricky shopping with a baby,' Esther said with relief.

'Don't I know it, love! You were impossible to keep entertained in a pram. There was always far too much you wanted to do rather than just sit around. Nothing's changed much, has it?' she joked, and within a short while, Kelly and Esther were skipping down the apartment block staircase and out onto the busy street.

The boutique where Esther had found her gown for the marriage blessing was only a few streets away and, once inside, they were greeted with excitement from the ladies who had heard all about the coming friend, Kelly, who was to act as *la marraine* for the christening of the bride's son at the joint ceremony.

'I think you ladies would like a glass of champagne to celebrate, yes?' she asked, without even waiting for a reply before pouring two glasses and handing them over.

They brought out Esther's dress, and she stepped into it so they could check they had the fitting just right. It was full-length and ivory, with a fitted bodice and long sleeves, all made with the same lace that covered the long, flowing skirt. Esther loved the way the dress fitted around her luscious new curves, and Kelly cried just a little when the assistant attached a comb to Esther's hair with a short veil draping over her shoulders.

'Oh, Esther, you really do look absolutely stunning,' she said, clapping her hands to her mouth then wiping the tear from her eye.

'You don't think it's too much? Not too "traditional wedding" sort of thing, after the back-to-front way we're doing everything?' Esther asked, biting her lip.

'It is perfect. You and Jules and Fabien are perfect together. And everything is happening in exactly the perfect order,' Kelly said firmly and with a broad smile.

'Now then, what about the shoes?' Kelly asked.

* * *

On the night before they left Paris, Jules went out with his mates and co-workers from Paris for a stag party, and Esther went out with Kelly for dinner and a drink while Lucy stayed home with her grandson.

'Are you sure you don't mind not coming, Mum?' asked Esther.

'Are you serious? There is nowhere else I'd rather be than spending a night alone with my darling boy, especially before we head off into Normandy for the noise and bustle of time with all of Jules' family. They'll want to get their hands on Fabien then, so I'll make the most of my time alone with him now,' she said as she held him in her arms at the door to the apartment.

'Have fun, girls,' she said, holding up Fabien's chubby little hand for a wave before she shut the door.

The next morning was a busy one of packing the car with everything they would need for the church service and for around a week altogether spent at the farm. There was just enough room to cram all the bags and baby bits and pieces into the boot, and Esther was thankful that baby Julien had moved out of his cot and into a little bed now, so his cot had been moved to the room that she and Jules would share on the farm and they didn't need to bring their portacot. Lucy and Kelly were going to stay at a little *pension* in the town centre, as the rooms at the farm were filling up, and Kelly's husband Jordan was coming to join them in time for the ceremony.

'Oh, here they all are!' cried *Grand-mère*, who'd been sitting at her little outdoor table for their arrival. She was just saying goodbye to a friend who'd come up from the town to collect milk.

'Monique, you must stay and meet my new great-grandson,' she said with such pride it made Esther's heart swell.

Jules got everyone settled in and had a cup of coffee with them all before setting off.

'I need to get up to Cherbourg to meet the ferry now, *Maman*,' he called across the throng in the kitchen and set off out to the back garden where Esther was sitting with Giselle and the children, to kiss her goodbye.

'We'll be home for dinner, but make sure they remember to save us some food in case we are running late,' he joked, knowing full well that food was one thing that would never run dry for the next week of family gatherings and celebrations.

Esther spent a little while organising all their clothes, hanging up her dress and Jules' suit carefully, and settling Fabien for an afternoon nap, while Monsieur Joubert drove her mum and Kelly into town so they could have a rest in their *pension* rooms before coming back again for dinner. While Fabien was resting, and Jules was still out collecting Grandad, she took the chance to lie down for a nap herself. The next couple of days were bound to be tiring, but she was so excited she wondered if she'd be able to sleep. She couldn't wait for the moment when the priest suggested the groom could kiss his bride, right there at the altar where they'd first kissed. Esther chuckled with happiness. She had a lot to be thankful for, she thought.

* * *

*Grand-mère* was in the kitchen, alone for the first time in hours, when she heard Jules pull into the farmyard. She looked around her for Esther, or her daughter-in-law, but realised everyone was elsewhere in this rambling old farmhouse. She dried her hands on her apron and went out to greet the men, just as Jules was pulling the old man's small suitcase from the boot of his car.

'Ah, here's one of them already,' Jules cried, signalling his grandmother. '*Grand-mère,* meet Esther's grandad, George,' he said with a big smile before hurrying on. 'Do you mind if I leave you two alone for a little while? I just have a phone call I need to make,' he said, pulling his Motorola flip phone from his pocket and walking over to the other side of the farmyard, running his hands through his hair as he began to talk rapidly.

The two great-grandparents stared at one another a few moments longer than was polite, but it was *Grand-mère* who had done a real double take and almost stumbled as the mixture of déjà vu and shock threatened to overtake her.

'George?' she whispered at last.

## 27

SAINTE-MÈRE-ÉGLISE, OCTOBER 1999

Marie-Claire boiled milk on the stove for coffee and took her time making two bowls of hot chocolate and slicing some fresh bread. She carried the breakfast to the kitchen table and set one helping for herself and the other for George.

'Please, forgive my bad manners yesterday, Mr Holt. And I hope I can explain,' she said, as they started to eat. 'You see, I knew a man called George, back in the war, and just recently I was reminded of him. He died, of course – so many of them died – but something about seeing you and hearing your name...' She trailed off and waved a hand as if to dismiss the wanderings of her elderly mind. 'It reminded me of him, and it was as if I saw him before me,' she explained.

'No need to apologise, Madame Joubert. I know exactly what you mean, and I must say I am half expecting to see ghosts here as well,' he said, and she looked up at him sharply in surprise.

'I've been here before, you see, to Sainte-Mère-Église. I came in on the landing craft on Utah Beach, and we fought our way here and battled it out with the Germans to win this town back,' he said.

'*Mon Dieu*, this is really true? I was there myself. I fought in the town, from the café-bar and then from the other side of the square,' she said, shaking her head in disbelief.

'You really are the Marie-Claire I heard of then? I've wondered that, all these years since our Esther started coming here. You see, I met a man – a good man and a great leader – near the beaches. Jean-Baptiste was his name. In a lull, when we were talking about the town of Sainte-Mère-Église, where we were headed, he told some of us about a brave woman who would help in the battle for the town. He told us that you saved many Jewish families from the Nazis. I wondered if I would meet you then, but of course, it was such a mess here,' he said, and they both allowed their minds to wander back to the terror of that battle.

'Jean-Baptiste died that day, you know,' she said. 'My own husband almost died too. He worked with Jean-Baptiste, as I did, in the resistance. But my husband, Louis Joubert, was saved by a man called George Baker. A very good man, and I've been thinking about him a lot just recently. When I saw you yesterday, and heard your name...'

'I can understand your confusion – and that it might have been a shock, bringing those memories back. How did we get through it all, hey?' George asked, and Marie-Claire simply shrugged.

'We had no choice. We had to survive, and some of us chose to survive better by fighting back. And we won,' she said with a broad smile. 'And look what our beautiful grandchildren have now, as a result.'

At the ceremony in the church later that morning, everybody was dressed to reflect the gorgeous early autumn day. The flowers that Madame Joubert had arranged inside the church looked magnificent, and Jules cried when he saw his bride walk down the aisle on her grandad's arm. Elodie scattered petals everywhere, and Fabien slept through the entirety of his christening, waking only when he felt the cold shock of water on his forehead.

While the young couple were having some private photos taken, the family milled about the church and square and Marie-Claire found George looking up at the stained-glass window with the parachutes, and reading the plaque in honour of the man who'd been caught on the steeple – the other George.

'I had no idea he was anyone I knew, when I saw him caught up there during the battle, you know? It was only much later when Louis came back, and we shared our stories from that terrible night that he told me what had happened to him, and how George had sacrificed himself, and helped Louis get away alive. He was a very good man,' she said, and grew thoughtful for a time. Eventually, she turned and spoke to George Holt again.

'We are all very thankful to you and all the Allies, for what you did, George,' she said, tapping his arm. He looked into her face and took her arm in his.

'Marie-Claire, we all did it together. And the Allies couldn't have achieved what happened on D-Day without the incredible strength and courage of resistance fighters like you, Jean-Baptiste and Louis. We were a team,' he said, patting her arm and walking with her out of the church.

## 28

### SAINTE-MÈRE-ÉGLISE, DECEMBER 1999

Hugo and Jules leant across the kitchen table which was strewn with printed profit and loss sheets, maps, hand-scrawled notes, and a few pages of artistic impressions of a variety of gîte styles. On the other side of the table, Giselle and Esther were deep in conversation about the best way to market their new business venture. They'd written a few drafts of a sales pitch and were trying out different angles.

'Whichever way we sell it, I think it's a great idea,' Madame Joubert said as she came in to make a pot of coffee for everyone.

'Papa and I are ready to slow down, and as neither of you two are interested in farming the old way,' she said with a look of mock horror to Giselle and Jules, 'it's a great way to keep the family business going and move it forward into the new millennium. But I think the visitors to *les gîtes* will still want to see cows and the milking, so they get something of a farm experience.'

'Yes, I think you're right, *Maman*,' said Esther. 'Staying in a gîte on a farm will be much more attractive and special to English families and French from the cities if they can experience some of the farm life. They'll want to taste our delicious milk, and there's nothing like a breakfast of milky hot chocolate with croissants,' she said, drifting back to her first experience in Sainte-Mère-Église.

'I know a lot of farmers around the place are turning their barns into holiday gîtes now. It seems to be working for them,' Madame Joubert said as she handed round the coffee. 'And you four young people certainly have the brains for it, put together.'

This much was true, and made the whole idea seem perfect. Jules had a business and economics degree and many years of experience in property development. Esther had also studied commerce, and was trained in translation between French and English, as well as having worked at the Chambers of Commerce in both Poole and Cherbourg. Hugo was an accountant and had built up some great contacts all over Normandy. And Giselle had worked in interior design in both Normandy and Paris before stopping work to have her children. They made a great team.

'And don't forget your old mother and grandmother,' Marie-Claire had chimed in at one stage. 'We are both very skilled cooks, and perhaps we could set up a little restaurant here on the farm somewhere,' she'd suggested. An on-site restaurant in close walking distance for the gîtes was a brilliant idea. The gîtes were planned to be created partly by converting some barns in neighbouring fields, with a couple of new builds made to look as though they had always been there. The plan was for four separate holiday gîtes in total. Plus, there was the conversion of the barn in the farmyard to deal with.

Esther and Jules loved being on the farm, for Fabien's sake. It was so lovely to see him being adored by his loving grandparents and great-grandmother, and Jules and Esther could see him growing up to be like a brother to Elodie and Julien. After their stay in Sainte-Mère-Église back in October, and when the English visitors had gone home again, Jules and Esther had returned to the apartment in Paris, and both felt the loss of family while they were there. The business that Jules worked for had forged ahead with the use of the internet which was becoming more and more common in business settings, and he'd found ways to work from the farm. But this new idea might release them to live on the Joubert farm full-time, and so Marie-Claire had suggested the full conversion of the barn into a home for them.

'We could certainly plan a small restaurant in the downstairs of the barn conversion, fronting the road, or perhaps a crêperie?' suggested Jules in response to his grandmother's idea, and it soon became part of the firm plans.

But Esther felt there was more to be done with this suggestion and that the matriarch of the family had a great skill in both cooking and writing. Perhaps the gîtes and restaurant business could become something even more than that – a place where people could holiday and learn to cook delicious French cuisine at the same time, under the direction of the Joubert women. Part of their stay could include a book of recipes, written by *Grand-mère*, along with her beautifully descriptive writing about the ingredients and provinces which inspired the food.

So one morning she caught *Grand-mère* while everyone else was busy, and Fabien was taking his morning nap. Talking quickly, she was so excited, she pulled out the old cookery journal from the drawer to rave over *Grand-mère's* brilliant writing and enticing recipes, and she laid out her idea to the older lady who smiled warmly in response.

'Esther, what you are suggesting is something that I have wanted to do for over sixty years now. I started planning to write a recipe book long before I even met Jules' grandfather, you know. I've been a cook, and I've written about food most of my life. I've run a café-bar, and a crêperie, and I love to help people learn about food.'

Over the next few weeks, the team worked on the business plan together and Jules made an application for a loan so they could begin stage one: converting the barn into the business base, manager's residence, and restaurant-cum-cookery school.

It was during this time that Marie-Claire found a chance to creep into the barn one afternoon when nobody noticed. She looked furtively over her shoulder, just as she used to do before climbing the hayloft ladder and going up to the hideout during the war. But this time it was because she knew her family would be worried for her safety. It was certainly more of a struggle than it had been nearly sixty years earlier, but Marie-Claire soon found she was at the top – a little puffed, but unharmed. She made her way across the hayloft and into the hideout, the door of which seemed to have been permanently removed. Once inside, she gasped to see it was unchanged.

There was the low bed with the old mattress, the bucket in the corner and, yes, if she bent a little lower she could see the old radio they once used to transmit messages still in its place under the bed, and the retractable aerial leading up through the roof. She sat down heavily on the bed, and ran her hand over the mattress, watching the dust motes that danced in the spears of light that peeped through the tiny holes in the wall, and she remembered them all: George Baker, and Rachel Epstein. Marguerite and Adeline. Jean-Baptiste and Louis.

All this would be gone soon, removed and destroyed to make way for the beautiful new home that Esther and Jules were creating here for their family. Marie-Claire lay down on the bed and faced the wall, closing her eyes and touching the timber barn wall beside her, and she cried a little. Then she pulled the folded recipe page from her pocket, and read at a whisper the poem by Paul Verlaine, and the note she'd secretly written to George. She folded it up into a tiny square and searched until she found a hole in the mattress where she could bury it deep inside.

Leaving the hideout, she took one last look over her shoulder and breathed her goodbye, carefully making her way back down the hayloft ladder and out into the light of the farmyard once more.

By February, the loan was in place, the barn conversion had begun, and Jules and Esther took a trip to Poole to spend time with her family, and allow Esther to wrap up her employment at the Chamber of Commerce. She had taken six months' maternity leave with the option to return, but now with these developments they had decided their main home would be on the farm, and her working role would be in the new holiday gîte business.

'Esther, I have to say, I'm not surprised. Your new life is so full of possibility and adventure! But you know how much we'll miss you here, don't you?' her boss had said as they met in the offices at Upton House. 'Please don't see this as a door that you're closing and let me know anytime you'd like to come back,' he'd said.

'To be honest, I will probably be in touch sooner than you think – from the other side, as it were. I've been talking with the Chambre de Commerce de Cherbourg, and Monsieur le Maire is very keen to work with us on our new project.'

Later that morning, Jules took Fabien to visit his Poole grandma and great-grandad after dropping Esther off so she could catch up with Kelly for lunch in The Clipper restaurant, in the Dolphin Centre.

'Hello, sweetie,' smiled Kelly as she gave her friend a kiss on the cheek, and then laughed as Esther kissed her other cheek as well, in the French style. 'I miss having you around, but it's so lovely that you get back here so often,' she said as they found a table in a cosy back corner.

'Have you finished work at the newspaper for your maternity leave yet?' asked Esther when they'd ordered their lunch.

'No, I've got a few more days to go, and I've been busy writing a few extra articles that they'll publish after I'm gone. And I plan to go back part-time and write from home when the baby is a few months old. Let's just hope he or she is a good sleeper!' she laughed.

'Sometime later in the year, I'll have a great scoop for you, Kelly,' said Esther with a grin and told her friend all the plans for the new holiday gîte business. 'There will definitely be a free holiday in it for you, for review purposes, and of course a restaurant and cooking class review,' Esther added, and went on to tell her all the exciting new plans.

'Mmm, sounds wonderful! I'll be up for that, no problem. And you say that the old *grand-mère* is a cook?' she asked.

'Yes, apparently she trained as a young woman in the south of France, and used her cooking skills as part of a cover in the resistance during the war. It seems so hard to believe that such a sweet old lady could have been in the thick of all that fighting, but she was. She has quite a sad story, actually,' Esther said, and told Kelly everything she knew about Marie-Claire's early years during the war.

'That is so tragic, Esther. Imagine the shock of losing both her husband and baby boy, both on the same night, and still having the courage to go on and fight for her country like she did. What a woman,' she said, before growing thoughtful.

'And you say the surname was Dubois? Antoine Dubois?' Kelly asked, her face crumpled in puzzlement. 'I can't believe they can be connected, and I know it's a common name, but I think I might have heard of that part of the family,' Kelly said.

'It's probably a different family altogether, Kel, and it is a very common French name. Besides that, the family line died out with this little boy in 1940,' Esther said, taking a sip of her wine and smiling at Dave, the waiter who delivered their meals to the table.

'But what if it didn't, Esther? What if the boy – Antoine – made it all the way to the south of France, as planned?' Kelly pushed.

'Well, he didn't. He died when his train was hit in a bombing raid, just outside of Paris,' said Esther, shrugging and getting stuck into her meal.

'Did his mother – Marie-Claire – did she see the body?' asked Kelly persistently.

Esther put down her knife and fork and turned to have a good look into the face of her friend.

'What are you getting at, Kelly?' she asked. Kelly took a deep breath before she explained.

'I have this friend, who works in the library. She had an old colleague who went to France and married a man called Jean-Pierre Dubois. They live on the Côte d'Azur in a little town called Saint-Christophe,' she started, and Esther picked up her cutlery and began to eat again, sensing this would be a long story.

'Apparently, this man's father – Antoine Dubois – arrived in Saint-Christophe in 1940 on a train from Paris, with friends of his parents. They were due to follow on, but never turned up and couldn't be traced. He was just two years old at the time,' Kelly explained, and Esther stopped the loaded fork inches from her mouth, and put it down on the plate again. She took a deep breath.

'That is an uncanny coincidence, Kel. How big is this town, Saint-Christophe?' she asked.

'Quite small, apparently – just a little local seaside fishing harbour that has a pretty beach and bay, so it's become popular with tourists. But the local population is fairly small, I gather. Esther, you don't think it's possible that baby Antoine made it to safety after all, do you?'

Esther thought about all the possibilities. Paris in 1940 would have been hell, and the mass exodus would have confused everything. What if it wasn't Antoine's train that had been hit after all, and he'd survived?

'I could ask *Grand-mère*, I suppose,' Esther said, thinking out loud. 'But it could be such an intrusion. I'll have to think about how to bring it up naturally. Leave it with me, Kelly, and I'll talk it through with Jules. It's worth investigating. What if this was the same Antoine, and he's still alive? She would have grandchildren in Saint-Christophe that she doesn't even know about!'

\* \* \*

'It's such a coincidence,' said Jules later that night when Esther told her everything she'd learned from Kelly. 'But it does sound possible it might be the same person. I will talk to *Papa*, and see what he says. But I think he will say you might as well ask her yourself. She's a tough old girl, and not prone to high emotion. Her losses and experiences in the war must have had something to do with that,' Jules had responded.

When they headed back to the farm again, Esther waited for a moment when she might ask *Grand-mère* about Antoine. One afternoon, the chance came when the great-grandmother was cuddling Fabien, who was now six months old and growing into a strong wriggler, almost ready to crawl. But he would sit in her arms and lie still, falling sleepy, while he watched the flames of the fire, and she sang to him. When he fell asleep and she gently rocked him, *Grand-mère* kissed him and whispered her love to him.

Esther had been watching from the doorway, and smiled at Marie-Claire when she looked up and saw her there. She sat in the opposite chair and settled in by the fire.

'You're so good with him, *Grand-mère*. He knows he can trust you,' she said.

'Ah well, I've nursed a few babies on my knee over the years, *chérie*. Perhaps he knows he is in safe hands,' Marie-Claire chuckled, and Esther carefully thought about what she would say next.

'I know it was a long time ago – a lifetime, really – but I'm sure it must make you remember Antoine, nursing Fabien. Does he look like your son at all?' she asked.

Marie-Claire closed her eyes momentarily before answering.

'All these children have looked a little like Antoine, in some way. When Louis and I had our daughter, and then our son – Jules' father – both had a look of Antoine around their eyes. But I was busy being their mother and didn't notice any similar characteristics. And then the grandchildren, they also reminded me of him, and Giselle had the same fair hair. But Jules, he was all Joubert in his looks, apart from the dimples!' She laughed, and the women sat in the quiet together for a minute.

'Since I've had Fabien, and especially after you told me all about how you lost Antoine, I've often wondered... When you heard the news that he'd died in that train derailment, did you... were you able to go and see him? Was it possible to hold a funeral? Is he buried somewhere in Sainte-Mère-Église?' Esther asked, and held her breath, instantly worried that she had pushed too far into Marie-Claire's tragic past.

The old woman took a deep breath and let out a shuddering sigh.

'No, it wasn't possible to go and see the train wreck. The war made everything difficult, and there was no way to get there. I only heard the news through my friends who had helped me on the night I escaped Paris. They were working with the underground resistance, you see, and they had contacts who told them about the wreck. They knew the train Antoine had been on, and heard that there were only a few adults who survived. No children,' she said, giving a little shrug. 'But I'm glad I can remember him as the happy, healthy little boy he was and didn't have to see his broken body.'

'*Grand-mère,* I'm not sure where to begin, but I think I may have learned of a little more detail about what happened to Antoine,' she began, and watched as the old lady's face went through multiple emotions.

'What do you mean, what happened to him?' she asked, and Esther explained everything that Kelly had told her. When she'd finished sharing everything, Marie-Claire looked into the fire and her breath quickened so much that Fabien stirred. She patted him back into deep sleep and held him close, then wiped a stray tear from her eye.

'Do you really think it is possible that he made it there alive? That he's been there all this time, and I didn't know it?' she whispered with a croaky voice, and then Esther braced herself to deliver the next bit of information they'd discovered.

'Apparently Antoine grew up there and married. He had two children – Yvette and Jean-Pierre. But very sadly, both he and his wife passed away about ten years ago. The children now have children of their own – more great-grandchildren for you, if this Antoine is your boy, *Grand-mère,*' Esther finished.

'To think he might have grown up there without me, after all, and never knew that his mother thought he had died!' she said, looking overwhelmed and bewildered. 'I never contacted my family after the war, of course. I parted on bad terms with my parents when I married Benjamin and once I had my life here with Louis, I didn't ever want to see them again. And those distant cousins in Saint-Christophe, the Laurents? I think I was so lost in my grief after losing Benjamin and Antoine, that I just wanted to forget everything we had planned for our new life.'

'It might have been another Antoine Dubois, of course,' suggested Esther. 'But the similarities do seem very strong,' she said, and Marie-Claire nodded.

Later that night Esther contacted Kelly, who got hold of her friend from the library and put the two women in touch with each other. Esther agreed to write everything she knew so it could be passed to the woman in Saint-Christophe – Felicity Dubois.

Within a few days, Esther's phone rang and she took the call from Felicity, who was very glad to hold such a complex conversation in English with Esther. She had spoken with her husband and sister-in-law. They were very keen to meet and invited Marie-Claire and the family to visit, but she had another suggestion first.

'I've had a bit of experience with tracing heritage myself, and I recommend getting a DNA test done through one of the family history research societies. That will tell us quite conclusively if my husband and your grandmother-in-law are related,' Felicity said.

A month later, Marie-Claire received the letter they'd all been waiting for, and she opened it at the kitchen table, while the family looked on. She didn't need to say any words to tell them what it said. The news was written on her tear-stained face.

And so, plans began to form for a family trip in the summer to the south coast, to visit Saint-Christophe.

## 29

SAINT-CHRISTOPHE, CÔTE D'AZUR, JUNE 2000

Marie-Claire looked along the line of airplane seats beside her, where some of her brightest and best treasures were waiting with her for take-off. She had been so blessed in this life: incredibly blessed. And now, after all these years when she'd never imagined there was any hope of reconnecting with Benjamin and Antoine, she was on her way to meet her grandchildren. *Who could have imagined this, for the end to my life's story*, she thought to herself.

As the plane raced south on the very short flight from Caen to Nice, Marie-Claire remembered back to when she had first arrived in Caen, almost sixty years earlier, on that dreadful night in 1940. If she hadn't met Jean-Baptiste, what would have happened to her? And if her new friends hadn't told her that Antoine was dead, what would she have done? Might she have made it south and found him again, after all?

But then, if she'd done that, she would never have met Louis, or Adeline, Marguerite or George. And perhaps none of those Jewish families she had helped to escape would have survived. No, she decided firmly. There really was no point thinking about all the 'what-ifs' of her life. It was as it was, and everything must have happened for a reason. There was no other way to process it all. How could she regret her life in Normandy, and her beautiful, growing Joubert family?

Fabien was as good as a small baby can be on a flight all the way south, but as the plane started its descent, he started to cry. Esther and Jules took turns at comforting him and trying to get him to drink from a bottle to help him swallow the pain away.

When they got off the plane, Jules went to organise the train tickets that would take them into Saint-Christophe, where Felicity had said she would meet them. The amazing blue seas of the Côte d'Azur sped by as the train flew westwards and, soon, they were on the platform of the station in the little town beside the sea.

Felicity, Jean-Pierre, and Yvette were there to meet them all and Marie-Claire stayed back, fumbling with her bag and giving her attention to Fabien in his pram. She suddenly felt sick at the thought of meeting these grandchildren she had only discovered a few months ago were living.

'Marie-Claire?' said Jean-Pierre, quietly stepping closer to where she stood with the pram underneath the big tree on the station platform. 'Madame Joubert? Or may I call you *Grandmère*?' he asked tentatively.

She hesitated, confused at first by the options of what they might each want to call her. And she realised now with a disappointment that rained heavily on the hole in her heart left by Antoine and Benjamin, that some tiny, inexplicable and unreasonable part of her soul had imagined she might see both her lost loves here: Benjamin and Antoine – smiling, alive, and happy to see her. She scoffed at the silly old woman she was for her runaway emotions, and reminded herself of the mantra that had helped her get through life. *Be grateful for the blessings you have today.*

Soon, and before she could make a reply, any hint of awkwardness was blown away when four children, two older and two very much younger, ran into her, wrapping their small arms around her legs.

'*Grand-mère, Grand-mère!*' they cried, jumping up and down with excitement, making her laugh out loud. She bent down to them and when they turned their faces up to hers, and she saw both Antoine and Benjamin in their eyes, she choked and held a hand to her mouth.

'Oh, my dears, you are all so lovely! Thank you for this kind welcome. You make me feel like a queen!' she said through tears, and she couldn't decide if it was for joy or sadness.

And then all the adults greeted her with hugs and kisses like the long-time lost grandmother she was to them.

'Please, you can all call me *Grand-mère,*' she said. 'It is what everyone in Sainte-Mère-Église calls me, so I will know it is me that you want.' She laughed, and this new, wider family all joined in, while they organised bags and cars and took the Joubert family to the apartment overlooking the waterfront that they had booked.

Felicity and Esther soon hit it off, bonding over the similarities of their lives. Within a few minutes they had gone over the basics. They had both grown up in Poole, both married Frenchmen, and both settled with them in France. And of course, inevitably for their age, they both had grandparents with tales from the war.

Marie-Claire listened as the two women chattered away in English which was almost too fast for her to pick up, but she got most of it, and smiled to herself as she heard them becoming friends.

That evening, they all met for dinner at Felicity and Jean-Pierre's home, and Marie-Claire was seated at the table between Jean-Pierre and Yvette – her two brand-new and no longer unfamiliar grandchildren. Her own son sat opposite Jean-Pierre, and it warmed her to see how well the two men got along. Her son was a farmer from the north, with rural manners, and her grandson was a baker from the south, and yet this family tie had brought them together. Jules had also been a huge hit with their new family and soon he was sharing with them news of the developing gîte business.

'The barn conversion is nearly finished, so Esther and I will be moving in with Fabien in a few weeks' time. And then we can work on opening the restaurant. *Maman* and *Grand-mère* are both excellent cooks, and will be running the on-site cookery school and restaurant together, won't you?' he asked them, and they shyly batted away any praise.

'Everything I learned, I learned from my mother-in-law, and she learned it here in Saint-Christophe, didn't you, *Maman*?' Madame Joubert prompted, trying to help Marie-Claire talk about her past now that so much of it was being spread out for her.

'Yes, I learned to cook at your great-uncle's restaurant,' she said to Jean-Pierre and Yvette. 'I used to come here on holidays when I was a girl, and I worked in the restaurant with your grandparents. This is why we were coming here with Antoine – Benjamin and I – to escape Paris,' she said and then her expression saddened with clouds of the past again.

Yvette reached across and squeezed her new-found grandmother's hand.

'You did the right thing. The best thing. You and Benjamin were incredibly brave to try what you did, getting out of Paris then. I can't imagine what would have happened to you if you'd stayed until later in the war,' she said, and that prompted Marie-Claire to tell the story of all the Jewish families she'd helped to get out of Sainte-Mère-Église in 1942. The younger family members were in awe of their grandmother and her courage.

'And our father had the most wonderful life, growing up here on the coast. The war was, from what we can gather, difficult for those few years, of course. Even this far south there was a lot of trouble. And the D-Day landings that took place here on this coast were heavily retaliated by the German battlements positioned along the beaches,' Jean-Pierre explained.

'Really? I had no idea there were Allied landings this far south,' Esther said.

'Yes, it was a little after the landings in Normandy, which were in early June 1944, of course. In August the Allies arrived for the Provence landings along the Esterel Côte d'Azur region here. And there were fierce battles. Many more people died here at that time than throughout the rest of the war, I believe, and also many of our old buildings were lost,' Yvette continued.

'But once the war was over, little Antoine Dubois continued to live life as part of the family, and he learned to be a baker, which is where I get it from. So being an excellent cook certainly runs in the family, *Grand-mère*,' said Jean-Pierre, and they all laughed.

'I'm sorry not to have met my brother, Jean-Pierre, and Yvette. But I feel that we are getting to know him through your stories, is that not right, *Maman*?' Jules' father said.

* * *

By the end of the week, the Joubert and Dubois families felt they had known each other forever, and soon a firm plan was made for a trip north to stay in the new gîtes once they were fully operational. Esther had talked with Felicity about her help to advertise the holiday home venture here on the south coast, which she felt sure she could do through the successful little café-bookshop that she ran in town.

'Talking of town, didn't you want to go for another good walk around the shops, *Grand-mère*?' asked Jules. 'This afternoon, we are all taking that boat trip into Saint-Tropez that you didn't want to come on – unless you've changed your mind?'

'No, no, you all go together. And I will care for baby Fabien, if you like? I'm sure it will be easier for you to enjoy a boat trip without the pram. I can take him walking in the town and he can help me choose presents for everyone,' she laughed.

At three o'clock, everyone set off into town where they were due to catch the boat out for their evening cruise and dinner in Saint-Tropez. Yvette dropped Marie-Claire and Fabien into the town centre and showed her where she could find the boutique, when she was tired and wanted a lift home again – or if she needed help with Fabien.

The streets of Saint-Christophe were delightful, with narrow twists and turns and all kinds of surprising little shops and restaurants. Yvette had showed her the café-bookshop which Felicity had set up and it was open now with a young boy serving inside, while Felicity was out enjoying the evening boat trip with her new-found cousins.

In time, Marie-Claire found the place where she had worked as a young girl – at least, she felt sure it was the same building, but it looked very different now. It seemed to be a kind of jazz bar now, and there was a woman setting out extra tables and chairs for the evening. She glanced into the pram, and saw that Fabien was sleeping soundly.

'Are you open for coffee?' Marie-Claire asked the waitress who welcomed her to a comfortable table, and went to make up her order. When she came back, the woman peered into the pram and crooned about the beautiful baby admiringly.

'He's my great-grandson – one of my great-grandsons, I should say.' Marie-Claire laughed to think how much her family had grown now.

'You are very blessed, Madame,' said the waitress and left Marie-Claire to drink her coffee in peace and watch the sleeping face of Fabien as he breathed. She counted every blessing of her life, thankful for each one.

The next morning – their last in Saint-Christophe – the Joubert and Dubois families spent on the beach, enjoying the sand and sun, and giving Fabien his first paddle in the warm waters of the Mediterranean. Marie-Claire sat in a chair under a beach umbrella with her bare feet in the sand, and, after lunch, went for a little walk along the shore where the great-grandchildren were all playing and building castles.

She could foresee a bright future of holidays spent here on this beach, and of entertaining the Dubois side of the family in Sainte-Mère-Église in the new gîtes, and her heart bubbled with gratitude. She looked out across the bay and thought of Benjamin, and her dear darling Louis, of Jean-Baptiste, and Adeline, and of Antoine and all those she had lost in the dark days of war. And she thought of George Baker too, and how she had lost him but how he had sacrificed his life so that her Louis would be saved. So much had been lost, and yet now her life was full again with love and laughter, children and grandchildren.

Marie-Claire beamed as Jules carried her chair down to the water's edge so she could sit with the children and watch them laugh and play.

'Look at what we did, my friends,' she whispered to the memory of her team in *la Résistance*. 'Just look at what we fought for and won back for them all.'

\* \* \*

## MORE FROM RACHEL SWEASEY

Another book from Rachel Sweasey, *The Island Girls*, is available to order now here:

https://mybook.to/IslandGirlsBackAd

# AUTHOR'S NOTES

As with all the stories I have written, this fictional tale is twisted together with historical facts. But some of the details in those facts have been changed to suit this story.

The most prominent of these is in the history of Sainte-Mère-Église, in Normandy. There was indeed a paratrooper whose parachute was caught on the church steeple during the D-Day landings, and the poor man did hang there for some time, playing dead, before he was eventually taken down. He was captured by German soldiers, but escaped soon after. His name was John Steele, and he was part of the US 3rd Battalion, 505th Parachute Infantry Regiment. His story has been immortalised through the movie, *The Longest Day*, and there is a parachute memorial at the church, which is called the Église Notre-Dame de-l'Assomption. Sainte-Mère-Église was also one of the very first villages in France to be liberated by the Allies.

Another fact that I wove into this story was of the small plane that was stolen from the Germans by two young Frenchmen and flown from an airfield near Caen to England. This, and their experience on landing, happened almost exactly as I've told it in this book, according to history.

The poem 'Chanson d'automne' by Paul Verlaine was used by BBC Radio Londres in a signal to the French Resistance that Operation Overlord – which we all now know as D-Day – was about to begin. This was the call to arms for resistance workers to begin sabotaging railway lines.

There is a little bit of personal history here too. When I was a teenager at school in Poole, I went on a French exchange trip to visit my pen pal who lived on a farm. I did not know until I arrived that there was no bathroom, and only a primitive water pump for water. The cooking was all managed on a wood-fired range, and I had heavenly hot chocolate made with the creamy farm milk, with fresh bread, for breakfast each day. That memory has stayed with me for forty years and almost everything about the Joubert farm is based on that place which was in Saint-Pierre-Église, Normandy.

Fort Henry at Studland is a real landmark still existing and there were exercises held on the beaches which were watched by Winston Churchill, King George VI and General Dwight D. Eisenhower. Hundreds of landing craft for the D-Day operation were built in Poole shipyards at the rate of one per day at one stage, and a vast number of American troops were billeted in Swanage before they set off on the Allied rescue mission to win France back from the Nazi regime. All those who gave their lives for our freedom will never be forgotten.

# ACKNOWLEDGEMENTS

Thank you to everyone who has helped me with this novel including, as always, the famous Poole historians Andrew Hawkes and Rodney Legg for their fabulous books of historical photographs of Poole.

The book, *Suite française* by Irène Némirovsky, was a great source of information around the mass exodus from Paris after the occupation in 1940 and the terrible treatment of Jews, as well as *Paris '44: The Shame and the Glory* by Patrick Bishop.

Others who've helped with historical details and enthusiastic support are Peter Norton, Dave Stone, and all my family in Poole. Thank you, Alison, for checking my French, and to my own guys in Brisbane who graciously allow me to disappear into book-writing oblivion and cheer me on, always. I'm grateful for my brilliant editor Rachel Faulkner-Willcocks and all her advice, and the support of all at Boldwood Books as well as my ever-enthusiastic agent, Vicki Marsden at High Spot Literary. Thank you.

## ABOUT THE AUTHOR

**Rachel Sweasey** is a debut historical fiction novelist. She lives in Australia, where she was born to English parents, but bases her fiction in Poole where she grew up, which provides inspiration for her WWII stories.

Sign up to Rachel Sweasey's mailing list here for news, competitions and updates on future books.

Visit Rachel's website: www.rachelsweasey.com

Follow Rachel on social media:

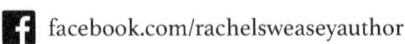 facebook.com/rachelsweaseyauthor

## ALSO BY RACHEL SWEASEY

The Last Boat Home

The Island Girls

The Girl From Normandy

# Letters from
## *the past*

Discover page-turning
historical novels from
your favourite authors
and be transported
back in time

*Join our book club
Facebook group*

https://bit.ly/SixpenceGroup

*Sign up to our
newsletter*

https://bit.ly/LettersFrom
PastNews

# Boldwood

Boldwood Books is an award-winning fiction publishing company seeking out the best stories from around the world.

**Find out more at www.boldwoodbooks.com**

Join our reader community for brilliant books, competitions and offers!

Follow us

@BoldwoodBooks

@TheBoldBookClub

Sign up to our weekly deals newsletter

https://bit.ly/BoldwoodBNewsletter

Printed in Dunstable, United Kingdom